TEN YEAR DANCE

A NOVEL

ARA GRIGORIAN

Love, Laugh, Learn
M E D I A

Love, Laugh, Learn Media

First Printing, 2017
Second Printing, 2023

Paperback ISBN-13: 978-0-9906919-4-5
Hardcover ISBN-13: 978-1-7324621-6-8

www.AraGrigorian.com

To my wife, my spiritual north star who puts up with this addiction of mine. You are my rock, my "the one."

To my boys — I love you. And when you finally fall asleep, I adore you :)

Mimik, my late grandmother, whose personality and attitude plays a role in this story. You showed me that it was okay to cry over a song, a memory, or a hurt. You also gave me my first beer — but that'll remain between us.

Above all, Him, for the gift of storytelling.

Part I

Friends

ONE

— SOPHIE —

Today

IT'S BEEN SIX months since Seth moved out of our home. To be accurate, it's been six months since I asked him to move out of *my* home.

Today, I take the next step.

My heart beats with an irregular cadence. My throat is constricted because any minute now, I'll receive confirmation that the divorce papers have been handed to him.

He won't be happy. But that's his problem, not mine. At least that's what I keep telling myself.

I scan the parking lot one more time. Pete, my best friend, isn't here yet. Just once, I wish he'd be early; or on time for that matter. I don't want to be alone right now.

I study my phone, confirming I have enough juice and at least a few bars of connectivity. I don't want to miss the call. All looks good. I just have to be patient.

As usual.

Why I wasted six months waiting to demand a divorce, I'll never know.

Truth be told, looking back on my life, I can accurately say that my life's theme can be boiled down to a simple headline: the art and science of a life wasted.

Wasted time on doing nothing when I could have cherished the limited time I had with my parents.

Wasted time crushing over a boy in middle school who barely noticed me.

Wasted time loving a boy who could never love me.

And to top it off, wasted time on a marriage that never should have been.

I step out of my car and grab my tennis bag. Might as well warm up while I wait for Pete. He doesn't know that today's the big day. He's been asking and I've been deflecting. If he'd known, he would've been with me all day, I'm sure of it... but I didn't tell him. Maybe because I wanted to give myself the out clause, in case I changed my mind. Like the last three times. But the wheels are already turning. No stopping it now.

I'd love to believe that when the sheriff hands Seth the documents, he won't get angry or hurt. He will know, because everyone knew, that we're just wrong for each other. He'll respect my decision and he'll move on with his life.

I can hope for this, but I know better. Because I know him and what he's capable of. For that reason, I'll have to be careful. I'll need to surround myself with friends.

I place my bag on the bench and begin to stretch. Gingerly. My ribs are still somewhat tender. *It doesn't matter now. It's almost over.*

My phone rings. I reach for it and snatch it off the bench. The call I've been anticipating. The one I've been dreading.

"Hey Sophie," Frank, my buddy since high school says. He's also a sheriff which is a benefit I've recently come to value. "It's done. Just got a call from the serving officer."

I take a deep powerful breath, but my exhale is shaky. "Thanks, Frank."

"Is Pete with you?"

"Not yet. Any minute now," I say, but I know better. Mister give-or-take-fifteen is always on the wrong side of the equation.

Frank is silent for a few moments. "Let me know if he's running late. You shouldn't be alone."

"I'm fine, Frank," I say and as I utter the words, I feel the release. The weight that was sitting on my chest is lifted. I know I'll be fine.

I hang up, thankful that I have a circle of friends who'll give up anything to help me. But I need one in particular right now. I text Pete. Just once, could he be ahead of the game and not make me wait? I really need my closest friend here, with me.

TWO

— PETE —

THE SHERIFF DELIVERED the divorce papers. It's done.

My heart slams against my ribs. Did she finally decide to leave that toxic relationship for good? I swerve to the curb to read Sophie's text again. Maybe I read it wrong. Maybe my wishful mind added words that aren't there.

The sheriff delivered the divorce papers. It's done.

Halle-freakin-lujah! I'm elated for her, but also worried. That imbalanced jerk is capable of anything.

I'm proud of you! I reply.

I'm not proud of myself... I hope you're on your way. I reserved court two, she writes. *Don't be late.*

I pull away from the curb and accelerate toward the country club. She shouldn't be left alone now that Seth knows she's serious.

A few minutes later I park next to her black-on-black Mini. I'm about to step out of my car when a text from the woman I'm dating, Natalie, gives me pause. I glance from the display to the country club tennis courts thirty feet away. Sophie is waiting for me, stretching, preparing to embarrass me yet again.

A cool breeze glides through the convertible.

I read Natalie's message. *Look at this beauty. It would be perfect!*

She has attached a picture of a property where one day in the distant future I can build my dream home—the one that has somehow become her dream home, too. How long have we been together now? Two? Three months? Even though that's a record for me, she's jumping to too many conclusions too soon.

I squint at the image she swiped from a realtor's website. Yeah, she's found a good one, overlooking a glimmering lake. The house is crap which makes it ideal. I could tear it down and rebuild it to match my designs, my vision. Just a few more years at this pace—and focus—and I'll have what I've wanted.

Very nice, I reply, and hit the 'send' button.

Should we check it out together next time I'm in L.A.?

We? Together? *Maybe.*

Let's talk about it when I fly down this Friday. I'll call you later with my flight plans. XO.

In truth, the next time she's in town, we may have a very different conversation. Don't get me wrong, she's great. Just not for me.

I glance up. Sophie is running laps around the court now. Still the All-American athlete she was in school. Only difference is she's in even better shape now. Which leads to one conclusion—she's going to hurt me. Again. I can practically feel the pain.

Watching her now, I can't help but beam. She's free: only paperwork away from finally being untethered from Seth. A relationship that never made sense is finally coming to an end.

I slide out of the car and grab the tennis racquet from my trunk. I don't know why I let her talk me into these things. After sixteen years you'd think I'd be able to say no to her once.

At least it's a perfect evening. A faint breeze, minimal smog—by Los Angeles standards, anyway—and a handful of birds chirping from the tree branches as the last rays of light fade behind the leaves. I study the open top of my convertible, then glance at the birds.

"No spray crapping in my car, kids," I tell them as I roll up the top.

I stroll onto the court just as Sophie rounds the corner and heads toward me. "Hey, Soph."

She slows down as she reaches me. Her golden-cinnamon eyes latch onto mine. The breeze lifts her red hair. "You're late, Pete. Again."

"I am an advocate for delaying pain and humiliation."

She grins and her dimples appear, reminding me why I never say no to her. She's awesome. I chose well back in sixth grade. My best friend then, my best friend now.

"Dork." She punches my arm.

I hold her arm gently. "Soph, are you okay?"

She shrugs. "I think so—that is, until Seth starts calling and leaving incoherent drunken messages."

"He had to know it was coming. You guys were separated."

She eyes me. "You give him way too much credit. He expected me to come to my senses. Like all the other times."

We stare at each other for a few moments. "You did the right thing. You know that, don't you?"

She studies me. "I've never quit before. Ever." The last word catches in her throat.

I fold her into my chest. "You did not quit. You *tried*. For much longer than you should have."

Her taught body softens.

"Now what?" I ask.

"Learn how to breathe again. Care for myself. Begin to choose me first."

I kiss the top of her head. "Welcome to the singles club," I whisper.

She pulls back. "You broke up with Natalie?"

I shake my head. "No, but you know what I mean."

"You're still with her, but you already assume it'll be over soon..." She steps away, shaking her head.

I shrug. "It just doesn't feel right."

"It's this cavalier attitude of yours about relationships that'll leave you alone and unloved." She walks toward her tennis bag.

I decide not to remind her where her idealistic notions of love have left her. "You love me," I say. "Who else do I need?"

"Yes, I love both you and my pit bull," she says as she draws her blood-red racquet out of the bag and executes practice swings with ferocity, generating a thunderous roar as it slices through the air. "But in my dog's case"—she eyes me—"I had him fixed."

My leg muscles spasm and my hand instinctively reaches down to protect my vitals. "You're sick... And dangerous."

She glances at me with her divine smile. "And you're still the same snot-nosed twelve-year-old I met in sixth grade. C'mon, let's play."

THREE

— PETE —

"STOP POUTING, PETROS. You're going to love your new school," Mom said.

How could she use 'love' and 'school' in the same sentence? How could she even think I'd like this place? We left my friends and home in Chicago for Hollywood. All my buddies thought it was so cool and that I was lucky. I may have only been twelve, but I knew better.

"Will you at least give it a chance?" she asked.

Did I have a choice? "Whatever," I said.

We strolled through the streets of the Hancock Park neighborhood to my new school. With each step, my chest tightened. I had no one here. Not a friend, not a cousin, nothing. No one to walk up to and nod, "'Sup?" or ask, "Can you believe summer's over?"

I'd seen enough movies to know that L.A. kids weren't the friendliest bunch. My life had transformed into a cliché Disney movie. All that was missing was for Mom and Dad to start singing. In my case, they'd break into a Greek dance.

"Look at the campus, Petros. Isn't it impressive?" she said, pointing to the two-story building. "That's the high school," she said. "Only a few more years. No need to change schools, find new friends, or—"

"Okay, Mom. I got it. And I told you, call me Pete."

She glanced at me. "Am I embarrassing you?"

"Yes."

She laughed. "Always the comedian. Your classmates are going to love you."

"Mom, seriously. I got this. You don't have to come with me."

"Don't you want me to help you find your first class and locker?"

My eyes must have gone wild because she laughed again.

"Okay, I'll hang out here until you're inside."

"Fine, fine," I said and picked up my pace. I shoved my trembling hands inside my pockets and hoped for the best. Be cool, that's all I had to do. I was from Chicago, after all. We defined cool.

"Petros," Mom called. I spun to her. "Aren't you going to give me a kiss?"

I pivoted and ran.

DURING LUNCH, I studied the various cliques that seemed to have devised unique touches to stand out despite their school uniforms. The athletes moved with a swagger, showing off their loud, colorful (and expensive) sneakers. The rockers' shirts were untucked, their Vans sneakers clean, and their longish hair movie perfect. The fashionistas wore scarves wrapped in intricate patterns and their uniforms seemed to fit them perfectly.

I glanced at my outfit. I was a wallflower. Or maybe a wallweed.

I didn't belong to any one of those groups. Mom had dressed me like a geek.

"Everyone will dress the same," she had promised. Wrong again.

"You wanna play ball?" I heard someone say. I turned. The kid from the athletic bunch was talking to me. He was tall with brown hair and blond streaks.

Why would he ask me? Maybe fooled by my height? It didn't matter. This was great, or possibly terrible. I didn't know the first thing about basketball, but I wanted to fit in.

"Sure," I said and joined the group of five other guys.

A girl was already on the court taking shots—and making all of them. Her thick, reddish hair was bound into a ponytail. She spun, leapt, and took another shot. That went in, too. Man, she was good.

"Get off the court, Sophie," a short guy from our group said.

She glanced at him then took another shot from further away. The ball went directly through the hoop and the net produced a snapping sound.

"Make me," she said.

"Nice shot," said the kid who had invited me to play. Then he gave Sophie a high five.

"Thanks, Robby." Her tanned face turned a bit red.

"Get off," the short guy repeated.

"Seth, why don't you admit that you're scared of being schooled by a girl," she said.

Involuntarily, I laughed. She glanced at me and grinned.

Seth eyed me then spun back to Sophie. "I'm not scared of you," he said, nearly in a whine.

"Good. You and me. One on one, after you guys play."

A chorus of *oohs* and *ahhs* followed as she sauntered off the court, dribbling the ball between her legs. She leaned against the chain link fence and watched us.

He spun away from her and yelled, "Three on three."

I nodded, clueless as to what that even meant.

With the start of the game came a lot of talking. I tried to follow the clipped conversations, to understand how best to win. How difficult could it be to play basketball? For all I knew, I was a natural. I was coordinated after all—always a good dancer. If I showed skills then I would earn some desperately needed street cred. Heart always trumps talent, my dad would say.

Unfortunately, from the instant I touched the ball, it became obvious I was talentless and heartless.

"Dude, don't try to dribble. Just pass the ball," Seth demanded. I wanted to please, so I did as instructed, but every pass was immediately stolen.

"Damn it, dude. You suck!" he yelled.

My focus shifted from winning to stopping the bleeding. The seconds dragged, Chinese-water-torture-style. I wanted it to end, wondering why the cursed bell wasn't ringing. Kids were yelling at me, telling me to do more of one thing, less of another. I looked over at Sophie. She had one eye shut, teeth clenched—an expression of pain. Now I was sweating. And worrying. And hoping for it all to end.

Wasn't lunch almost over?

I spun around, searching for a clock when something slammed into my face. The cold, stinging impact shook my skull. I stumbled, unsure what had happened. Then it registered. The basketball had hit me directly in the nose.

I began to black out. Sounds were disconnected and nonsensical until laughter cut through the clouds. The piercing sound came from a blurry Seth, laughing and pointing at me. He must've thrown the ball at my face on purpose. Then something warm slid over my lips.

Blood? I raised my hands to my nose then froze. Drooling down my face was a concoction of tears, saliva, a hint of blood, and snot. A lot of snot.

"Look!" Seth pointed, laughing uncontrollably. "His boogers are all over the place."

I covered my face.

Not on my first day. Not like this.

"You're such an ass, Seth," Sophie yelled and took a step toward him.

"Not cool," the blond-streaked kid, Robby, said.

Through my fingers, I gaped at Seth, plotting how one day I would kill that little bastard. That's when a blond goddess panned into view.

"What's the matter with you?" she asked Seth.

"Claire, mind your own business," he said.

She got in his face and said something.

"Screw off!" Seth said then shoved her.

She closed the gap with one wide step and kicked him in the shin, so hard that he doubled over, both hands clasping his shin, hopping around like the idiot he was.

She stepped up to me, her friends in tow. I pressed my hands into my face, watching her through my makeshift mask.

"Are you okay?" she asked. Angelic green eyes were trained on mine. And even though my nose was congested, the scent of vanilla enveloped me.

I nodded, afraid to speak.

She turned to a guy who was with her friends. "Erik, can you take him to the bathroom?"

"Sure," he said, tugging me toward one of the buildings. "That idiot is Seth by the way. He gives apes a bad name. Just don't feed the animals at the zoo and you'll be fine."

I glanced at Claire over my shoulder.

"Her name's Claire," Erik said, "also known as the Shin Kicker. Don't get on her bad side. She can be vengeful. But she can also be awesome."

Claire. A beautiful name. A beautiful face. Maybe California wasn't so bad after all.

"YOU OKAY, DUDE?" Sophie asked when I stepped out of the bathroom. She'd been waiting for me.

"Um, yeah. I'm okay."

I remained silent, unsure what else to say. I didn't hang out with girls much, so I studied my shoes instead.

"So, you're new here," she said.

"Yeah. We just moved here."

"Where from? The Valley?"

I glanced up. I didn't know what that meant. "I'm from Chicago."

Her eyes lit up. "Cool, did you ever meet Jordan?"

Jordan? "Oh, you mean flight Jordan?" I asked, happy that I recognized who she was talking about.

Her jaw slackened. "You mean *Air Jordan?*"

Crap. "Right. That's what I said."

She continued to stare, then grinned. "You don't know the first thing about basketball, do you?"

I shrugged. "I know the ball hurts if it hits your face."

She laughed. "You're funny."

I gave her a half smile and she produced the deepest dimples I had ever seen. We walked toward the lockers. Claire was there with her friends, laughing about something. With each movement of her head, the sun reflected off her hair. Almost like she glowed.

Erik caught my eye then nodded. I nodded back.

"Her name is Claire."

I turned to Sophie. "Oh. Yeah. Whatever."

"She's very pretty. And popular."

Yes, very pretty.

"The boy that helped you is Erik. He's nice."

Robby walked up to us. "Sorry, buddy. Seth can be a prick sometimes."

"Yeah, it's cool."

"See you around." He smiled at Sophie then walked away.

My focus turned to Claire, who had been watching Robby the whole time.

"He's Robby. He's also very nice."

"I think Claire likes him," I said, then turned to Sophie who was also tracking him.

"Yeah, probably," she said absently. From the look in her puppy eyes, it seemed Robby was the one all the girls liked.

I would have asked if she liked him, but it was just weird to talk about that stuff with a girl. Truth be told, I didn't need to ask. I finally understood a line my older sister, who had just started law school liked to say: some things are self-evident.

FOUR

— PETE —

Ninth Grade

WHILE MOST OF the kids hated social studies, I was awake and focused. Not on the classwork, or on the lecture delivered by the oldest living fossil, but on Claire, who sat in the row next to me just one seat ahead.

I waited patiently.

Any minute now.

Just then, she glanced over her shoulder. We made eye contact. She smiled then turned back.

Boom!

Something was definitely up. Over the last two weeks these glances and smiles had become common.

I tapped Raj's shoulder. "Dude," I whispered.

He shooed me away. Typical don't-disturb-me-in-class Raj. He and I were like blood brothers when it came to comic books, but when it came to matters of the heart, Raj was a satellite without an orbit. Completely useless.

I glanced at Frank instead. A small nod. He nodded back, then grinned. Oh yeah, he had seen the exchange with Claire. Evidence. I finally had a witness. If I was going to have a witness, Frank would be the ideal choice. Mister surfer dude who was always quick to point out all the girls who were in love with him. He was also the one who doubted Claire would find me remotely interesting.

"You're an artist. She likes athletes... like me."

How would he talk his way out of this one?

Up to now, none of them believed she was seeking me out. Not Raj, not Frank, not even Sophie who was always willing to put up with all my wishful dreams about Claire. I may have been dead wrong, but those looks had to mean something. Unfortunately, she also seemed to give Robby the same amount of attention.

But I wasn't about to let facts get in the way of my aspirations.

"Okay, time for an in-class project," the teacher said. We all moaned. "Here are the teams..."

I turned to Raj, certain that we'd be paired up again. Raj and I worked great together. He did all the work and I drew full-color diagrams. A perfect team. At least I thought so.

The teacher started calling out the teams.

"Claire and Pete," he said, "work together."

What?

I snapped toward Claire. She was already looking at me, one brow raised. "Bring your stuff here," she said.

"Plot twist," Frank coughed.

Raj and Sophie snorted and giggled. With best friends like them...

Erik, who always paired up with her, seemed bummed. He eyed me, I shrugged, then he winked at me. Always a good guy.

"Come on," Claire said.

Here we go, I thought. Just as I slid my desk next to hers, it snagged on the floor and tilted, nearly toppling me and the table over. I quickly recovered and prayed she hadn't seen the near disaster. I eased into my seat and moderated my breathing. The air around her was cool, like an orchard.

"You want?" She offered me some Altoids. Did my breath stink? I took one, almost spilling the contents of the tin can in the process.

Claire didn't waste time. She shared her ideas on how to tackle the project. As she spoke, I remained mesmerized, tracking her lips, studying her long fingers, inhaling her scent, and memorizing her handwriting.

The teacher came by and scanned our work. "Good, good," he said, and moved on to the next group.

Claire rested her hand on my arm. "Are you thinking of going to the dance thing?" she asked.

I ignored her searing touch and found the will to speak. "What dance thing?"

"The Winter Formal."

My throat tightened as I tried to find the right words. I picked the ones that I thought she wanted to hear. "I dunno," I said, because that was being cool—aloof. She wore Nirvana t-shirts on free dress days, so I had to be cool like her. And cool guys didn't go to dances, even though I loved to dance. This had to be a test. I prayed the words that were dribbling out of my mouth were the right ones. "Seems lame, don't you think?"

She nodded. "Yeah, exactly. I don't know why everyone's making such a big stink of it."

I had done well. I had passed her coolness test.

A FEW HOURS LATER, I was positive I had miserably failed her test.

"Why are you so quiet?" Sophie asked.

We were on the swings in my backyard. Her parents had come over for dinner and shortly after finishing, we were asked to go to the yard so they could discuss adult things.

"Oh, I don't know," I said.

"Let me take a wild guess: Claire. Again."

I nodded. I had thought long and hard about the meaning of Claire's question earlier during social studies. Had I misread her? Had she been opening the door, waiting for me to ask?

"You're a girl—" I started.

"Thanks for noticing."

"What I mean is, you probably understand girl stuff."

"The hole you're digging is getting deeper. You better spit out whatever it is you're fumbling through before I smack you."

"I think Claire may like me, but I don't know for sure, so I don't know what to do," I said.

"You need to be a bit more aggressive," Sophie said.

"What do you mean? Like grab her?"

"No dweeb, ask her if she wants to go to the mall, the movies, or something."

I frowned. That was not my style.

Sophie's eyes widened. "Oh, I know! The Winter Formal. Ask her to go with you."

"Ugh." I dropped my head.

"What?"

I told her. Sophie's reaction was immediate. "You asswipe! You better ask her first thing tomorrow."

"It's not that easy."

"It *is* that easy. She wouldn't have brought it up if she wasn't interested. Don't wait too long. Someone else will ask her."

"You think?"

"I know." She leaned in. "Don't create an opening for Robby. I want him to ask me, not her."

"He'd be stupid not to. You two are like the sporto twins."

She dropped her hand on my shoulder. "I've learned guys are generally stupid."

"You mean the other guys," I said. "Right?"

She smirked. "I mean guys."

ON THE FOLLOWING Monday I was ready. A weekend of planning had been just what I needed. I would ask Claire during sixth period.

She had not been making eye contact all day, but I didn't think that meant anything. She may have been upset at my lack of aggressiveness. I was going to change that up by end of day.

During lunch, Sophie dropped in the seat in front of me, hands covering her face.

"What's with you?" I asked

She glanced up, peering into my eyes. "Didn't you hear?"

"Hear what?"

She leaned forward. "Robby asked Claire to the dance last Friday."

A beat. "And?"

"She said yes."

I couldn't move for a few moments. "Your guy asked my girl?"

"Because *you* didn't ask her. You messed up for both of us. Thanks for nothing."

"I am such an idiot," I mumbled.

"Yes, you are. And for that, you and I will have to go together."

I eyed her. "Together? As in you and me?"

"Yes, and you better know how to dance. There's no way I'm staying home. We have to keep our eyes on those two before a date turns into a relationship."

———

I LEANED AGAINST THE WALL, on the lookout for Claire and Robby. I studied those brave few who had already started to dance. Pitiful. I was itching to get on the dance floor, to show them all my moves. But Sophie had not shown up yet.

The gym had been converted into a night club. The only light came from the strategically placed swirling lights and the DJ's automated lighting rack. Tables surrounded the large dance floor. Drinks and finger foods were monitored by the principal, teachers, and parent volunteers.

"I think she's looking at me," Frank said.

"Who?" I asked.

"Three o'clock," he said.

Raj and I spun in that direction.

"Don't make it so damn obvious," Frank said through gritted teeth.

"Tina?" Raj asked. "I can't see it. You're not her type."

"What's that supposed to mean?" Frank asked.

"She's an excellent student," Raj explained in his polite but aristocratic British-Indian accent.

Frank's face soured. "Why? Because I'm not?"

"Precisely," Raj said.

I laughed just as Sophie showed up. "Hey guys."

She looked really nice. Her unfortunate red mane had been straightened, reaching down below her shoulder blades. And the strapless top showed off her perpetually tanned shoulders.

"You look hot," Frank said.

"Dude!" both Raj and I said at the same time.

"Well it's nice of you to notice," she said.

"Yeah, you clean up real well," Frank said.

We sighed, then Raj and I slapped the back of his head.

Sophie grinned. "You guys are such baboons."

"Hi Raj," someone said.

We turned to the voice. Tina.

Raj froze, swallowed then blinked. "Hi," he croaked.

"You want to dance?" Tina asked him.

I could feel Frank's shock and disappointment.

Raj's brows shot up. His mouth moved, but words did not come out. The moments ticked by.

"Let's all go," Sophie said, coming to his rescue, then turned to one of her teammates from the basketball team, "Diana, come with us."

As a group we hit the small dance floor and took over. Some of us had the moves. Others—Raj—just bounced.

Sophie leaned into my ear. "Are they here yet?" she asked. Wow. She smelled so nice.

"No, not yet."

But as soon as I spoke those words, they came in, both looking like models from an overpriced magazine. I tracked their every move as they spoke to random friends. Eventually, they got on the dance floor.

Claire was a good dancer, but he sucked. He could barely keep the beat. This was my chance to make her feel jealous and stupid for going with Robby the jockstrap.

"Come on," I said to Sophie. I grabbed her hand and moved us closer to Cinderella and the toad. I just hoped Sophie could keep up with my awesomeness.

At that moment a Shakira song came on. When Sophie started, the room shifted to her. I found myself in a momentary trance. She moved her hips in ways I could barely describe. Her chest throbbed with the beat, her arms overhead. Her hair flowed with each movement. She moved like nobody's business.

I came to and tried my best to keep up. I was good. She was outstanding. This turned out better than I had hoped. Everyone was watching us—including Claire and Robby. And when the song turned to *Jump, Jive an' Wail* by the Brian Setzer Orchestra, she grabbed my hands and pulled my ear in.

"Can you swing?"

"No," I said.

"Okay good. Follow my lead."

We were spectacular. Okay, she was awesome, me by association. People made a circle around us, clapping and cheering. Even Claire and Robby joined the chorus.

After that, it became a team dance party. We danced forever, switching partners. We even made a move-your-groove-thing circle where many got a chance to jump in and show their best moves. That's when Erik joined us. Erik, arguably the best dancer among the guys, was epic. He danced with Sophie and Claire and half the girls in class. I made a mental note to get better at dancing. Girls apparently liked boys who knew how to dance. The rest of the guys, like Seth, were less impressed by Erik.

At eleven o'clock, Sophie and I were outside celebrating our victorious night while we waited for my brother, who was picking us up.

"Did you see how Robby was checking you out?" I asked.

She shrugged. "Claire was taken by your moves, too."

"Yeah, I was phenomenal."

"Hey guys," Erick said. "Did we or did we not rock that smelly gymnasium?"

"We danced the stink off that joint," Sophie said.

We gave each other high fives.

Erick squeezed between us and draped his arms across our shoulders. "You do know that everyone will be talking about tonight all weekend, right? We are the rockstars of the school now."

I liked the sound of that.

"There's my ride," he said as a white Range Rover stopped near us.

"Good night, dude," Sophie called out as he jumped into the car. He rolled down the window and flashed the 'hang loose' symbol: thumb and pinky spread wide open.

"He's awesome," Sophie said.

"Not as awesome as yours truly, but yeah, not bad."

My brother pulled up in his black Beamer. We jumped in the back seat.

"Sophie," Marcos said, his voice soft, measured. "We're going to go to your house, so you can grab a change of clothes and whatever else you need. You're sleeping over tonight."

"Why?" we asked in unison.

This was very odd. I'd had the guys sleep over before, but a girl sleeping over was weird. Even if it was Sophie.

Marcos rubbed his chin. "Your dad's in the hospital. Your mom's with him."

The air in the car turned cold. "Why? What happened?" she asked softly.

"I don't have the details. We'll know more tomorrow."

"I want to go to the hospital," she said, almost pleading. "I want to see my dad."

"Sweetie, your mom asked us to take you tomorrow. First thing, I promise. She insisted that you stay with us for tonight."

Sophie nodded. "Okay," she whispered.

I laid my arm across my best friend's back, and pulled her in. She didn't resist. Instead, she melted into me.

FIVE

— PETE —

ELEVENTH GRADE

I WAS ABOUT to throw up. I grabbed Frank's shoulder for support.

"There is an eighty-four percent probability of success," Raj said.

"Stop with the math, already," Frank said.

"She'll make it," Robby said. Claire held his hand with both of hers. "I know she will." Since the start of the playoffs, they had been hanging around our group regularly. And although I no longer obsessed over Claire, having her so close to us was both awesome—because she was great to look at—and dangerous—because sometimes I'd stare at her so long that Robby would pick up on it. But tonight, my focus was on one person: Sophie.

Outside, rain had flooded the streets. Inside, the gym was humid. I couldn't inhale.

But Sophie was calm. Sweat dripped off her chin with each dribble of the ball. Her jersey was soaking wet. Her oversized shorts had been tucked up just above her knees. The pink rubber-band expertly held her hair out of her face.

Thirty-four seconds left on the game clock.

We had a one point lead thanks to her first free-throw. She had one free-throw coming to stretch our lead to two points. The last game of the season. The CIF championship for small schools against the team that beat us by nineteen points the year before. Sophie had promised Coach they would win the championship this year. Maybe, just maybe, we'd have to call her Nostradamus soon.

She spun the ball in her hand, adjusted it so that the cross lines lined up with her fingers. She breathed in, bending her knees while simultaneously raising the sphere to her face. On the exhale, she released the ball with grace and without hesitation. The rotating dark brown ball traveled through a beautiful trajectory to the rim. A familiar snapping of the net followed.

Our crowd leapt in a wild roar.

She didn't react, just ran backward prepared to play defense, yelling out instructions to her teammates. Her number ten jersey glowed. The captain who had scored more than half the points was not ready to celebrate.

The seconds ticked away as the other team dribbled the ball up the court. They didn't have a timeout. Neither did we. I scanned the crowd. My mom and Sophie's mom were holding hands, yelling. My father on the other hand, looked like he was about to throw up, too.

I shifted my focus back to the court. Eighteen seconds left.

The other team's point guard pulled up to let the clock roll down before they started their set play. But when their point guard looked to her coach for instructions, Sophie leapt from five feet away. A Superman dive, arm outstretched, she punched the ball out of the hands of her opponent. The ball bounced into the back court.

Sophie and her counterpart scrambled for the ball.

"Get it!" we all yelled.

But Sophie had a different plan. She didn't have the angle to grab it, so instead she dove again, tapping it to her streaking teammate, Diana. She plucked the ball off the floor. One dribble, two, and she laid the ball off the backboard.

The horn blared.

We all jumped, charging the court.

My eyes never left Sophie. Hammering her chest with one fist, she pointed to the heavens with the other one, in honor of her dad, yelling God knew what.

I wanted to grab her, hug her, celebrate with her.

But Robby got to her first. He, Seth, Frank, and the rest of the boys' basketball team hoisted her up like the hero she was and marched her around the gym.

She and I made eye contact. She hammered her chest again, then pointed to me. Her radiant smile brought out the dimples we hadn't seen since her dad died.

"She's amazing," Claire said.

I turned. "Yes, she is."

"I wonder what I'll have to do to get Robby to hoist me up like that," Claire said.

I glanced at Claire. *Well, that's awkward.* Her eyes were trained on Sophie. Was there a hint of jealousy on her face?

"Hey guys, I'm going home," Erik said. "Pete, tell Soph that she will forever be Wonder Woman in my book." We pounded fists.

Claire turned to him. "Why? I'm sure everyone's going to go to the diner to celebrate."

Erik shook his head. "Yeah, love you guys and elated for Sophie and all, but hanging out with Seth and those goons isn't what I call a win."

I knew what he meant. Seth was too much to bear. And although Seth and I were not enemies per se, I knew that he'd been making fun of Erik when Claire wasn't around. His jealousy of Erik's innate ability to get surrounded by girls on demand was probably too much for Seth's little mind to handle. I liked Erik and although he wasn't part of our inner circle, he was always welcome. He was just one of those guys that could glide in and out without hesitation. Lately, he'd been spending more and more time with our group, which by definition meant that Claire was spending more time with us.

"Dude, come with me," I said. "I've only got Raj in the car."

He seemed to consider the offer. "Is Raj going to talk about astrophysics or something?"

We grinned at each other.

"Pete!"

We all turned. Sophie ran toward us. She leapt into my arms, wrapping her legs around my hips. Her body was tight into mine. She was a sweaty mess; perfect as always.

"We did it!" she yelled.

"You were awesome, Soph!"

She released the hold, dropped her legs to the floor then pulled my face to hers, planting a quick wet kiss on my lips. "That's for my biggest fan," she said, her smile brightening her eyes.

She spun around and galloped into a half-run march, yelling and punching the air as she reunited with her teammates. I remained planted, heart pounding in my ears, eliminating all noises.

"Well," Claire said. "I did not see that one coming."

Neither did I.

"Now I'm *definitely* coming with you," Erik said. "What the hell was that about?"

I wish I knew.

"Let's hope Seth didn't see that," Claire continued.

I glanced at her, unclear as to what she meant.

She grinned. "You haven't picked up on that? I think he likes her."

"She's far too smart to fall for that idiot," Erik said.

Seth? Was Claire sniffing glue? Erik was right. Even with his good looks, no one with half a brain would go out with him.

SIX

— PETE —

TWELFTH GRADE - BEFORE THE BIRTHDAY

ON THE MONDAY before Sophie's eighteenth birthday party, Claire and Robby broke up after being together for nearly three years. The machine that was the senior class rumor-mill delivered us the news. We all had our theories as to why, but no one seemed to know for sure. Whatever the reason, it was clear that Robby had not been expecting it, nor was he handling it well.

"Any credible rumors?" I asked Sophie as we walked back to campus from our favorite coffee joint.

"Not really," she said then grimaced. "Some idiot said it's because Claire got jealous of how much time Robby and I were spending together."

"No way. That's ridiculous."

She eyed me then punched my shoulder. "Thanks for the vote of confidence, *best friend*! Am I so improbable?"

I shrugged. "You know what I mean."

"No, in fact I don't."

Now I'd done it. Time to shift the focus. "You should ask Erik. He'll know."

"You ask him," she snapped.

"I sort of did, but I think he thought I was asking for selfish reasons."

"Yes, we all think you're selfish and transparent when it comes to Claire."

"Whatever."

She took a sip of her iced coffee. "If I feel like it I may ask him."

We entered campus. "Robby probably messed around with someone—typical for his type—even though he has the hottest girl in class."

She stared at me in disgust. "Don't be one of those birdbrains. He's not like that, and there's no evidence, so don't spread new rumors."

"Touchy much?"

When we reached the student lot, we saw Claire and Erik leaning against his neon blue Lexus IS, in a heated, emotionally charged conversation.

"Erik looks pissed," Sophie said. "I can't remember ever seeing him upset."

"What's that about?" I asked. "Do you think it has anything to do with the breakup?"

"God knows. But for Erik to be upset like that...it must be serious."

Not wanting to look like stalkers, we quietly slid into my car. I wasn't sure what was going on, but the last thing I wanted was to get wrapped up in other people's drama.

ON FRIDAY, the day before Sophie's birthday party, just as I walked toward my car in the student lot, someone tugged on my elbow. It was Claire.

"Hey, Claire, what's up?" I asked.

She shrugged, then gave a half smile. "Don't tell me you're the only one that hasn't heard."

No point in pretending or acting dumb. "I've heard," I said.

"Then you know how I'm doing," she said. She looked tired. The circles under her eyes were more pronounced from this close. "What are you up to? Any big plans this weekend?" She bit her lip and her feet were bouncing.

"Yeah, it's Sophie's birthday party."

"Oh that's right," she said, but I didn't buy her acting. She must have known.

"You're coming, right?" I asked.

She shook her head. "Doubt it. Not in a partying mood." Without warning she caressed my arm, as if straightening out my sweater. Her touch shot heat up my arm to my cheeks. "Do you want me to come?" She froze, her aqua-green eyes on mine.

She was absolutely, without any ambiguity, flirting with me. I hesitated, trying to find the words I wanted to say. Something cool and charming. "Hell yeah," is what came out.

She grinned then took a step back. "It's nice to be wanted. Well, have a good time without me." She hesitated and an eyebrow shot up. "On second thought, don't have a good time. Save that for me."

"Yeah. Okay. I'll try my best to not have a good time."

She winked, turned, and walked toward her car.

I wanted to dwell on that conversation and her scorching touch on my arm. I wanted to chase her down, take her out for coffee or something. But I had urgent matters on my hands: Sophie's birthday party preparations and a gift that wasn't ready yet.

SOPHIE and I surveyed the makeshift nightclub, the den we had transformed. All the furniture was in the garage. The perimeter of the large area was now filled with white folding chairs. The wet bar was empty, courtesy of my dad, even though my brother had promised a case of beer would be hidden in the shed for us. Through the speakers we blasted the mix we'd prepared the night before.

Sweat trickled down my back. I glanced at Sophie. She hadn't stopped grinning with approval since returning with her mom from the market.

"Pete," she said, "I'm not sure how to thank you. This is perfect."

"You can start by giving me that water bottle you were about to hand over," I said.

She glanced at her hand. "Oh, sorry." She tossed it, not bothering to see if she would hit the mark. She always did. She turned to me. "Why are you still here? Go home and shower, because you need one badly, and be here at seven. Don't be late. I want you here before the others arrive."

"I'll be here. But seven will be tight. I need to get ready."

She studied the wall-mounted clock. "It's not even noon yet. How much time do you need?"

"You can't rush good looks."

"I told you to stop sunbathing so much. Now you've gone stupid." She grabbed my sweaty shoulders and gave me a hug.

I pulled back. "I'm sweaty and stinky," I said.

"Hello Sweaty and Stinky. Go home and get ready. I need you here. On time."

I SPED TO RODEO DRIVE. The boutique had promised that Sophie's gift would be there by 1:00 p.m. They had been promising the same thing for weeks now.

When I stepped in, the sales lady brightened.

"It's here. I told you we'd come through for you."

I didn't bother to point out that she'd been dropping the ball for weeks.

"It's a beauty," she said as she opened the case.

33

I compared it to the picture I had. From the picture to the real thing, I scanned back and forth. I must have grinned like a kid because they had nailed it. That was the right item. The picture fell from my hand as I reached for the ornate leather wraparound wristband. The same one Shakira, Sophie's favorite singer, wore.

"You have great taste, Mr. Nicos."

I thought so too. But the only opinion that mattered in this case was Sophie's.

SEVEN

— PETE —

TWELFTH GRADE - THE BIRTHDAY

I ARRIVED TO Sophie's birthday at ten past seven. I opened the door and let myself in.

"It's me," I called out as I made my way to the den.

Sophie stepped out of the den at that same instant, smile brightening her face. "I'm so glad you came early," she said. "Look at you. You almost look presentable."

I would have responded, but all my words stopped mid-thought. She looked stunning. A brown one-piece velvet sheath dress hugged her body. The high heels made her just a couple of inches shorter than me. Her makeup must have been applied by one of the studios, because she looked smooth, like a porcelain doll. And her hair, what used to be her albatross in sixth grade, was now a beautiful mane of red.

"Holy shit, Soph. You look like someone out of a goddamn magazine."

Her eyes widened, then she blushed and raised her hands to her sides like a princess. "This old thing?"

I held out her gift. "Open it," I said. "Before the others get here."

She took the box from me and sat on a chair. She tore it open but paused when she saw the red felt container. She glanced up at me then lifted the lid.

Her eyes widened and her lips parted.

"Oh, Pete," she breathed. "It's gorgeous."

I sat next to her. "It's the one that—"

"Shakira's," she said. "I can't believe you got this for me." She lifted her eyes to mine.

"Anything for you," I said.

She embraced me, buried her face in my neck. I hugged back and breathed her in. My fingers tightened around her exposed shoulders. Tight, satin-like skin. My breathing became more shallow.

The doorbell rang.

We pulled away. She held my gaze. "This is the best gift ever."

"You better get the door."

She rose, closed the box and placed it inside a drawer.

"You'll need to save me a dance, okay?" I asked.

She grinned. "All night if you want," she said.

As our classmates arrived, it became evident that I was not the only one who was taken by her transformation. The girls hovered around her while the guys lingered in silence and stared at her like she was an alien life form.

She couldn't wipe the twinkle off her face that night. Not even a meteor shower would have out-shown her. She had blossomed into a beauty and was finally getting noticed.

The place got packed fast. Frank was there with some new girl and Raj was talking it up with the guys. By eight o'clock I went to the back yard, confirmed no one was there, then slipped into the shed. I grabbed a beer from the icebox, poured the liquid gold in my plastic cup, then slid out.

I took a long swallow and wondered if Robby would come. But based on the condition he was in, I guessed he probably wasn't in much of a party mood.

I would have to follow up with Claire on Monday. What I saw in our interaction after school told me that with Robby out of the picture, I was suddenly a person of interest. The question of "Why?" rose in my mind, but I quickly pushed it away.

I was about to take another sip of beer when I saw her. Claire and two of her friends walked in from the side gate. She wore a skirt, showing plenty of thigh, and a button-down top. She was dressed the part of a party animal, but her face betrayed no emotions. Her eyes searched, probably scanning for Robby, while her friends walked in with a bounce.

She came. Why? For me?

Maybe it was the trace levels of alcohol in my bloodstream or memories of the conversation we had at school. Whatever it was, I intercepted her before she and her friends went inside.

"Claire," I called out. All three of them turned to me. When Claire registered me, her mouth parted into a smile, then she turned to her friends. "Go on. I'll come in a bit."

They studied her. "Are you sure?"

"Yeah. I'm good with Pete."

I nearly grinned. I loved the sound of that.

She walked up to me. "Anyone else out here?"

"Just us."

She pointed to a spot further back in the yard. I followed her into the shadowy edges.

She glanced over her shoulder then slowed down. "Surprised to see me here?"

"Glad to see you here," I said.

"Me too," she said with a smile.

She sat on the cement bench and tapped the space next to her. "Please tell me Robby's not here," she said.

"No, I haven't seen him," I said as I sat. *Is that why she came?*

She breathed out. "Good."

Ouch. This wasn't a temporary break. She sounded relieved.

"What are you drinking?" she asked as she took the cup out of my hand. She studied it, eyed me, then took a sniff. "Beer? I thought you were all proper."

"Only on Wednesdays."

She took a big swallow before handing the cup back to me.

"Glad you changed your mind about coming," I said, then drank some.

"Me too." She took the cup and took another hit. "Is there more?" she asked.

"I'll get us two."

As I went toward the shed, she followed. I glanced over my shoulder, confirmed we were still alone, then snuck in, Claire right behind me. Light from the yard illuminated portions of the shed. I opened the cooler then took out two beers. I popped them open, ready to pour them into the cup when she took the can out of my hand.

"Let's drink it here." She raised the can to her mouth and took a long drag. I followed suit.

We clinked cans then drank some more.

"I hate beer," she said.

"Me too."

We both laughed then drank the rest quickly.

"Is it the bad taste that has me all tingly, or the alcohol?" she asked, then started laughing. She leaned into my chest, her lips only inches away from mine.

"I'm not sure," I stammered.

Her hand glided through my hair then rested on my neck. She rose on her toes, her eyes closed and her lips moved toward mine. Her mouth touched mine, spreading heat through my chest, back, and legs. Just as I was about to grab her waist and kiss back she slid away and stepped out of the shed.

I followed her, feeling a bit unbalanced. My heartbeat slammed my chest and my breathing shallowed. I wanted us to go back to the shed and continue what she started.

"What a beautiful night," she said.

Truth was that it was a cold night, which is why no one else was outside. But the alcohol and her lips had warmed me up completely.

She threw her head back, eyes closed, and took a deep breath. When she exhaled she opened her eyes. "Oh wow. It's a full moon tonight," she said.

"Is it?" My senses were a little dull. "I hear a full moon can make people a bit insane," I said.

"Come on, let's drive to a spot I know and stare at the moon. Maybe it'll make us go insane too."

I froze. "I can't," I said. "Sophie will be upset if I leave." What I didn't tell was that I was a bit tipsy and I had promised my brother that I wouldn't drive until at least two hours after drinking a beer.

She frowned. "Just for ten minutes? Please."

It turned out that with her, I had no will. That was the first time I broke a promise.

"WHERE TO?" I asked when she buckled in. "But not far because that foul tasting cheep ass beer my brother bought gave me a buzz."

She tucked the four beer cans under her seat then reached over and caressed my face. My skin must have been on fire, because sweat broke out at the nape of my neck.

She grinned. "Just drive."

So we drove, listening to a Maroon 5 CD. Although my eyelids felt heavy from the alcohol, that didn't stop me from stealing glances at her thighs and the skirt that continued to ride up with each turn.

We hadn't driven for more than a few minutes when she asked me to park on a poorly lit street where the view of the moon was unobstructed.

"Roll down your sun roof and we'll be able to see it perfectly."

She was right. The moon was beautiful. It seemed larger somehow, or maybe it was because I was actually studying it for the first time.

"C'mon," she said as she grabbed the beers then climbed to the back seat. I tracked her movement and her long creamy legs as she slid into the seats.

"She Will Be Loved" had just started playing.

"What are you waiting for?" she asked.

I unbuckled and did my best to get my large frame into the back without crushing her in the process.

I plopped down and was handed a can of beer. I snapped it open, we bumped cans and drained them.

"Horrible!" she said, then grabbed the last two and gave me one. I studied her long neck as she polished off another can of beer. I emptied mine too. I shook briefly from the horrid taste. Why was she in such a rush to get drunk? Now we were out of drinks and feeling the downward spiral of cheap alcohol.

With that, I sank into the seat and she leaned into me, resting her head on my chest. Her scent was all over me and I felt my heartbeat in my throat. The music blurred into the background. When I lay my arm around her shoulder, she squeezed into me, nudging me to lay sideways.

Her hair was inches from my face. I breathed her in and my heart rate picked up. I could feel my ears burning and my eyes blurring. Her head still on my chest, she glanced up into my eyes. She didn't utter a word, but spoke volumes directly into my heart.

She inched up and seared my lips with hers. Her tongue discovered mine and just when I brought her face closer, her hand landed on my thigh. My chest tightened. Her hand traveled up. My breathing shallow, I grabbed the back of her thigh and slid my hand up just below her butt.

She pulled away, grabbed my hips and yanked me toward her so that I could be flat across the back seats. As she rolled onto my lap, her mouth slammed against mine.

Her lips devoured my lips, her tongue forced its way in. We kissed, bit, and nipped, experiencing each other for the first time. She yanked my sweatshirt over my head and I unbuttoned her top. Her mouth found my ear then traveled down to my neck. With both hands, I slid her skirt up just as her hands slid to my waistline. Without hesitation, she unbuttoned my pants and her fingers glided in. Warmth traveled from my hips to my knees. My ab muscles spasmed.

This was really happening.

"Condom?" she breathed.

I froze. "No," I gasped. "I don't have anything."

She stared at me from inches above. Her hair hung loosely around her face. Even in the shadowy car, I could see her green eyes. She smiled. "I don't care," she whispered.

I didn't argue.

I didn't stop her.

She was my first.

The one I loved.

On that night, we became one.

JUST OVER AN HOUR LATER, we were back at Sophie's party. I shut off the engine then turned to Claire. She was staring at me, blinking rapidly, frowning.

"What's wrong?" I asked.

Her forehead relaxed. "Nothing. Nothing I guess."

But she didn't sound like nothing was wrong. Her eyes bounced around as she fumbled with her purse. "I better go first."

"We can't go together?" I asked.

"No. I don't know." She didn't make eye contact. Instead she squeezed her temples. "I need to think," she said then opened the door but didn't step out. After a momentary hesitation she glanced at me. "I enjoyed that," she whispered. "A lot."

"Me too."

She smiled then stepped out of the car. I watched her speed walk

ARA GRIGORIAN

toward Sophie's house. I gave her three minutes then headed for the party.

I could feel the emptiness already. I didn't want to leave her. I wanted to stay with her in my car forever. I wanted to go to her place or somewhere else. I wanted more of her.

My body was electrified and my thigh muscles were spent. But somehow I found the energy to sneak into the house, hoping Sophie had not seen me leaving with Claire. The music was loud and the bass thrummed through my body. This was supposed to be Sophie's big day, but instead, it had turned into mine.

I could still smell Claire on me. I scanned the crowd, looking for her. Were we a couple now? I slumped against the wall and thought about the implications. I was finally with Claire. After all these years, it had finally happened. But now what?

Sophie appeared in front of me. "What's wrong, Eeyore?" she asked, almost yelling over the music.

She wasn't mad. She didn't know that I had ditched her.

"I... umm," I started.

"Have you been drinking?" She glared at me. "I can smell it on you."

"Yeah. I had a couple." A perfect excuse.

Her face shifted from anger to frustration. "Sober up. You're supposed to help me celebrate my birthday. I need you here with me. You owe me a dance, remember?"

I grinned. "I do."

"Wait here," she said, then ran away. Seconds later she was back with the wristband in hand. "Can you clasp it for me?"

I wrapped it three times around her strong arm then clasped it.

She shook her wrist, causing the layers to come together. "Perfect," she said. "I'm going to wear this forever. A timeless reminder of what you did for me on my birthday." She kissed my cheek, hugged me hard, then stepped back.

I couldn't make eye contact with her because what I had done for her birthday was I'd skipped it, driven while drunk, and lost my virginity in the backseat of my car to the hottest girl in school. How could I ever tell her the truth?

"I better get back," she said. "You're coming, right?"

"Absolutely."

I stumbled into the kitchen, found a Redbull and drank it empty in seconds flat. A few minutes later, when I entered the dance area, Usher's *U Got it Bad* was playing. I listened to the lyrics and agreed with the sentiment. No, nobody wants to be alone. I wanted to be with Claire, badly. Like an addict, I wanted to taste her mouth, be with her again.

Through the sparse crowd of kids, I saw Sophie dancing with someone. I shifted to get a better view. Seth. Of all people, she was dancing with *Seth* and she seemed genuinely happy.

Behind them I saw Claire. She was staring at me directly. Just studying me.

I smiled at her.

At that, her lips instantly parted into a heavenly smile. We did not break eye contact until Erik showed up next to her. His face taught. I hadn't seen him earlier so he must have come when we were out. He said something to her, she nodded and stepped outside with him.

They spoke in the yard out of earshot. But I stole glances, hoping I could decipher what they were discussing. She shook her head and broke eye contact, focused on the ground. He just stared at her for a few moments then brought her into his chest. He held her gently until she looked up at him, said something to which he nodded. They left the party from the side gate. The same way she came in, she left.

EIGHT

— PETE —

ON SUNDAY, THE day after Sophie's party, when I went to her house to help clean up, I couldn't muster the courage to tell her the truth. For the first time ever, I'd lied to her. I did not tell her about what happened with Claire. I didn't talk about the sex, about the recklessness, or about living in the moment and enjoying every minute of it.

I lied to her for a second time that day when Claire texted me and I pretended it was one of the guys. I was lying to her. I didn't like doing that, but the need to be with Claire was strong, overpowering.

"Pick me up tonight at eleven o'clock by the willow tree."

I was by the willow tree at ten.

On Monday at school, everyone could tell something was happening between us. Sophie and the guys questioned me, but all I told them was that things were happening.

Claire texted me again that night and every subsequent night after. We couldn't get enough of each other.

We had been seeing each other for just under a week. As we lay exhausted in the back seat of my car, Claire asked, "Are you going to ask me to prom?"

I hesitated. Of course I wanted to, but weeks earlier, Sophie and I had agreed that we'd go together since both our first choices had been with other people at the time. Even so, I was sure Sophie would understand.

I cupped her face. "Claire, will you go to prom with me?"

She shrugged. "Yeah, I suppose."

I leaned in for a kiss but she stopped me. "But let's not make it public."

I think I understood. She had just broken up with Robby. She probably didn't want people to call her out. But I didn't like it. "How long are we going to hide us?"

She stared at me for a long moment, then said, "Not sure. Just not yet."

THE NEXT AFTERNOON, most of the senior class was going to go to the beach together. Claire and I kept our relationship a secret, but the need to be together made it harder and harder for us to be with our friends while pretending there was nothing going on.

While our classmates figured out who would go with whom, I decided to tell Sophie about the prom situation without giving away what was really happening.

"Soph, I've sort of asked Claire to prom."

Her gaze froze. "And?"

"She said yes."

Her eyes went wide. She quickly scanned the crowd for Claire and found her staring at us. Claire spun away. Sophie eyed me. "Is something happening with you two?"

I delivered my best line. "Not yet, but I hope to change that with my dazzling smile and dance moves when we're there."

She nodded because she believed me and I wanted to bury my

head for not being honest with her. "It was bound to happen." She smiled. "I'm happy for you."

"Are you sure you're okay? We said we'd go together—"

"Don't be silly. Of course it's okay. I'd never stand in the way of your fixation."

She always understood. "What will you do?"

She shifted. "Well, someone asked and I said no, but I guess I can always say yes."

I became hopeful. "Robby?" If he asked Sophie, then that meant he was no longer an obstacle for me.

"No, not Robby. Poor guy's a mess. He didn't even make it to my birthday."

"Then who?"

She lifted her chin slightly. "Seth."

"Are you kidding me?"

She narrowed her eyes. "I didn't say I'm dating him. He asked me to prom. He was fairly decent to me at my birthday, so it may turn out okay."

"Yeah, but Seth?"

"Yes, Seth. If you have such an issue with this then tell Claire you changed your mind and take me instead."

I hesitated.

"That's what I thought."

A large group of friends moved toward us. As everyone discussed which spot at Zuma Beach we'd camp out and who would get sandwiches on the way, I received a text from Claire. I scanned for her and saw her standing with Erik, next to his car.

"I'm going to say I want to take a ride in your car. When we get in, I'll pretend I forgot something. Then you and I will go off for a bit, mess around, then hit the road. Okay?"

"Hell yeah," I replied. Was she finally opening up to the idea of telling people we were a thing? I could only hope.

Everyone was talking over each other when Claire showed up.

"Pete, you mind if I hitch a ride with you? I want to check out your Beamer."

I fixed my eyes on her, forced myself to not turn to Erik or Sophie, who I knew were staring at us. "Sure, no problem," I said.

"Great," she said then turned to Erik. "You don't mind, do you? I'll drive back with you."

He gave her a nod. "Don't mind at all," he said, then glanced at me. He was reading me like well-worn underwear—transparent and obvious.

Just as we were all getting into our cars, Claire looked into her cinch sack and said, "Oh crap, I forgot something," then turned to me. "Can we stop by my house for a minute?"

"Sure," I said, and saw Erik's face.

He stared at us, shook his head, then stepped into his car and took off with the rest of our classmates.

She spun to me. "My house. Fast. No one's home."

THIRTY MINUTES LATER, we were back on the road, heading to the beach. The familiar afterglow was draped across us.

"I wish we didn't have to go to the beach," she said. "I wish we could just hide away from the others."

I stole a glance then focused on the windy road. "Why the secrecy? Why can't we just come out?" I wanted to be able to talk about it freely, tell my friends, come clean with Sophie.

She chewed on her nail. "Maybe after prom," she muttered.

Traffic slowed down on PCH. The traffic jam snaked around forever. "Great, now we're really going to be late," she said.

"Hey, at least we're together," I said just as her phone rang.

While she studied the name of the caller, my phone rang. Sophie.

We answered at the same time.

We heard the chaos at the same time.

Then the words that cut through the hysteria registered.

The world stopped in that instant.

An accident.

Erik.

Dead.

IN THE DAYS leading up to the funeral, rumors littered the hallways of our school. Some questioned if it had really been an accident. Our classmates came up with various imaginative scenarios and plausible conclusions. They said that he had been quiet lately, withdrawn, upset. I had not seen any of that. I'd seen a friend who seemed concerned for another friend. Apparently, Erik's family got wind of these rumors, because the day before the funeral, with permission from Erik's family, the school counselor and a representative from the sheriff's department gave us additional details about the accident. Erik was texting when he lost control of the car.

Erik had become part of a new and increasingly alarming statistic. An epidemic with no real cure.

It was the memory of him staring at us in disappointment that haunted me. For Claire, it was the knowledge that she had altered his destiny. If she had gone with him as planned, he would still be alive.

Then we heard another detail. He had been trying to text Claire. She went into hiding. Stopped answering texts and calls.

Days after the funeral, I returned to the cemetery. I'm not sure why, I just knew I had to go there. Guilt maybe. If not for what we'd decided to do, that urge to be together, Erik would not have texted her. He would still be alive, laughing, joking, dancing.

I knelt in front of his recently covered gravesite. That's where Claire found me.

"Can I join you?" she asked. I had not seen or spoken to her for days. She was pale, her hair a bit messy. She wore tattered sweatpants and held white lilies, baby carnations, and roses.

"Of course," I said.

Like a worshiper in front of an altar, she knelt on the grass next to me then placed the flowers in front of where the tombstone would one day be.

"I miss him," she said. "A lot." Tired tears rolled down her pale face. When she leaned into me, I held her. "I don't know what to do. My best friend is gone." Her body shook.

I tried to calm her, to sooth her, but I was barely able to control my own emotions.

"It's my fault," she said. "If only I—"

I turned her face to mine. "Don't do this. You can't change anything now. None of us can." But I knew she was right. It was our fault and the guilt was too big, the responsibility too onerous for me to take on. So I brought her closer, our lips a breath away. "We have to let it go," I whispered.

Tears streamed down her cheeks.

I ran my fingers through her hair. Her eyes locked on mine. We held each other's gaze as gravity closed the last inch until our lips met.

She pulled away. "I can't do this," she said as she staggered to her feet.

"Please stay." I stood.

She stepped backward, shaking her head. "I can't. I'm sorry."

She ran to her car, slid in, and skidded away.

CLAIRE RETURNED to school the next day, looking particularly distraught. During lunch she pulled me aside near the admin building.

"Pete, I need to tell you something. Something I've been meaning to tell you." She looked directly into my eyes for a long moment.

"Shoot," I said.

"I—" she started.

"Claire McIntyre, your mom is here." We both spun toward the voice. It was the school secretary. "Let's go," she said, her eyes hard, her hand waving Claire to follow.

Claire turned to me. "I guess I have to go."

"Call me," I said.

She whispered, "Not over the phone. We'll talk in person. Tonight at eleven? Same place?"

My heartbeat accelerated. It felt like years had passed since we had been together. "Okay," I said. "At eleven."

But we didn't talk later.

She didn't show up at eleven.

And she never returned to school.

One week after Erik's death, two weeks after we became lovers, Claire disappeared from my life.

NINE

— PETE —

WE'VE PLAYED TENNIS for barely thirty minutes and I'm already sprawled on the court, trying to catch my breath.

"Are you about to throw up?" Sophie asks.

I find the strength to shake my head. "I'm good."

"Maybe we should go back to basketball. At least you have the height for it," she says.

"Why are you trying to kill me?"

"It's spring. Just a few months from summer. You can't go to the beach with your body like that."

I squint at her. "What's wrong with my body?"

"That swimmer's body you built during college is disappearing on you. You need to get back into the groove of things."

"What are you trying to say?"

She shrugs. "You know... You've gone soft. And pale."

"I can't go pale. I'm Greek. My olive complexion is genetically encoded and—"

"Your olive complexion is a lemon complexion now. Trust me."

I try to stand, but my limbs are not interested. Sophie hoists me up, but grimaces momentarily, then gently touches her ribs.

"Are you okay?" I ask.

"Yeah, bruised my side at the office." She shakes it off then considers me. "When we first met I had so much hope for you."

"What's that supposed to mean?"

"You were tall, a Greek, and your first name was Pete. I thought you'd be like Pete Sampras and I'd finally be able to play tennis with someone who was good. After all this time, you still suck."

"First of all, that's racial profiling. Second—" My phone rings. "You just got lucky." I glance at the screen. It's Natalie. I moderate my wheezing and answer.

"Hey," she says, sounding dejected. "Turns out I won't fly down this weekend after all."

I step away from Sophie. "Why's that?"

"A potential acquisition on a tight timeline. This one might mess up my schedule for a few weeks."

"Don't worry about it," I say. "It's work, what can you do?"

"Nothing, I guess." A pause. "Why don't you fly up instead?"

"Not this weekend."

"Why not? You haven't been to San Francisco in weeks."

"We're going to take pictures of my Santa Barbara project this weekend."

"We?" she asks. "You and Sophie again?"

Here we go. I wish she'd understand that Sophie's like a sister. She knows Sophie was practically adopted by my parents after she lost both of hers, but that doesn't seem to make a difference. The fact that I have to defend my relationship is getting old.

"Yeah, me and Sophie," I say and add nothing more.

After we hang up something dawns on me. I'm not sad that Natalie won't be coming this weekend.

I should be.

But I'm not.

I run my hand through my hair. This one was different. But as expected, it's happening again. Just like all the others. Whether a weekend affair or a few weeks of dating, none last. The same script. Same ending.

I stroll over to Sophie, a bit off-center.

"Natalie?" she asks.

I nod.

"Did you tell her you're here with me?"

"Sure."

"Let's eat," she says. "I want to see what else you'll lie about."

CAFE BEEFSTRO IS NOT a trendy fusion restaurant in the Wilshire District. It's a deli-slash-restaurant-slash-coffee shop hidden on a lost corner of Wilshire Boulevard. The chairs are nearly comfortable and the wobbly tables always clean. We come here for the Mediterranean food, which reminds us of Yiayia's—my grandma's—Greek cooking. The smell of roasted meats, toasted breads, and freshly ground coffee induce immediate hunger pangs. The closer I get to thirty, the more I crave the foods that used to bore me.

We wave to the owner and he gives us two thumbs up. He knows what we want because we're fixtures here. Every Wednesday for lunch and sometimes for dinner—like today. A tradition that started during our senior year in high school.

Minutes later, after we've eliminated the hummus, our food arrives.

"Hi Pete," the waitress says.

"Hey," I say, unable to remember her name. "I love what you've done with your hair."

She blushes. "Thanks." She places my plate in front of me and practically drops Sophie's.

She strolls away as I grab the Gyro sandwich, prepared to devour it.

"Hi Pete," Sophie says in a low nasally voice. "You like my hairdo?"

I grin. "Are you jealous or something?"

She squints. "Homeboy, please! I'm used to your silly games, but at least don't make me gag right before I eat." She stops talking then tucks a loose strand of hair behind her ear. "I will give you this: you may not believe in love, but at least you've always been faithful to whoever you've been with."

I'm at a loss. How could Seth have cheated on her? She's perfect and he's flawed on a good day.

"Forget about Seth," I say. "He never deserved you."

She shakes her head. "I'm not so sure about that. Maybe I'm the one who doesn't deserve anyone."

"That's just silly."

"Is it?" Her phone rings. As she studies it, her jaw tightens. She drops it back in her purse.

"Anyway," she says and smiles with effort. "I'm famished."

Good. Let's move on from that topic. I raise my Gyro again.

"I assume you heard about the ten-year reunion?" Sophie asks.

My Gyro freezes mid-ascension. Tzatziki sauce drips onto the paper plate. "Who's having a reunion?"

"Our high school class. Who else?" She picks up a Kalamata olive and pops it in her mouth like popcorn. "In May," she says then licks her fingertips.

"Has it been ten years already?"

"Funny how math works like that." She lifts the chicken kebob sandwich and studies it for a moment before sinking her teeth into the toasted baguette. She chews slowly while I try to reconcile this information.

"Back when we were at Hancock Prep," she says, "I used to picture going to the tenth reunion all decked out, stepping out of a Porsche with Prince Charming at my side. I never thought ten years would go by so quickly."

"And with so little to show for."

She shrugs. "Yeah, well. There's that, too." Silence. "I can't believe I'm getting a divorce," she whispers. "It wasn't supposed to be like this."

"How was it supposed to be?"

"Fall in love. Stay in love. Respect. Be respected."

I lower the sandwich. "Maybe what you're going through is the new normal. Maybe I've been right after all. Love is another lie we've been sold."

"I can't believe that."

"No? Then why is it so hard for so many people to find a meaningful relationship? I know I'm not the only one. And what you're going through—hate to say it—but it was only a matter of time. Fifty-fifty chance of a divorce for all couples. That's a fact."

She leans forward. "Maybe because people don't marry the right person. Maybe they pick poorly."

I grin. "Are you going to get on your soapbox about 'the one' concept?"

"Why not? Why is that so impossible to believe?"

"You and Yiayia... at least she's eighty. What's your excuse? God has not pre-selected 'the one' that was meant for me. And even if I bought the theory, where is she?"

She shrugs, pops another olive in her mouth. "You probably screwed up somewhere and lost your chance." Her face twists in a pout. "And I guess I did, too."

We eat silently for a few moments. "There was Claire..." I say.

"Ugh! All these years without hearing her name and you had to screw up a clean record."

"It's your fault. Talking about reunions and lost chances. Objectively speaking, she was my girl—my 'one.' And her sporto boyfriend was supposed to be yours."

She rolls her eyes. "Robby and I were friends." But she won't look at me. She knows there was always a bit of wishful thinking with him.

"Maybe he'll be at the reunion," I say then shake my head. "They can't be serious about the reunion thing."

"They must be. They have an event page set up on Facebook and there's interest already."

"Seriously?"

"You must have received the invite. Check your email. And will you please check your Facebook account once in a while? I've posted a bunch of pictures of the gang."

"Sure, one of these days. So explain this to me: why would anyone go to a reunion after just ten years? I get twenty. But ten is a nothing. You go to college, graduate, get a job and bam! It's been ten years. I don't get it."

"Maybe to show everyone how awesome they've turned out."

She has a point there. We would shine among those has-beens.

"Or maybe to find closure after a rough end to our senior year," she continues.

That wasn't a rough end. That was torture. As for closure—wait. What's today's date?

"Or maybe," she adds, "genuine interest to reconnect and relive some of the good old days."

I don't like the sound of this. "What good old days? Sophie, you're not considering going, are you?" Her answer could have life-long implications. Countries have gone to war over lesser trespasses.

"Nah, I don't think so." She pops another olive in her mouth. "I take it you won't go?"

"All the people I want to see, I already see."

"Hmm," she says, then takes another bite.

My right eye twitches. "What are you hmm-ing about?"

"Oh, I don't know. There must be a couple of people you'd like to see. Or at least see how they've turned out."

"Like...?"

"How about Diana?"

An uncontrollable chill shakes me. "My prom date? Are you insane? She's bound to show up with a shotgun. Why would I want to see her?"

"Maybe you'd like to apologize?"

"For what? We were not together. It was a fake date. And furthermore, it was your brilliant idea. So if anyone's going to apologize, it should be you to me."

I went with Diana because the person who should've been my date disappeared without trace or warning. That's what Sophie's really driving at. She wants to know if I've finally laid Claire's ghost to rest. Hard to completely forget the girl you thought was the one.

In that moment, the long-forgotten emptiness and depression I felt all those years ago bores itself into my gut. Back then, with each passing day, each unanswered text, my lack of worthlessness was confirmed.

Whatever. She's barely a memory now. I've moved on.

For the most part.

Suddenly, tomorrow's significance dawns on me. "Soph, not sure if you realized, but tomorrow is—"

"I know," she interrupts. "Erik's tenth anniversary."

IT'S dark when we leave Cafe BeefStro. A good day. The start of her new life.

"Do you want to meet me at the cemetery tomorrow morning?" Sophie asks.

"Sure. 8:00 a.m.?"

"Yeah, that's—" she stops in front of her car. Her mouth is agape as she studies her car. "Son of a..."

"What?" I step closer to her. That's when I see it.

Engraved on the hood of her car is *B I T C H.*

I spin around, looking for him. "Do you see him?" I want to tear his head off.

"Leave it," she says.

I turn to her. "Leave it? Bull!" I pull out my phone and call Frank.

"Pete. What's up?" Frank says.

"I need help," I say. "A sheriff had Sophie's divorce papers delivered today—"

"I know, I had it arranged through my department."

"Well, we were just having dinner and the jackass vandalized her car."

"Is he still there?"

"Don't know."

"Did you see him doing it?"

I close my eyes. "No. What can we do?"

"The first thing we're going to do is agree that we'll do everything within the boundaries of the law," he says.

"Fine. Fine. What are the options?"

"We'll get an immediate restraining order. He's reacting and being dumb. Take pictures, shoot them over, so we can get a permanent order placed."

"Okay great. But is she safe?"

Long pause. "She needs to be careful. I'll have one of my buddies from LAPD get a patrol car by her place tonight."

I hang up and turn to Sophie just as she opens her car door. "Sophie, I'm not feeling good about this."

She's looks at me. "Follow me home. I have Pit there. He's a solid guard dog. Come on."

Ten minutes later we're at her house. Everything seems to be in order. No sign of anything.

"I don't like you being alone."

Pit barks at me when I say that.

"Don't offend him," she says, kneeling down, rubbing his massive head.

I lean down too. "Pit, I'm counting on you."

Pit's long tongue comes out and slobbers all over Sophie's perfect cheek. Just then, an LAPD cruiser slows down in front of her house. We walk out to greet the officers.

"Are you Sophie Perez?" the officer asks.

"Yes."

"Is everything okay? Any issues?"

"None."

"Good. We'll be driving by for the next couple of days."

After they drive off, I text Frank. *You've finally proven to be useful.*

Go screw yourself, he replies.

The support structure is in place and solid.

TEN

— PETE —

I SHUT OFF THE ENGINE, grab the flowers, then step out of the car.

I glance toward the familiar white church nestled in the Hollywood Hills. From here, it appears embraced by the wooly clouds. Slivers of sunlight struggle to break through, but the clouds will probably win this match.

Faint threads from the past converge as I stroll the cemetery grounds. Sophie said the reunion might bring closure. She's wrong. Erik will still be dead.

As I near his tombstone, I scan the others, thinking there is no logic to life and death. Some pass too soon, some live a full life. Some only had parents, while other enjoyed their grandchildren. The rules of this game are unclear. Unfair.

I find the polished marble tombstone.

"Erik Sorensen, 1988-2006, He left us too soon."

Kneeling, I touch Erik's engraved name. "Rest in peace, Erik." I lay down the flowers.

From behind, I hear footsteps. I turn to find a florist delivering a massive bouquet.

"Excuse me," the Hispanic man says as he lays them next to mine.

I glance at the flowers after he leaves. White lilies, baby carnations, and roses. Something about them nudges at an old memory.

My eyes widen and my heart rate accelerates. Those are the exact flowers Claire had brought with her to the cemetery a few days after Erik's funeral.

I eye the delivery guy who is climbing into his van now, then reach for the arrangement and read the card.

"*Rest in peace. Love Always. C.*"

C.

As in Claire?

I sprint toward the van and wave down the driver. He rolls down the window.

"Yes?"

"Can you tell me who sent those flowers?"

"Sorry, I can't."

"I'm not asking for a phone number, or anything like that. Just a name."

He stares at me.

"Please," I say.

He studies his clipboard then hands it to me.

"No name," he says. "Only initials. C. M."

Claire. McIntyre.

I stroll back to the site and consider the implications of her return.

"Hey," Sophie says from behind me. She's also clutching flowers. She glances at the two bouquets. "Are the lilies yours?"

"No. But it's from someone we both know."

"Who?"

I don't respond.

She kneels and reads the card. "Who's C?" she asks.

"Claire."

Her eyes go wide. "How do you know?"

"I checked the delivery slip. C. M. I don't need to be Sherlock to piece it together."

Her eyes drift to the flowers. We're both silent for a few moments.

"Does this mean she's back?" she says. "After all these years?"

"I don't know," I say. "And I don't care. Let's get coffee."

———

WE SIT on the outside patio of the coffee shop, nursing our piping hot cups. We've been silent. Lost in the past.

"Do you really think those flowers were from Claire?" she asks.

"Don't care. Not going to dwell on it. Claire is the past and the past can stay in the past."

Her eyes harden. "I see. So if Claire shows up right now, what happens to Natalie? Or anyone for that matter."

I hesitate. "I'm not interested in hypothetical discussions." But images of Claire's face and her bare body in my car litter my mind.

"Then why can't you accept what you already have. You're always looking elsewhere."

"I don't even know what that means. And I don't get why you're so vested in this."

"No, I suppose you wouldn't." She rises.

"Where are you going?"

"The office. I feel the need to sue someone."

"Hi, Sophie," we hear from behind us.

Sophie turns to the voice and a huge grin appears on her face. "Hey, are you headed to the office?" she asks. The guy wears a tailored suit and a Hollywood smile to match the considerable amount of hair gel on his head. He holds two cups of coffee.

"Sure am," he says.

She strolls to him, almost as if I'm not even here.

"Goodbye, Sophie," I yell out. "Take care."

They both glance at me. "Oh, sorry. See you later," she says while he barely even notices me.

They head to their cars, laughing and smiling. Happy people in Happy Land. He has a Porsche. Is his name Prince Charming by any chance?

I sink back into my chair and take a long sip.

C. M.

Where has she been all these years?

ELEVEN

— SOPHIE —

SETH LEFT ME more deranged messages. I save them all digitally, as requested by my attorney. It'll help next month when we have to go in front of a judge to request the temporary order be changed to a full-fledged restraint order. I wish there was a way to accelerate the divorce process. I want out.

Hard to believe I'm doing this.

Hard to believe I waited so long.

Los caprichos se pagan, my father used to say. *Stubbornness carries a heavy cost.* But Seth chose his path. He left me no choice.

He's ill. When he's medicated and receiving regular therapy, he's a good guy. Sweet in fact. When he's off, he's impulsive, unreliable, mean, and downright dangerous.

My hand instinctively caresses my ribs. I never told Pete, Frank, or Raj. It would have only made things worse.

My desk phone rings. It's my executive assistant.

"I have Jack on the phone for you again," she says. "Should I tell him you're not available?"

I'm getting tired of this guy. An account manager from a vendor who wants to do business with us but is unwilling to meet our terms. A man who prefers working with men.

"Put him through," I say. I put the call on speaker phone and spin my chair toward the window. I study the activity on the studio's lot.

"Sophie," he says. His stern tone already pisses me off.

"Hi Jack," I say.

"I need you to approve the changes. ASAP! Your sourcing department is dragging their feet. I have rarely seen this level of incompetence. So open up that email of yours, reply to all, and make it clear that we're good to go."

I say nothing, waiting it out.

"Sophie? Are you there?"

I crack my knuckles. "Yup."

"Well, are you going to send that email or not?"

"Of course not."

He gasps. "What—?"

"Jack, I think you're slightly confused here. I am in the legal department. We draw up the contracts. We develop the T&C's. We spend valuable brain power to assure our interests and those of our clients are properly addressed when we work with any partner. Our 'incompetent sourcing department' has done exactly what they're supposed to do. Stop vendors from getting into deals that are counter intuitive."

"We've worked for years with—"

"Yes, yes, Jack, I know. For years and years. I understand the Lakers box seats were a favorite gift in the past. We've stopped special favors and instead hold up contracts as the basis for partnerships. So back to the issue that's confusing you: we will not accept your modified terms. You will either accept what we've clearly laid out, or you will not. This was an open bid for competitors. Just because you may have done work with us in the past—under questionable terms—does not give you an incumbent's advantage. In fact, you should be aware that your competitors seem to have a better handle on what we're looking for. We're looking for a partner, not a special arrangement. So why don't you get on your email, hit reply all, and tell my 'incompetent sourcing department' whether you want to be part of the bid or you want to exclude yourself?"

Silence. *However, in this case, I doubt it's a negotiating technique.*

"Did my phone break up?" I ask. "Did any of my message get lost in translation?"

"No," he says, his voice low.

"Excellent. Always a pleasure talking to you."

I hang up.

"That was absolutely brilliant."

I spin my chair toward the front door. My boss is leaning against the door jamb. A huge grin stretches her face.

"Didn't even hear you walk in," I say.

"I was walking by and when I heard his voice, I decided to give you support," she says. "Apparently you didn't need any."

I grin. "Yeah, his type doesn't intimidate me."

"That's exactly why they want you," she says.

I sit up. "Seriously? They said yes?"

She nods. "I got confirmation from personnel. If you want the role, it's yours."

This was not supposed to happen. I asked a couple of weeks ago, then forgot all about it. Now that it's mine if I want it, the reality of the choice weighs on me. Can I actually go through with it?

"Wow," I finally say. "I can't believe they went for it."

She grins. "I've got a lot of pull," she says.

My guess is that they looked at my file and realized I can be an asset in the office.

"I have to digest this."

"Do it, but don't graze on it. Life happens fast. You got to jump on it when it's there."

When she leaves, I turn my attention to new contracts and commercial agreements for new feature films, but I can barely focus on my work. Each time I read the red-line changes, my attention drifts and I have to re-read it. I don't have the clarity of mind needed to be effective, so I do what any self-respecting professional does: I check the status of the world on Twitter, Instagram, and finally, Facebook.

I notice a new friend request. I click and the face that greets me does something wonderful to my heart. Robby.

Not just Robby, but the drop dead gorgeous version of him. How could he have gotten even better looking? How did we fall out of contact? We were so close, but after high school he dropped off the map and I got lost in my world. I go to his page and try to stalk his pictures. Only a couple are accessible because we're not friends yet. But the couple that are there are swoon worthy.

His hair is short now—almost a buzz cut—and darker. No more light brown. He is all dark chocolate. But his square jaw and angular features are etched in stone. I study his neck. You can tell a lot about a guy from the neck muscles. And his hands. He's in better shape than ever.

The next picture explains a lot more. He's a couple of years younger if the date stamp is correct. He's a Marine. Or was. His profile shows "US Marines" in the "Past" category. Now, he works at "Self Employed," whatever that means.

I realize I'm leaning into the screen. I may or may not be smiling like a teenager watching her favorite boy band dancing.

I breathe deep then pull away.

"He wants to be friends, we can be friends." I click on "Confirm" and lean back. "It's official. We're friends."

A thought dawns on me. *Is he going to the reunion?*

Facebook Messenger chirps. I have a message. From Robby.

Sophie! How the hell are you?

I take a deep breath and jump in.

I'm great, I write, and for a minute I actually believe it.

I missed you.

Is that right? *I missed you, too.*

Did I hear this right? You and Seth got married? Then he adds, *Congrats.*

Well, we're going through a divorce.

I wait for his response. But nothing comes through for a few moments.

Thank God! His loss. Can't wait to see you. I'll be going to the reunion. Are you going?

I cringe. *I doubt it.*

Reconsider. I'd love to see you. Are you still in L.A.? I'm in San Diego. We should try to get together before the reunion. See what I did there? I'm trying to see you twice.

My heartbeat bounces around. I realize I'm grinning and swiveling in my chair. Is that music I hear coming from the universe? I don't know why I'm so excited. After middle school I never thought of him romantically. Maybe I like the fact that hot Robby is flirting with me. Maybe I'm not a washed-up mess after all.

Just as I'm about to play the game, my phone rings. I scan the number. My neighbor.

TWELVE

— PETE —

I GO TO work, hoping to find escape in paper and pencils and design software. My assistant glances at me as I quickly slide into my office and close the door. Glass walls look impressive in an architectural firm, but if it's privacy I was hoping for, this is the wrong place.

I slouch behind my drafting table and study the partial view from my quasi-office. The space next to mine has a perfect view of the ocean which makes that one a real office. After five years of solid results, I'd thought that corner office would be mine. I was wrong. The professional ass-kisser got the nod instead.

A light knock on the glass and the door opens. "Pete, I left two messages on your desk," Sandy says. She's my assistant designer, protégé, and full-time pain-in-the-ass.

"Thanks."

"Also, the editor called again. She still wants to interview you."

"Right. I'll have to get back to her."

She crosses her arms. Here we go. "Why are you putting it off? This is a great opportunity for you—not the firm, but you."

She's talented and smart. Which makes her a free-spirit—which is good. She's also ballsy—which is not so good when the target of her nut cracking is me.

"I'm not putting it off. I'm just busy."

"You're wasting time and I can't understand why you're delaying the inevitable. If you took advantage of some of these opportunities, you'd have everything you'd need to go solo."

"Sandy, I thought we agreed I'm the boss."

"You are the boss, and I've learned more from you in the past six months than all those years in college combined, but you're still wrong," she says, steps further in, then shuts the door behind her.

"Something else on your mind?" I ask, knowing she has another out-of-the-box idea.

"Quit. Go solo. I'll join you."

I drop to my stool. Was I as naive as her when I first came out of college? "In order to start a business, one needs capital."

"I know people."

I frown. "And customers."

"Like I said, I know people."

I throw my hands in the air. "Then let's meet some of these people."

Sandy glows. "Awesome!" she says and leaves the office.

Well, that was too easy. She's delusional but at least she's happy for now. I study her as she grabs her cell phone and runs outside. Is she serious? What if she does know people?

Unlikely.

I sink in my chair and scan my personal emails. More than fifty new messages in my inbox but only one seems to pulsate with heat. The one from Facebook. I thought all of those went to my Junk Mail. I cautiously open it and read the message. "Invitation: Hancock Prep, Class of '07 Reunion."

After a two-second deliberation, I delete the message and return to my drafting table. Not interested.

I glance at the drawings on the table then turn my attention to the row of twelve old-school *Staedtler* mechanical pencils. Number seven's tip is blunt. I sharpen it, inspect it, then blow off the specs of graphite from its tip before placing it back in the stainless-steel container. I touch the tips, assuring they are perfectly aligned. Much better. I can focus on my work again.

A couple hours later, my inbox chimes with an email from Sophie. *"In case you didn't get it... or inadvertently deleted it :)"* It's the same Facebook invitation I deleted.

If I didn't know better, I'd think she wants to go to the reunion.

Fine. One innocent glance at the names and posted messages won't hurt. I click on the link, I'm in.

On the top banner there are indicators telling me that I have twenty-six friend requests, thirteen private messages, and dozens of notifications. Why so many? This is why I stopped checking. Some good stuff lost in the noise. I nearly click the notifications but remind myself to remain focused. Reunion.

I dig in and before I know it, I have spent nearly half an hour stalking the eighteen people who have confirmed attendance.

Eighteen out of a graduating class of fifty-seven.

We should have been fifty-nine. But Erik died and Claire disappeared weeks before prom. That's how things go sometimes.

I gaze at the notifications in red. The mouse pointer hovers over them just as my cell phone rings. Sophie.

"What's up—?"

"Neighbor called. Someone threw a brick through my window. Can you meet me at my place?" Her voice is strained, near a breaking point. Not because she's scared. She's angry.

I shut off my computer and rise. "On my way."

THIRTEEN

— PETE —

THE DAMAGE IS CONSIDERABLY WORSE than what Sophie told me on the phone. A squad car is there, and so is Frank. She's talking to an LAPD officer. When Frank sees me he approaches me.

"What the hell, Frank?" I say.

"He was smart about it. Made it look like a robbery," he says.

"And Pit? I thought pit bulls are guard dogs."

"Educated guess: Pit didn't attack because he knows Seth. He was probably taken to the bedroom, the place was trashed, then the dog was let out again."

"How about prints?"

Frank shrugged. "They would be meaningless. Of course his prints would be in the house. He lived here."

We both turn to Sophie, who is visibly shaken.

"I'm going to kill that bastard," I say.

"Don't do anything stupid. Let the police do their job. He's irrational. He'll screw up."

I don't want him to screw up. I want to take all my anger out on him. He's ill. Switches from the nicest guy to a rainbow-colored prick. But even for him, this is a new low.

Sophie shakes the officer's hand then stumbles toward us. "Thanks for coming, Pete," Sophie says. Her eyes are blood shot.

I give her a hug. I don't know what to say. She must feel violated.

"What can I do?" I ask. "Name it."

She pulls away. "Can you hang here until the investigators are done?"

"Yes, of course," I say.

"I'll call Pam and we'll help you clean up," Frank says.

She puts her hand on his wide shoulder. "Thank you," she says but her voice cracks. She collects herself. "I want to see how Pit's doing. I left him at my neighbor's."

We watch her walk away.

"She can't be alone," I say.

"Nope," Frank agrees. I can feel him eyeing me. "Any ideas?"

"I have an idea. I need her to agree."

We're silent.

"And how will Natalie take it?" he asks.

I turn to him. "Irrelevant. This is Sophie we're talking about."

"And how will *you* handle it?"

I don't have an answer that will shut him down because he knows. He saw. So I give him the only honest answer I have. "I'm a big boy now."

He peels his eyes off me. "That's what I'm afraid of."

"YOU CAN'T BE SERIOUS," Natalie says.

"Why wouldn't I be serious?" I try my best to remain calm.

"Pete, don't you think what you're proposing is a bit odd and frankly inappropriate? She's a young woman. A very attractive young woman. She's still married, and you have a girlfriend. Me, in case you've forgotten."

"I've known her since we were kids. She's my best friend."

"And she's a woman. Guys and girls—particularly attractive ones —can't be... you know."

"Natalie, I didn't say this to hurt you or to get into a debate. I was just letting you know."

There's silence on the phone.

"You weren't asking. You were telling," she says, more to herself.

"This is Sophie. She means the world to me. I will do everything I can to help her."

More silence.

"I wonder if you'll ever feel that way about me," she says but I don't think she wants a response. Even though I have one.

"I'm sorry this hurts you," I say. "I have to do the right thing."

"It seems the right thing for you is the wrong thing for me. I don't want you to do this. If you do, then I know where I stand in this relationship. Sleep on that, Pete. Goodbye."

I don't have to sleep on it. I know the answer. "Goodbye, Natalie."

I hang up then step out of my car. That's that, I guess. Not what I had planned. But it was inevitable.

FOURTEEN

— SOPHIE —

I STEP AWAY from the cleanup effort. Pam, Frank's girlfriend, has been helping. She may only be a hair over five feet, but she's fast and driven. I want her on my side during a zombie apocalypse.

I dial my friend Linda.

"Hey *chica*! How are you?" Linda asks.

"Well... not great."

"Did Seth do something to you?" He voice has an edge that I welcome. She's as hot-blooded as they come.

"Not to me. But he trashed my home."

"I'll be right over," she says.

"No, you don't have to do that. I've got cops here, my friends, and even one who's a sheriff. I'm good, but I have a favor to ask."

"Anything."

"Can me and Pit stay with you tonight?"

"Absolutely," she says before I've completed my request. "I'll prepare the guest room and aerate a couple of bottles of red wine."

"You're the best."

"Only when I want to be," she says. "See you soon."

I hang up then join my friends as Frank ties the last trash bag.

"You can't stay here tonight," Pam says. "Stay with me."

"Thanks, but I've already asked a friend if I can sleep over," Sophie says.

"Who?" Frank and Pete ask.

I smirk. They're funny when they become protective. "Someone I know from the gym. She's a good friend."

"What's her name and where does she live?" Frank asks. He pulls out his notepad.

"Her name is Linda Reyes, she has a black belt, and lives in Calabasas. Don't worry sheriff, she's clean," I say then crack a smile that I hope will satisfy them all.

"Calabasas is a good neighborhood," Frank admits. "But you need a long-term plan."

I shrug. "I haven't thought that far ahead."

"I have," Pete say. "You can stay with me."

Words don't form in my mouth. Instead I study his eyes for a few moments, then shake my head. "No, that won't work."

"Why not?" Frank and Pete ask I'm unison. They must have planned this together. My heart thrums in my ears. Or was this Pete's idea?

"Pete, you haven't thought through what you're saying. Natalie... you know how she feels about our friendship."

"It's been handled," he says.

I frown, studying him. Where is this coming from? Chivalry or something else? "What does 'handled' mean? You told her and she said fine, no problem?"

"It means your safety and comfort are more important than anything else. Like I said, it's been handled."

"Staying with Pete does make more sense," Pam says. "He's just a couple of blocks away. You can't commute every day from Calabasas to the studio."

"I was thinking of just a night or two," I say. "Then back home, business as usual."

"I was thinking until Seth is controlled," Pete says.

76

"I agree," Frank adds. "Even if he doesn't try this again, it is infinitely wiser for you to be with someone else."

I chuckle as I turn to Pete. "Then I may become your permanent guest."

"I'm okay with that."

"You're insane," I say.

"Yes, he is," Frank says, "but in this case, I think it's a great idea."

I shake my head. I should want this. It's simple and convenient, but also risky. "Guys, I'm too tired and wound up to be having this conversation. I need to rest, think things through, then plan the next step."

"Fine," Pete says. "Stay with your friend tonight. Tomorrow we discuss this plan, okay?"

I stare into his eyes. "Okay. Tomorrow we discuss it."

FIFTEEN

— SOPHIE —

"HE ASKED YOU to move in with him?" Linda asks.

We're nestled on her plush couch, each holding a glass of Argentinean wine. Her long black hair is tied into a pony tail; the silver in her large gray eyes shine; and her lips remain parted. She's a beautiful woman who has made a decision to never marry or get serious. Just like Pete. But if she chose to, she could have a line of suitors spanning a few blocks.

"Yeah, he did. I was not expecting it at all. Completely from left field."

Linda slides her long legs beneath her. Her grin is unmistakable. For someone who doesn't believe in relationships, she's very eager to know more. Maybe we're all romantics at heart.

"What will you do?"

"I don't know."

"But this is Pete. Your best friend. The one you told me about."

"Yes."

"What do you think it means? I mean, for someone to ask you to move in..."

"He's just acting out of chivalry. We've lived together before."

"What?" Linda's eyes widen even more. She grabs the bottle of Malbec and pours more into our glasses. "Go on."

I smile. "It's not what you think. Three years after my dad died, my mom passed away. I was in college at the time. Pete's parents took me in. I lived with them until I finished undergrad school."

"Oh," Linda says, disappointed. "So nothing happened with you two?"

I feel my ears redden. "No. Not really."

Linda smiles. "Tell me *that* part."

I laugh then take a big gulp of wine. "We shared a Jack and Jill bathroom. I was in one room, in between was the bathroom and he was in the other room. So each of us could get into the bathroom from our own bedrooms."

"Nice!"

"I accidentally walked in once when he was undressing to take a shower. We both got embarrassed and agreed to lock the door when the other was in." I hesitate.

"But..."

"But we didn't. Not once. And a few times we 'accidentally' walked in at the wrong time."

"No way!"

I blush. "We were silly horny kids."

"Did you guys ever... mess around?"

"No," I say firmly. Because that one time was just a little nothing. And that other time at Raj's wedding... well, that was a little more than a little nothing. But neither are worth mentioning to Linda.

I HAVE NOT SLEPT all night. I continue to imagine Seth is outside Linda's home, waiting for the opportunity to hurt me. I see his face in every shadow.

Pit pushes his muzzle into my hip. He wants me to cuddle with him. Apparently, he's feeling traumatized by what happened to us.

How did I end up with the world's softest pit bull? I give him a kiss and he makes an odd sound. The type of noise I'd expect from a horse.

I slide off the bed and stroll into the den. From the glass sliding door I scan the stars and the moon. It's a beautiful evening. The stars don't have the slightest clue what I'm going through. What did Albert Camus call it? The benign indifference of the universe? Sounds about right. The universe doesn't give a rip about me.

Pete does.

And so do the rest of my friends. But Pete wants me to be there with him. He wants to be close to make sure I'm okay.

I sneak into Linda's office and admire her autographed tennis racquet once again. I study for the hundredth time all the pictures she has with, in my not-so-humble opinion, the best and most under-rated tennis player in the world. I can't believe she knows Gemma Lennon. If I play it cool, maybe Linda will introduce me to her. I'm not one to go all fan-girl, but Gemma's story, the fact that she was orphan, and her drive to make it on her terms, is down-right inspiring.

When I step out of the office, I hear the familiar chirp of my phone. Another message from Seth? I shiver as I pull out the cellular from my purse. There are a bunch of messages from all my friends. The latest one is from Pete.

I can't sleep. You're on my mind.

Should I move in with him? How will that work? That night at Raj's wedding...things got a little too close.

I run my hand through my hair as I exit the messages and go to my email app. I find the email from my boss.

Like I said, it's yours if you want it. The studio's UK division is waiting for you. Take it from me, if you really want to create a separation that's safe, you need to move away. And when you're ready to return, we'll process your transfer. But I need to know soon. They want to fill the role.

How can I leave everything I have here? At the same time, how can I possibly stay under this type of threat?

I'm about to turn off my phone when I notice I have a Facebook message from Robby.

I hope you're okay. Whatever is happening I hope you know you can call on me. Anything. Anytime. Here's my cell.

Am I reading into it, or is Robby interested? I recall all those years in middle school when I had hoped, but he'd done nothing. Not even a kiss. We were kids then. He's all man now. And he seems to have taken an interest in me.

I scroll through my pictures on Facebook. I nod as I flip through the images I've posted. There are a few that show off more of my body than I probably would have wanted. Is that what he saw? Is that what he wants?

Maybe.

I turn off my phone and throw it inside my purse.

UK...

No one knows about this option. Not even Pete. But I had to plan for what I suspected would happen once I filed for divorce. If Seth does what he's supposed to, then he could have a chance at happiness. Just not with me.

I drink a glass of water and remember the eighteen months I lived with Pete's family before I went off to law school. Anything was possible back then. That's when Seth and I started dating. That was also when Pete became galvanized in his views about relationships and love.

I remember those late nights when one of us couldn't sleep so we'd go into the other person's room and talk about nothing and anything. But the best part was when we'd cuddle up and fall asleep together.

Those were the best days.

I'd like to have that again. Truth be told, that's exactly what I need.

I pick up my phone and send a text to Pete.

SIXTEEN

— PETE —

MY PHONE CHIMES. I stretch for it on my nightstand.

It's from Sophie.

I'll stay with you.

"Yes!" I yell out loud. I don't recall ever reading something so beautiful in my life. I sit up in bed, ready to reply when another text comes through from her.

Just promise to be open.

I rub my eyes. What is she talking about?

Open to what? I ask

To anything.

I hesitate, but there's no point. I want her here. *I promise.*

Part 11

Roommates

SEVENTEEN

— PETE —

I PULL UP in front of Sophie's house, ready to help her move whatever she needs moved to my place. A sparkling black pickup truck is parked in her driveway and a few boxes and two large suitcases are already in the bed.

I hop out and jog to her door. At that instant, a tall woman steps out holding a box. She's an imposing figure. Long black hair, powerful arms and shoulders, long tanned legs. She's studying me with the probing eyes of someone who has authority even though she's younger than I am.

"Hi," I say.

She scrutinizes me for another moment, then her forehead relaxes and she smiles. "You must be Pete," she says. Her voice is just as powerful as her demeanor.

"Yes, I am. Linda, right? Let me help you with that," I say.

She pulls from me. "No need, I'm good." She strides to her truck then slides the box on the bed. She hops on top and adjusts it next to the others. She jumps off the truck and steps up to me. "Sorry about that. I'm weird about getting help." She grins. "And yes, I am Linda." She puts out her hand. I shake it. Firm grip.

Did Sophie say she's a black belt? I'm suddenly feeling less male.

"Oh good, you're here," Sophie says from behind us. "Did you guys meet?"

"Just," Linda says.

"What can I get?" I ask.

"We're done," she says then gives me a peck on the cheek. "Always late to the party. Let's go."

Pit ambles out and stumbles toward Linda's truck. He waits by the passenger door, his stump of a tail gyrating.

Sophie bolts her front door then runs to Linda's car.

I guess I'm driving alone.

I PULL my car into the garage just as Linda's truck pulls into the driveway. Both doors open and two beautiful women step out. Pit saunters down, his tongue nearly caressing the ground.

"This is a beautiful home," Linda says. She's studying my little Craftsman.

I join them. "Thank you."

"Pete restored this himself," Sophie says. "He's a gifted architect and designer."

Linda nods in approval. "Very nice." She claps her hands together and says, "Let's do this."

With that, we jump into action. I'm tempted to yell, "Yes, drill sergeant!"

I grab the suitcases and drag them to the guest room. I never went back to sleep after she told me she'd move in with me. I cleaned up the spare bedroom, washed bed sheets, cleared out the closet, and added a few touches from mom's attic to make Sophie feel at home.

"Pete!" Sophie says when she walks in. "Are those the same posters from my room at your parent's house?" She's smiling so broadly that I fear she may not be able to close her lips again.

I grin. "What do you think?"

She drops the box she was carrying and hugs me. "Just like the good old days," she says.

I hug back, hard. The scent from her hair invades my senses. I practically lift her off her feet. I've made a lot of choices in my life—this has to be the best one yet.

Shuffling feet cause me to open my eyes. Linda is looking at us, a smirk on her face. I've been holding Sophie a bit longer than I should have. I let go.

"Welcome home," I whisper.

When I study Sophie's face, she's blushing. I bet I am, too.

A COUPLE OF HOURS LATER, we've moved in all that she bought, including various kitchen appliances that look like the type of contractions people use to make healthy foods.

"All right, *chica*," Linda says. "I'll be off."

"I'm ordering pizza," I say. "Stay and have lunch with us."

"I'd love to, but can't."

She leans down to Sophie and kisses her on both cheeks. "Call me later."

They embrace. When she steps up to me I think she'll kiss me on my cheeks also, but instead, she gives me her hand.

We go outside to see her off and Pit runs after her. When she opens the door, Pit jumps in and sits in the passenger seat.

"Get out of there, Pit," Sophie says. "We're staying." But Pit doesn't make a move. "Out." Instead of jumping out he plops down, making himself more comfortable.

"He does have good taste," I say.

Both Linda and Sophie eye me.

"I just mean... you know..." I decide it's best I shut my mouth.

"Do you want to stay with me a while?" Linda asks Pit.

Pit turns to her and has the look of a love-starved... umm... pup, I guess.

"You two-timing mutt," Sophie says.

He glances at her, makes a sound then turns to Linda again.

"Do you mind if I keep him for the weekend?" Linda asks.

"If he gives you trouble—"

"Don't worry. I can handle all dogs."

I can't help but think she's talking about the human species, not canine.

The truck rolls out, Linda taps the horn, and off she goes. Pit stares at us from the passenger window.

"So... what's her story?"

Sophie glances at me. "She's not interested."

I take a step back. "I'm offended. I'll have you know I'm not interested in her either."

She shakes her head. "So predictable."

"I am not. I wouldn't go out with her."

Sophie crosses her arms. "And why's that?"

"Because she can kick my ass in two seconds flat."

"She can," Sophie agrees. "That's how I met her."

"She kicked your ass?"

Sophie swats my head then marches toward the house. I follow. "We met at the gym. Some guy was hitting on me. Following me around the gym."

Anger and concern find their way into my throat.

"Linda intervened and told the guy to back off. She had been beating away at a heavy punching bag. You should've seen her. The tape from her gloves was partially hanging loose. Her shoulders and arms were pumped, and long, wet strands of her hair hung loosely from her pony tail."

For a moment I visualize this. Glowing light from behind her and the theme of Rocky playing in the background.

"The dork who had been hitting on me was sensible enough to listen. That's when I knew she could easily become my new best friend."

She walks off.

I'm planted.

"Wait. Hold on! I thought *I'm* your best friend."

She glances at me over her shoulder, a devilish eyebrow raised. "I'm all for a meritocracy. I'll give you a chance to prove yourself."

SOPHIE HAS SPENT the last ten minutes looking though my pantry and now she's scrutinizing my refrigerator. I feel like the United Nations nuclear auditor has entered my home and the verdict will have dire consequences.

She gently shuts the refrigerator but doesn't turn toward me immediately. She hesitates.

"What?" I ask.

She breathes deeply then turns. "I'm going to the market."

"Why? We have plenty of stuff."

She stares at me, looking like a parent trying to explain something trivial to her three-year-old.

"Yes, you do have stuff. Seven. Seven different types of cereals— each with a different cartoon character on the box."

"I like what I like."

"Four. Four boxes of Chinese takeout that have started to move again."

"Vicious lie!"

"Three. Three apples that if checked for firmness, will implode and a plume of green gas will kill us in seconds flat."

I study her for a moment then rush to the pantry. "Eight!" I say. "Eight boxes of Macaroni and Cheese!" I cross my arms. "What do you say to that?"

WE'RE at a supermarket that I don't think I've ever entered.

The place is packed with women who almost exclusively wear

yoga pants and tight tops. I'm not complaining. It's a nice place to hang out and people watch, but I question the foods they have. I don't see any cereals with cartoon characters on them.

I'm following Sophie with the cart. She continues to load it, making us look like hoarders. Who can eat this much food? If we can actually call it food. Some of the things sound like a disease in a box. Wheat Germ? Seriously?

We reach the butcher and she orders salmon. "Wild caught," she clarifies, whatever that means.

As the cashier rings us up, I notice that after a couple of items we're already north of $100. At this rate, the bill will top $200.

"$303.76," the cashier says. I take out my debit card, but Sophie hands her three large and an Abraham.

"What are you doing?" I ask. "I'm paying for this."

"Apparently you're not."

"You're about to piss me off," I say. "You're my guest."

"And I am very grateful, but this is the stuff I want to eat. If after you try them you decide you like them, you can start buying it, too."

I shiver. "Don't expect me to eat no germ. I'll go for the salmon and the strawberries but all this other stuff... they can't be good for you."

The cashier, a pretty brunette, glances at Sophie. They start laughing.

"Haters," I say.

"THAT WAS AWESOME," I finally admit. And I mean it. In all these years, Sophie has never cooked for me. We always order out. This was a real treat.

"You're welcome," she says as she hands me the last washed dish.

"Here's the plan for tonight," I say as I dry the plate. "Ice cream, coffee, and we rent a movie."

She glances at her watch. Water droplets fall from her long fingers. "I'm actually really exhausted."

"You're killing me!"

"And we have an early start tomorrow," she says, as she takes the dish towel from me and dries her hands.

"We do? What's going on in the morning?"

She heads toward her room and I follow.

"We're going to take pictures of your Santa Barbara home tomorrow, right?"

"Yeah..."

"We should take pictures at sunrise." We stop in front of her bedroom door. "My instinct is that this house will take on a life of its own if we capture it at the right time of the day."

"That means we have to leave early... very early."

"Exactly. So you'd do best to get a good night's sleep." She steps across the threshold into her room.

"Okay..." I say, but I don't want to sleep. I want us to hang out. "Fine," I mutter.

She's about to close the door when she stops, spins, and embraces me. Her head nestles into my neck. I hug her back.

"Thank you, Pete," she whispers. Her warm breath rests on my neck.

I kiss the top of her head. "Thank you for coming."

She lifts her head and plants a kiss on my cheek.

"Good night," she says, then enters her room and shuts the door.

I stand affixed for a few moments, my emotions rumbling. I hope I know what I'm doing. Because the thoughts that are going through my mind are dangerous ones.

EIGHTEEN

— PETE —

IT'S FOUR IN the morning. I feel half-human. My face is swollen, my eyelids, barely slits. As spent as I feel, there is a tremor of excitement running through me, threatening to burst. Sophie and I will be visiting my latest finished project in Santa Barbara in a couple of hours.

When I see my homes through the pictures she takes, I feel a sense of accomplishment. She may be a lawyer, but she's also a gifted photographer. Her pictures transform the homes I design into works of art. So when she says photo shoot at sunrise, I trust her instinct. And when I see Sophie's reaction, that's when I'm complete. That's when I no longer feel like a fraud. After all these years, her validation still means a lot.

The warm shower helps, but I'm still pissy when I step out of my room. Thankfully, the scent of fresh coffee—Sophie's epic Colombian blend no less—gives me hope for the day.

"Good morning," she says. "Hungry?"

"No."

"Coffee?" she holds out the large cup.

"Hmm," is all I produce. I accept the cup and sip the coffee as she takes my hand and walks me to the garage.

As we pull out of the garage, I drop the top of the convertible, then accelerate our way onto Pacific Coast Highway.

"What a beautiful day," she says.

Eventually, I'll agree. Right now, I focus on the coffee and traffic.

A few moments into the ride, she grabs my iPhone and scrolls through the music selection.

"Sure, go ahead. I'm not listening to this," I say.

Unfazed, she continues to scroll. "What happened to you? You used to have good taste in music."

"No, in the past, you'd tell me what to buy and I would."

"You showed so much promise." She smiles, her dimples on full display, a reminder of how I will always remember her—a twelve-year-old firecracker. "Now look at you," she continues. "Country music. Really, dude?"

"You did *not* just go after country music!"

"You're Greek! Since when is this your thing?"

She wants to get in the mud, we'll get in the mud. "I would have played Ranchero music in honor of your heritage, but figured you already woke up to that—"

A direct chop to my ribs. I don't learn. She's a badass.

"Oh good," she says and sets the phone down. She's found what she was looking for—Shakira. Unfortunately, she sings along. Her voice is an off-tune onslaught which can drop grown men to their knees.

"Seriously? That song's so sixth grade," I say.

"Seventh, actually. Sure brings back memories." Sophie sinks into the headrest. Her honey-red mane swirls with the wind and music.

"What's on your mind?" I ask.

She turns to me, strands of her hair wrestling with the wind. "Robby contacted me."

I snap to her. "What for?"

"Just to say hi."

I study her for a few moments, nod, then focus on the road again.

"Also..." she starts, "he asked if I'm going to the reunion."

Her words register. "But you told him you're not, right?"

She offers a faint smile.

"Oh, come on, Sophie! You promised."

"I did no such thing."

"Well, it sounded like a promise."

"Not to me. I was on the fence."

Here we go. If she goes, then all the pressure will fall on me. She'll totally expect me to go and will annoy me until I buckle. I've been there each time she's jumped on some idea or another. This will not end well for me. Another thought pollutes my mind. Why is Robby seeking her out? Why now?

"How can you do this to me?" I ask.

"First of all, I haven't decided yet. Second, I didn't do it to you, I did it to me."

Does she like him or something? "But now you'll bust my balls about going."

She rakes her hair behind her ears then peers over her sunglasses. "What do you say? It might be fun."

"Or it might be like gouging my eyes out with a blunt spoon."

"You're being closed-minded." She turns her gaze to the Malibu cliffs.

Is this what she meant when she asked me to be open? "I didn't say no."

She spins to me, grinning.

"But I didn't say yes, either."

The smile disappears.

WE TURN onto the winding slate driveway, purr up the slight incline, and park in front of the cavernous entrance. Sophie's gaze has not shifted from the property. I've visualized this home's lines, cuts, and angles for so long that the distinction between drawing and reality is blurred for me.

Connie, the homeowner, opens the oversized double doors. She's beaming. I step out of the car and hurry up the short walkway toward Connie and give her a peck on the cheek.

"I'm sorry for the early start," I say.

Sophie's face is a mask, no hint of approval or disapproval. Nothing.

"Are you kidding? I can't wait for you to see what the interior designer did," Connie says. "I barely slept because of the anticipation."

Sophie grabs her gear, twists her hair into a ponytail, then slides on her old, weathered HPA baseball cap. Embroidered on it is her last name, Perez, and the number ten. Her jersey number, the only one that was retired by our school's athletic department.

"I'm glad I took your advice on the custom-built furniture," Connie says.

Sophie's weapon of choice in hand, she marches off to the top of the hill. I never ask what she plans, nor tell her what to do. She disappears behind the home, into the thick trees.

I'm about to step inside with Connie when her daughter shows up on the front porch, holding a dollhouse larger than her in her arms. She lowers the toy house in front of me. She's in her PJs, her hair a mess.

"Why are you awake so early?" Connie asks.

"Mister Pete, you fixed the big house. Can you fix my doll house, too?" she asks.

"Oh, sweetie, I told you, Dad will take care of it later," Connie says.

"It's not a problem," I say then sit on the granite porch next to her.

"Okay, fine. I'll make coffee and bring it out," Connie says.

"So what's wrong with your house?"

"The walls and the roofs don't fit anymore. I can't close it."

I study the dollhouse. More complex than I thought. This is no discount aisle toy.

"Can you fix it for me?" she asks. Her pale blue eyes are hopeful.

"I think so," I say.

She grins then scoots next to me.

She tells me about all the adventures her toys have had in the house as I study the roofline, the walls, and where the floors meet. It's a classic design, probably lifted from a typical Art Deco home.

It's a simple alignment problem. Like a puzzle, I see how all the pieces should work. I've seen it thousands of times. I've studied it, drawn it, and have even... I pause. Something registers just as the toy walls click into place.

"Thanks, Mister Pete." She grabs the toy by the handle and trudges inside, yelling, "He fixed it, Mom."

I step backward, my eyes locked on the real home's roofline and frame.

No, I'm being paranoid. Sure, there are some shared elements between my home and the dollhouse, but for the most part—Christ, what am I saying? Is that what I design? A child's toy for adults?

I march to the edge of the property and study the house more carefully. In my mind's eye, the drawing I drafted superimposes itself over the actual home. I practically see the walls expand and expose the inner details as I had conceived them. As the components merge, the patterns emerge, uncovering the unique elements. The house appears as if it were born of the ground and surrounding natural stones and boulders. The sharp edges and diagonal lines are original and beautiful. It all fits. It works.

But something still bothers me. There are elements that are tried and reused and dull. I need to up my game. I can't repeat the patterns of old designs continually. No replicas. No more.

"The coffee is ready," Connie calls out.

I make my way inside, wondering if Sophie has also noticed this. When she's taking pictures, she must see the same details I do. She must think I'm a hack now.

Like the designs of my homes, I think about the life choices I've been making. Have I been repeating the same mistakes over and over?

———

CONNIE and I are in the kitchen drinking coffee when Sophie shows up, but she doesn't speak or make eye contact. My worst fears are materializing. She hates the house.

I eye her.

She nods.

I rise. "She's done," I say. "Thanks for letting us invade your home."

"No problem at all. Hey, Sophie," Connie calls out, "have some fresh coffee before you guys head out."

"When will you officially leave L.A. and move here?" I ask.

Connie pours a mug and slides it to Sophie. "Not until summer," she says. "Less disruption from school. We really love Hancock Prep but this has always been our dream location."

"I can understand why," Sophie says.

"Sophie, I noticed you're wearing an HPA cap," she says. "Did you also attend HPA?"

"Yes. Pete and I were classmates," Sophie says.

"Ten years, right? Are you guys having a reunion?"

"It's been announced," Sophie says.

Connie studies each of us. "You're going, right?"

"Maybe," I say.

"Are you kidding me? Just a couple of years back was my twentieth, and you bet I went. I didn't attend the tenth, but if I was sitting in your shoes, I'd be counting the days."

Sophie chuckles. "You didn't go to your tenth. Why do you think we should go?"

Connie's jaw slackens. "Seriously? Look at you two. You guys are gorgeous."

"I see," Sophie says.

"Oh, I'd go all right." She's nodding, as if there's music she's rapping to. "I went there to show them all what I'd turned into. Success, money, a great husband, and a Maserati. Take that, Shelly," she says, flipping the bird.

My eyes go wide. "Shelly?" I ask.

Connie laughs. "Sorry. She always thought she was all that. So I showed her."

"But at the tenth..." Sophie starts.

"Not exactly where I wanted to be in my life." She wraps an arm around Sophie's shoulder. "But if I looked like you, I'd go there and make 'em all drool."

WE HEAD to our favorite breakfast spot in Santa Barbara. As I park the car, Sophie wraps up transferring pictures from her camera to the iPad. During the drive down she didn't say anything. I feel deflated. Of all people, I always want her to love what I design.

Minutes later, we're seated for breakfast when she closes the tablet's cover and acknowledges my existence again. "It's beautiful," she says.

A stupid grin reshapes my face. Normal breathing resumes and my lungs suddenly remember how to intake the coastal air. "Thank you. I'm glad you liked it."

"I don't like it. I love it. This is your best one yet. I wish it was mine, not hers. I wish I could live in it until I die." She grabs my arm. "I'm so proud of you."

Only Sophie can make me feel relevant. All the accolades and awards mean something, granted, but if you're in this business long enough, you accumulate those. Sophie, however, always speaks the truth. She calls things as she sees them, and she's usually dead accurate.

"When will you quit your stupid job and go solo?"

So much for dead accurate. "Can I see the pictures now?"

She hesitates, enters her password, touches a few things on the iPad, then hands it to me. "Only the Santa Barbara album."

"When will you let me see your other work?"

"Not today. Santa Barbara album only."

"When then?"

"When you're ready."

"I'm ready now."

"I'll tell you when you're ready."

I've lost this argument before, but it never hurts to test the waters. I don't understand her unwavering position.

With each image, I start to feel better about myself. I feel—dare I say—talented. Her pictures are brilliant.

"iPad, please," she says.

"Paranoid much?" I cough.

She gives me a dirty look, but takes her tablet and slips it into her bag. "What did you think about what Connie said about the reunion?" she asks.

"I didn't. I get it. I do. But I'm not interested. To what end? There's nothing there for me."

"How do you know? Isn't that part of the fun?"

"Fun?" I ask. "Will you admit that you're hoping something will happen with Robby?"

She shakes her head. "Pete, honestly, I don't have a clue what I'm hoping for. I'm in the middle of a divorce. A bad relationship that has made me reconsider what my future would look like. I used to imagine kids, a nice house, vacations. Now, I'm realizing this might be it. I'm twenty-eight. Almost thirty. Blink and I'm forty. I'll focus on my career. Do more, earn more, and hope for happiness."

"You're sounding like me," I say, but I'm not happy about this. I never thought she'd give up.

"You've influenced me, I guess. Took a while, but it was bound to happen."

If she only knew why I gave up on love and relationships... If she only knew she was the reason.

NINETEEN

— PETE —

"WELCOME TO THE Los Angeles International Airport," the flight attendant said. "The local time is 8:05 in the morning and the temperature is..."

I leapt out of my seat, grabbed my carryon and hurried off the plane. After a two-week trip with my class to visit architectural landmarks of the west, I was ready to get back home.

I texted Sophie: *I just landed.*

I swerved my way through the crowds then picked up my pace. I was going to see Sophie again. Finally.

It happened on the third night when we were in Scottsdale. The depression had hit me hard. At first I thought I was ill, maybe because of the Arizona desert heat. I wasn't homesick per se. I had always looked forward to being away from my parents. Particularly since my university was fifteen minutes from home, it had been very hard to justify getting an apartment. This was supposed to be the fun getaway. I'd even planned to spend some quality time with some of my classmates

100

with whom I'd been flirting all year. But messing around wasn't even on my radar.

I didn't have a fever. I just lacked motivation. I was the last to breakfast and never completed my meals. I didn't know what it was. But when I received a text from Sophie saying she missed me, I realized what it was. I missed her, too.

I hated being away from her.

Over the past six months since she'd moved in, our friendship had evolved into something I couldn't explain. When she was home from school I'd stop doing whatever I was doing to just hang with her.

"Want to go to the library?" she'd asked.

"Sure," I'd say, even though what I needed to do was work on drawings.

"Ice cream?" she'd suggest.

"Let's go," even though I knew the dairy would do horrible things to my digestion.

I wanted to spend time with her, all the time.

It dawned on me during my time away—I was in love. In love with my best friend.

It seemed improbable, wrong even. But there it was.

I had lost sleep over the ensuing days, wondering how she felt. I thought about how we sometimes fooled around and flirted. I thought of the first time she came to my room because she wanted to talk. How she fell asleep in my bed, cuddled next to me. How that one time when she was going to kiss my cheek, she kissed the side of my mouth, leaving an imprint of her lips on mine.

Now I was minutes away from seeing her. My phone chimed. *We missed you! We're at the luggage pick up.*

I had to talk to her. Somehow find the courage to tell her. If she didn't feel the same then the risk was greater than I cared to calculate. But I had to know. I needed her to know.

I scanned the crowds, trying to find her. She found me first. She waved, practically hopping in place.

"Soph!" I said and ran to her.

She jumped into my one-arm embrace and wrapped her arms tight, squeezing me. My face in her hair, I inhaled the scent that I had missed.

She released her hold. "How was it?"

"Great," I said, referring more to the hug than my trip. "How are you?"

"I have news," she said. Her eyes were wide with excitement.

"Go on," I said as she took my hand and walked me toward the luggage carousel.

"Last week," she said, "you'd never guess who I bumped into."

"Who?"

She grinned then nodded toward the carousel. I turned my gaze. "Seth," she said.

I spun back to her. "Seth? Seth Davis?"

She nodded. "He's a different Seth. He's amazing."

"Amazing?" I couldn't even understand what these words meant. Was this a joke? Was I being punked?

"There he is," she said.

I turned. Seth with a shaven head, trim, and muscular. And the oddest thing on his face: a smile. A genuine smile.

"Is this it?" he asked holding up a red suitcase.

"That's the one," Sophie said. "Thanks."

He rolled it over then put out his hand. "Man, it's so nice to see you," he said.

I paused for a few beats then extended my hand. "Seth, you look different," I mumbled.

He rubbed his head and grinned. "You noticed" Seth extended his left arm, into which Sophie slid. He held her with a tenderness and care I had never seen from him. I didn't know what to say. I studied Sophie. She was all smiles.

"So... you guys..." I started. "Wow..."

"We bumped into each other at the movies," she said. "Then a few of us went to Norm's Diner. Next thing you know it's just us. Talking."

"Well, that's... fantastic."

"Let's get you back home," Seth said. "You must be exhausted."

I blinked. Swallowed. "You have no clue."

"HOW?" I asked Sophie. There were so many phrases that could have followed that simple question.

How did this happen?

How could you fall for him?

How is it that the guy who made you feel depressed on prom day, the guy who you abandoned even before the after party, is now someone you date?

And most importantly, how could you not realize that I'm in love with you?

I didn't have the words or the energy to ask all those questions. She was with him. She had even kissed him when he left. Had she slept with him already?

"I can't explain it. When we bumped into each other, I was ready to run the other way."

"But..."

"But there was something about him. Like his energy was different."

"Energy?" I wanted to yell at her for buying into the crap that Yiayia had been spewing. The energy of God. The energy that binds people together.

"I'm telling you. I felt it. Later that night he opened his heart. His little brother—do you remember him?"

"Sure"

She hesitated. "Poor kid committed suicide."

I recoiled. "Oh God." I ran my hand over my face. "Why? What happened?"

"Bullied. Can you believe it?"

"The guy who bullied everyone..."

"Is the guy who lost his own little brother. That broke him. Humbled him."

I nodded. I could see how life could do that. "So now... you two..."

"I'm in love," she said.

Loss's talons dug into my heart, yanking, not gently, not carefully but with the ferocity of a dying sun.

I found a smile. "I'm happy for you," I uttered, and fought gravity which wanted to force me to my knees. I embraced Sophie and cursed Yiayia for making me believe in love, in the idea of "the one." I had found the one—twice. And each time, they had torn my heart out with a smile.

No more. No more pain. I would not be so weak as to ever let someone hurt me again.

TWENTY

— SOPHIE —

Today

I WAKE UP to a throbbing neck ache. I've fallen asleep in Pete's car at a weird angle. We're headed home after making a day of it in Santa Barbara. The Pier, State Street, lunch, and shopping. A perfect day. Now, the sun is making its descent behind the rolling hills as dusk takes center stage. I glance at Pete who's running his fingers through his thick black hair, helplessly trying to reverse the windblown effect. When the light hits just right, I catch an unfamiliar glint. Is that a hint of gray?

I STILL REMEMBER the first time he discovered a bit of puberty-induced facial hair in seventh grade and the first time he tried to hide pimples by poorly applying his mom's makeup in ninth grade. Before my eyes, he has transformed into a man.

I need to tell him what Frank told me yesterday. There were a couple of chances earlier, but I hesitated, not sure how he'd take it. In the past, news about Claire has derailed him. Which is what might happen again, once he hears the latest developments.

"Let's take a walk," I say when Pete pulls into the garage.

He shrugs. "Sure."

It's a nice evening, but that's not the reason for the walk. I'm taking him somewhere specific. I need to witness his reaction.

I clear my throat. "Something I wanted to tell you," I start, but his phone chimes with a text message.

He's studying his phone, frowning.

"What's wrong?" I ask.

"What kind of assistant sets up a meeting for tomorrow."

"On a Sunday? Why would Sandy do that?"

"A potential client she believes will help me pull away from the firm and start my own studio."

"That's awesome," I say. I wish he would trust himself and take some risks.

He eyes me. "Don't get too excited. I doubt anything will come of it. Plus, hanging my future on one job is too much of a risk. I'll convince the client to work with my firm instead."

"Well that's plain idiotic. Didn't they pass you up for the promotion? You don't need those myopic fools. Sometimes all you need is one shot to leap off. What if this one's it?"

"Somehow I doubt Sandy has found the one. Either way, I can't on Sunday. We'll have to reschedule."

We take a left then another right. He's too busy reading his emails to realize where I'm taking him.

"Is it over with Natalie?" I ask.

He glances at me for a moment. "Yeah."

He doesn't appear broken up over this. His relationships are on auto replay, it seems. He continues working on his phone.

"Another one that didn't work."

"I wanted to make it work with Natalie. Who wouldn't, she's great. But something was missing. I just can't put my finger on it."

But I can. I know all too well why all his relationships have stalled.

After another block, the house comes into view. I stop. So does Pete, but his gaze remains fixed on his phone.

"Would you like to hear the latest rumor?" I ask.

He focuses on me. "Sure."

I point to the house on the other side of the street. His gaze shifts then his eyes widen. His mouth has gone slack.

"Word is that Claire is coming back," I say gently.

Outside the home that Claire and her family had vacated all those years ago is a crew of contractors cleaning up for the night: garage door open, a handful of people inside putting away tools; a team is loading a van with old carpeting material. The McIntyres never sold the house when they moved away. I suppose they hadn't needed to.

"Ah man," Pete whispers.

His expression reveals what I have always suspected. He is so not over Claire.

WE DON'T STAY LONG. He's antsy. I don't argue.

With Claire's return on his mind, I go for the big question as we head back home. "So what do you say? Reunion. Me and you."

He hesitates this time. "I'm still a no."

"You do know that the rest of the gang will go. Jen will be all over this. Same with Pam."

"I doubt Raj and Frank would be interested—and it's their reunion, not the significant others."

"Which planet do you live on? You think if the ladies want to go, the guys will be able to stop them? Especially Jen? Please. I'll call tomorrow and get them to commit."

Pete's right eye twitches. I know this is hard on him, but sometimes we have to force the issue. Before the breakthrough, there is a breakdown.

He studies me. "You want to go because of Robby. Admit it."

"Of course I want to see Robby," I say as he opens the door. "Wouldn't you go if Claire said she'd be there?"

In his eyes I see the answer that he is unwilling to utter. Is he wondering if Claire will come? I don't know the answer, but I will do everything I can to find and convince Claire to attend. We all need closure.

I hold his arm, forcing him to stop. "I asked you to be open," I say. "Let's have fun with this. We'll go wild. It's only a few weeks away. We'll get tanned, toned, and all shmexy."

He laughs, but there is no agreement on his face. "To what end?" he asks.

"Does there have to be an end goal? Can't it be just for fun? We go dancing together. Is there an end goal?" I ask, but feel my face warm up. Maybe there is a bit of hope.

He breaks eye contact. "I'll think about it," he says.

I hope he does.

TWENTY-ONE

— PETE —

I FLIP THE light switches in the great room of my home. The Craftsman look comes alive when the light glowing through the stained-glass lamps reflects off the deeply stained wood furniture.

"I'm going to take a shower," Sophie says. "A long one."

Perfect. That'll give me the time I need to do what I have to do. Sophie may have defected, but the rest of the guys might still be salvageable. I pause. Why do I want to convince them not to go? What's the big deal? Let them go. Who cares?

But what if Claire is there?

What if Robby is interested in Sophie?

I shake my head. Why am I behaving like the teenage version of me? I need a drink. I grab a beer just as Sophie steps out of her room, a change of clothes in her hand.

"Don't disturb," she says.

"You wish."

She grunts before she closes the bathroom door.

I take a long swallow of the amber liquid then run to my office and grab the phone. There are two calls I have to place before Sophie comes out.

"Frank, are you—?"

"Hey, Raj. Can you believe—?"

By the time I hang up for the second time, all my hopes for a coup are shattered. They all want to go. Sophie has already won, even without trying.

The good old days, Sophie said. Apparently I'm the odd man out. They're all romanticizing the past. Frank reminisced about his near-death experience with the seaweed on Senior Ditch Day at the beach, and Raj reminded me of how we first met over a debate on whether Spiderman could really beat the Hulk if web came to smash. He was wrong then and he's wrong now. At least Peter Parker got a few hotties in his time. The Hulk... not so much. Also, how could I go against my namesake?

I check Facebook. Ignoring the increased notification count, I go straight for the latest posts to the reunion site. Twenty-eight have confirmed now. They've picked up ten people in a few days, reaching the tipping point.

One by one I check out the profiles of my ex-classmates. Like an avalanche, little memories roll down the hill I have tried to forget. From kindergarten all the way through twelfth grade, someone has systematically scanned and posted images from the yearbooks. All the class pictures, individual headshots, and impromptu pictures are now on Facebook.

I glance at the dozens of notifications, private messages, and friend requests and consider diving into them, but change gears when my cell phone chirps. A text from Sophie.

WTF? I can hear the bath water running. "Are you texting me from the bathroom now?" I yell.

"I said, don't disturb," she yells back.

I read her text.

I just want to say I know what you tried to pull off with the guys. And that you're pitiful. That's all.

Sometimes I wonder if the guys will ever side with me.

I search the reunion site and find the pictures I've been looking for.

I study Claire's scanned grainy picture from sixth grade. That is exactly how I remember her. Medium length blonde with nearly white streaks; Ocean green eyes; freckles on her nose; and a crooked smile—the kind that doesn't really want to commit to happiness, but is open to the possibility.

Does she have a Facebook account? I quickly search it up. A handful of names match, but none of the faces are hers.

I grab another beer and realize I'm hungry. I shouldn't drink too much, but the occasion calls for alcohol.

I pull down a few Hancock Prep yearbooks and go to the living room. I play an appropriate playlist then crack open the sixth-grade yearbook. Like the gates of an abandoned home, the book creaks and the pungent smell of old paper delivers a pang to the pit of my stomach.

I read the brief notes from my classmates.

You're cool. Keep in touch.

Nice to meet you this year—

Lakers Rule!

And a one-page essay by Raj, arguing that Iron Man was not made of Iron, but an alloy and therefore should have been named Alloy-Man.

I guzzle the beer and in the background pick up the lyrics from a Chris Isaak song. Yes, those days were hard days, lonely days.

I toss the yearbook on the floor and grab the ninth-grade yearbook from the pile. I flip through the pages and find the note from Claire.

I'm glad we grew closer. You rock! Luv, Claire.

I had been so close in ninth grade. But I'd hesitated and Robby stepped in. I screwed it up for both me and Sophie. She may have a chance with him, but why would Claire show up now? To pick up where she left things off? To get Robby back? To come clean? Would history repeat itself?

The thought of possibly being with Claire again brings back

memories of those amazing nights in my car. After what we had, how could she just leave and not call me? What could've been so bad?

One thing's for sure, Robby is tracking Sophie. I don't like it. The thought of those two together makes me uneasy. As much as I'd like to not go, I may have to, just to keep an eye on them. More importantly, I need to keep Sophie safe from Seth. I'm sure he's aware of the reunion.

The doorbell rings, causing me to yelp. I check my watch. It's almost 8:00 p.m.

"I ordered delivery," Sophie yells from the bathroom. "I'm almost done!"

"Good call," I say and stumble to the door.

I open the door and grab the bags. "Already paid for," the delivery guy says, so I hand him a $5 tip. The spices from the Thai food drive my senses toward craving.

I spin to the great room when Sophie steps out of the bathroom. I freeze.

Her hair is wet and she's wearing an oversized t-shirt with the Wonder Woman logo on it. Her left shoulder is exposed and the shirt drapes to mid-thigh. Her bare, powerful, tanned legs glow. *Is that thin t-shirt the only thing covering her?* Her movements are in slow motion.

"That smells good," Sophie says, waking me from my delirium. She takes her dirty clothes to the laundry room. I watch her movement, knowing I shouldn't.

It's the damn beers. I'm tipsy and confused. *Stay focused.*

As she comes toward me, she locks onto my eyes. She fingers the bottom edge of her shirt and for an instant I think she's about to tug it off.

"Wait," I say just as I notice she's wearing shorts. Itsy bitsy shorts. She's just fanning her body... not getting undressed.

"What?" she asks, studying me like I'm insane. She's right.

"Nothing, I... I've been thinking about the whole reunion thing," I say as I place the food cartons on the kitchen table.

"And?" She steps toward me.

I face her. "And I figured I don't want you to go alone. So we'll go together."

She launches at me, clutching me in a bear hug. She presses her damp body into mine. "Thank you for being open," she says.

She releases the hold and gives me a huge smile. "This'll be so much fun."

I like it when she's happy, but the warm sensation I'm feeling after that hug hasn't dissipated. I can still feel her body. I can still smell her mango-scented shampoo.

"We can start tomorrow morning," she says.

I snap out of my trance. "Start what?"

"The makeover."

What have I agreed to?

I WASH my hands and face, then stare into the mirror. *What the hell's the matter with you? You asked her to come here to keep her safe and now you're mentally undressing her.*

I wander back into the great room. The food is spread on the coffee table. Plates and forks neatly set on napkins.

"And what were you doing with this?" She holds up the yearbook like a TSA agent with a five-ounce bottle of shampoo.

"Nothing bad."

"I bet." She sits on the couch and opens the yearbook to the personal messages. I take a step toward her just as her finger nearly touches Claire's little message. "I had forgotten about this note."

I sit next to her and look over her bare shoulder. "Me too," I lie.

"Do you remember how pitiful you sounded when you tried to decipher the meaning of this note?"

"I wasn't pitiful. I had a legitimate question."

"Legitimate? You wondered if instead of 'L-u-v' she really meant to write 'L-o-v-e.' That's pitiful."

"It was a valid possibility."

"For an obsessed boy, maybe. She was already Robby's girl by then."

I eye Sophie as she flips through the pages of the yearbook.

"We look so young," Sophie says.

I glance at Sophie's picture. "Other than your afro, not much has changed with you," I say.

She eyes me. "Thin ice, buddy. Very thin ice."

"Just sayin'."

"Very. Thin."

Sophie flips pages, then her finger lands on pictures from the Winter Formal. Robby and Claire dancing.

"There is a lot I want to fix at the reunion," she whispers.

I glance at her. *Does she mean with Robby?*

She finds a picture of us dancing at the ninth grade Winter Formal. "We were pretty awesome that night," Sophie says. "I'm glad we went together. No one expected you to be such a good dancer, me included."

"My brother's motto: if you can't play the guitar, learn how to dance."

"Surprisingly good advice, coming from Marcos." She gives me the evil eye. "You totally used me that night," she says.

"How dare you accuse me?"

She's grinning. "You were so damn obvious in the way you wanted to dance near Claire and Robby. You knew the poor guy didn't have an ounce of groove in him."

"I have no recollection."

"It's okay. I used you too," she says. "Not that it worked, but I tried." She flips the page and we're both silent for a few moments. "Oh, Erik," she sighs as we both stare at the face of the boy that was so full of life.

I take the yearbook out of Sophie's hands. "Let's set this bad boy to rest."

She dabs at the corner of her eye.

"I've recorded a bunch of *Kitchen Nightmares* episodes. You want to watch?"

"Yes, absolutely. He's so hot."

"Who?"

"Chef Ramsay. I love how he gets all emotional."

"That makes him hot? I can do that."

"Yeah, not so much."

TWENTY-TWO

— PETE —

MY ALARM GOES OFF, but I have no desire to get out of bed. I didn't sleep much because my mind was filled with all the wrong thoughts. I kept thinking of Sophie. In the same way I did when she lived at my parent's house.

I drag my bones out of bed and wash up. I'll watch some TV, hopefully some good History Channel shows, and veg the rest of the day. My Sunday routine is a work of science.

As I reach my door, I hear music, or something that sounds like music. I open the door and step out.

It *is* music. Spa music.

I take a few more steps and see Sophie. On a Yoga mat in the den. Looking hot and powerful. All my thoughts from the night before come crushing into me again.

I can't help but stare at her. She's holding a wide stance, her right knee is bent in front, the left straight back. Her left hand is reaching back, gently touching her calf, while her right hand is stretching straight up. Her eyes focus on the heavens.

Call a sculptor. Get the clay before it's too late. She is a goddess.

When she transitions out of her pose, she notices me.

"Good morning," she says as she graciously changes pose. She does something that looks like a push up, holds that position, then drops her lower body, her hips nearly touching the floor while she raises her upper body, arms straight. Her body is in a full stretch. Like something a cat would do.

"Does that hurt?" I ask.

She says nothing for a few moments then returns to the push-up pose again. Her feet leap toward her hands and she rises.

She grabs the towel and tosses it on her shoulder, then grabs the water bottle. She's facing me, drinking the water greedily, but her perfectly-formed body doesn't waver. She's not tired. She looks like she's just starting.

"Initially," she starts, "it will hurt. But as the body learns how to stretch and hold the various poses, as you strengthen your core, you'll be able to sustain any type of physical activity for the long haul."

I grin. "I'm all for sustained physical activities."

An eyebrow shoots up. She takes a couple of steps up to me and stands inches away. "Is that so?" she asks, a smile teases her lips.

My heart rate picks up. She's sweating, blood is pumping through her veins, and her body has never looked more fit. "Uh-huh," is what comes out of my mouth, but my throat is suddenly dry.

She places a hand on my shoulder. "Let's find out," she says, then grabs my arm and pulls me to the yoga mat.

"Oh, come on. I don't want to do this."

"Don't be such a wimp. Just a few movements."

"I'm not dressed properly. I need yoga pants."

"You're already wearing shorts. Good enough."

She man-handles me, positioning me on the mat. "Okay, get on your knees."

"I feel objectified," I say just as she gets me on the floor.

"The first pose is called the plank. It's like the end of the push up," she says.

"Oh yeah, I know this one." I do the push up and hold it when I get to the top position. "There," I say and lower myself to the floor.

"What was that?"

"The plank."

"Get back up and stay there."

I do as requested. But within three seconds, I feel the tremors. "Now?" I grunt out.

"Hold it. Not yet," she says. "And lower your butt, for the love of all things decent. It's sticking up like you're calling for attention."

I lower it.

"More," she says then pushes my butt down.

But that's the straw. I collapse to the floor. I'm breathing heavily; I roll to my back. She's above me, staring down. Even in this position she looks amazing.

"You're pitiful."

"Thanks."

"Get up, we'll try another one."

I try to argue, but it's no use. She gets me in a position that she calls upward dog. This is the same one I saw her doing—head high, my crotch nearly touching the floor. I'm able to hold this one better.

"Good. Now we switch to downward dog." She grabs my hips and starts pulling me up. "Lower your head as I move your hips upward. Don't move your feet. You'll take an upside down V pose."

This is hard and getting harder. Not only because it takes more strength and control, but because she's holding my hips. Her strong hands have wrapped themselves completely around my waist. What the hell is going on with me? I feel the current. I feel things I shouldn't be feeling with her.

I drop. "Okay, that was good." I slide away from her.

"No way, Pete. We agreed we'll get all *purrty* for the party. Put on sneakers and get hydrated. We're going for a run."

"What are we running away from?"

WE RUN—AND walk—for nearly forty minutes. I'm a sweaty mess. I can barely breathe and my sides are tearing up. I'm convinced I'll have scar tissue. Why did I stop swimming?

I stumble to the front porch and take a long pause. My hands are on my knees, my face down, and my eyes closed. I'm breathing deeply because I'm convinced these are my last breaths.

Sophie drops her arm on my back and leans down to eye-level with me. "I'm so proud of you. You made it."

"I'm about to die."

"No, you're just starting to live. Let's go in and take a shower."

My head snaps up.

She opens the door and marches toward her room. *She didn't mean what I think she meant, right? Of course not. What kind of sick depraved person am I?*

She enters her room, grabs a change of clothes then goes to the guest bathroom.

"I'm going to pick up Pit from Linda's," she says.

"I'll go with you."

She eyes me. "You don't have to."

"I don't have to, or you don't want me to?" I ask.

"If you're going to come, please don't embarrass me," she says then closes the bathroom door.

I march toward my room which has an en suite. I peel off my clothes and take a look at my body, wondering if I'm already ripped.

Apparently, I'm not. My swimming days during college have helped me keep a decent form. But I no longer have the lean cuts I used to have. Maybe Sophie's right.

The water from the guest shower turns on. I also turn mine on. The two showers share a wall.

"Can you hear me?" Sophie yells through the wall.

I step into the shower and lean into the wall. "Yeah."

"Is the water going to get all cold now?"

"No, I had all the piping redone. This home is all modern with a tankless water heater."

"Whatever," she says. "You're such a geek."

I want to preoccupy my thoughts with plumbing and water heaters because I know too well that she's on the other side of the wall. Naked.

I hear a sound from the other side. I focus.

She's singing *Sway* by Dean Martin, and without warning I am transported in time to Raj's wedding.

TWENTY-THREE

— PETE —

BY THE TIME the limo arrived at the reception hall, we were already done for.

Sophie was the bridesmaid at Jen and Raj's wedding, and I was the best man.

Recently, Sophie asked Seth to move out as part of their official separation path. But the last few weeks before things became official, Sophie had been in hiding, almost withdrawn from the rest of the team. Because of this seclusion, when the champagne bottle in the limo was opened, she was the first to down her portion. The two of us finished off the second bottle.

Even before the booze hit my blood stream, I had been stealing glances all night. Sophie had a definite aura of fire around her. And she didn't do anything to subdue the hungry eyes of everyone there. She played her "A" game. From the way she moved, to the way she touched me. She was flirting. I was sure of it. As sure as a drunken man could be.

She wore a tailor-made one-piece turquoise dress and super high heels. Up to that point, we were buzzed. Then we saw the tequila bottle at our table. That became our downfall.

A Greek and a Mexican sitting in front of a tequila bottle. There was only one thing that could be done. We asked for lime wedges and drank one shot after another of *Patron Silver Anejo*. We drank toasts to the happy couple, but the happy couple was on the dance floor, out of earshot. I was drunk by the fifth toast, but Sophie kept going strong. She was in a rush to lose control, much like Claire years earlier in my car.

By the time we emptied the bottle, she was yanking me off the chair toward the dance floor. She smelled so nice, her skin soft, and her whispery voice tickled my ear.

"I love this song," she said.

Dino crooned about two lovers swaying to the ocean breeze.

"You look very beautiful today," I said.

"Just today?"

"No. No. Every day you're beautiful." The room was spinning. "But today you are more beautifuler."

"I don't think that's a word," she said.

"It should be. It definitely should be. I invented a word for you."

And with that drunken conversation, she laid her head on my shoulder and danced. We danced for what felt like days.

"I need air," she said sometime later.

I took her hand and walked her through the crowd of dancers to the balcony overlooking the San Fernando Valley.

When she hugged her arms, I slid off my Tux coat and draped it around her shoulders.

"Thanks," she said as she stared at the glittering view.

I leaned forward on the wrought iron gate, Sophie slipped her arm through the crook of my elbow and placed her head on my shoulder.

I didn't lean on the gate to be cool. My head was spinning and I was worried that my knees would buckle any minute. But having Sophie next to me made up for all that.

"The view is so mesmerizing," she whispered.

"*You're* mesmerizing," I responded.

She glanced up at me and smiled. "Is that right?" she asked but when she blinked her eyes didn't open.

In that moment, I studied her face, her soft forehead, long eyelashes, small nose, and full lips.

I leaned in, held her face with both hands and did what I had to do. I kissed her.

She didn't resist, she didn't hesitate. Her mouth accepted mine. I straightened, gently pulling her face tighter. My jacket slid off her back and hit the ground. She tasted like lime and agave. Her lips enveloped mine.

Just then, the glass door opened.

The roar of the party *whooshed* out.

We both spun to the door. Her foot got tangled with my jacket on the floor and she went down. I tried to help but went down with her.

She was on her back on top of my jacket and I was on top of her, trying my best to not crush her.

Sophie threw her head back and laughed.

I maneuvered my way around her, barely able to control my laughter.

"That was sad," she said.

"Are you guys okay?" a guy with a deep voice asked.

I had to focus on the person who had interrupted us. "Frank?"

"Yeah, dipshit, it's Frank."

He helped her up just as Pam came outside. "Are you okay?" she asked Sophie.

Sophie was still laughing and swerving.

"Take her to the restroom, please," Frank said.

"Looks like someone's been locking lips with a bottle," Pam said.

Sophie stopped laughing, turned to me, then snorted and laughed again.

I got to my feet and was wiping myself down when I felt Frank's stare.

"What?" I asked.

He closed the space between us and took me by my shoulder and walked me to a corner.

"What are you doing with Sophie?" he asked.

Suddenly, I felt sober. "Nothing," I uttered.

"Good. Remember she's still married."

"She's separated."

"What if they reconcile? It happens."

I stared at him. "But I like her."

"Then respect her and don't mess up. Particularly when both of you are drunk."

He was right. What the hell had I been thinking?

I nodded. "Thanks man, I'm glad you came when you did." I stumbled toward the glass doors.

"Remember, this is Sophie, not one of your usuals. If you're going to do it, do it right. She deserves that."

But as we walked away, even in the state I was in, I knew he didn't really understand me. When I was kissing Sophie, sex was not on my mind. At least that was not the *primary* thought on my mind.

I thought about how perfect she felt. And how wonderful her lips were. I didn't want us to stop. What I wanted was for her to divorce Seth.

TWENTY-FOUR

— SOPHIE —

Today

UNDER THE DOWNPOUR of the shower, I sing a song that Pete and I always dance to. It's a dance that we have perfected. A song where we meld when we're together. Just like at Raj's wedding.

Being here has the potential of going down as the biggest mistake I've ever committed—and that says a lot when I look at my resume of disasters. But I can't help it. I continue to think of him.

And although I make fun of him for not being in shape, I can't help but think of him, naked, only inches away. Even so, the crevasse between us may be insurmountable. Because no matter what I try, to him, I am always his sister—his buddy.

TWENTY-FIVE

— PETE —

NEARLY A WEEK has passed since Sophie moved in. I'm wrapping up for the day and not a moment too soon. I've been assigned to a very dull project. When the project is boring, the work is ten times more difficult. All I want is to go home, get a beer—or five —and veg with Sophie. It's nice to know she'll be home when I arrive. A smart move for sure. In fact, having her there makes the end of day something to look forward to.

"Knock, knock."

I jolt. It's Sophie.

"Hey, Soph. What brings you here?"

"Let's go to the mall, then dinner," she says. Not a question. A command.

"I don't know. I'm exhausted," I say.

"Please," she says.

I can never deny her. "Fine, but you're buying."

WHEN WE ENTER NORDSTROM, I mentally prepare to do the typical guy-friend thing and tell her if one dress looks better than the other. "That's it," I'll say. Or, "Wow, amazing." But I'm not up for doing this now. What I need is a drink.

"Okay, wait here. I'll get someone," Sophie says and marches away.

I look around for a place to sit when I notice men's clothing around us. I rewind our earlier discussion.

"Pete, this is Geoffrey. He's responsible for your makeover," she says. A colorful little Hispanic man stands next to her, beaming.

"My what?"

"Well, we certainly have a blank canvas to start with," he says. Both Sophie and Geoffrey laugh.

"I don't need a makeover. I have plenty of clothes."

"Pete, be quiet. You need to stand out next month."

"I do stand out."

Sophie turns to Geoffrey, who is shaking his head, a look of distaste plastered over his tanned face and bleached white teeth.

"Oh for cryin' out loud." And with that, I am measured, fondled, squeezed, and manhandled, for the next hour.

"Too plain—"

"Not enough character—"

"Too outlandish—"

"Not enough color—"

"Too... something—"

I'm a castrated bull being paraded in front of the butchers. I am no longer involved in the conversation and start wearing whatever they hand me.

"Oh, I don't know, Miss Sophie. He looks a little..." Geoffrey starts, then they both giggle.

"I hate my life," I mumble as I slog back to the dressing room.

I button up the latest shirt. "No more after this." I throw on the suit coat and storm out. "Hear me loud and clear," I say as I approach them. "I am done."

Sophie rises slowly while Geoffrey beams and clasps his hands. She steps up to me, smiling beside Geoffrey who looks like a proud cat observing his latest catch.

"What?" I ask.

Sophie adjusts my collar and brushes the lapel of my coat. She gently slaps my cheek, punctuating each word. "You. Look. Incredible."

I take a step back and scan my getup.

"You think?"

"I do," she says. "Well done, Geoffrey."

"This one was difficult," Geoffrey says. "But we did well, Miss Sophie. We did very well."

Is he crying?

SOPHIE'S in good spirits over dinner, proud and content.

"Five weeks to go. Have you heard anything new?" I ask.

"Funny you should ask." She clears her throat. "You remember Pat?"

I search my memory. "Pat, *el presidente?* Our class's fearless leader? The one who agreed to everything the administration wanted and threw us all under the bus?"

She frowns. "Yes, him."

"Nope. I have no idea who you're talking about."

She gives me a face. "All right smart ass. Hardy har har. Anyway, he's reached out to me asking for help with pictures that I may have from the yearbook collection and personal pictures and videos. I've been helping here and there, and we were discussing something."

"Something?"

"Yes, we had a question for you."

"We?"

"Yes. Pat and I."

I don't like the sound of this.

"Pat asked if you could be the evening's emcee."

"Me? Emcee? What are you guys smoking? I'm no emcee. Those people barely remember me."

"You're wrong. They all remember you as the guy that made us all laugh."

"Laugh with, or at?"

"Stop. Did you forget Homecoming? How you took the mic out of the coach's hand and had both sides on the field splitting a kidney?"

"That was because I had a beer, courtesy of Marcos."

"How about the Halloween party senior year?"

"More beer."

"Then we'll just have to juice you up before the reunion," Sophie says. "Pat loved the idea."

"They barely even know me."

"Everyone knew you. You just like believing you didn't matter. You were always epic. You never bothered to notice how people really saw you."

We're quiet for a few moments. "Fine," I say.

"Thanks, I appreciate it."

"Hey, that's the least I could do for my bestest friend."

She seems to be contemplating something. "Do you recall why and when we became besties?"

"Of course. Seventh grade."

"Go on."

"It was my infamous haircut. One Saturday, my dad was so tired with my hair that he woke me, then dragged me to Supercuts and forced me to slash my long hair, converting me into a geek."

I remember hating dad, hating my hair, hating the girl at Supercuts who chewed strawberry-scented gum while she destroyed my "look."

"Then on Monday, when I came to school, everyone made fun of me. But then I got a note... from you. It was written on the back of your Hello Kitty daily calendar sheet. You said, 'Your hair looks great.'"

Sophie has been listening intently. When I'm done, she shakes her head. "Close, but that wasn't it."

I frown. "What do you think did it?"

Her eyes turn glassy for a moment. "It was seventh grade and it was about hair, you're right about that. But it was Seth's insults about my hair, calling me the red chili and hot tamale. By math class, he got me to tears. I was going to deck him when you stood, calmly strolled up to him, and punched him in the nose. Do you remember that?"

"Of course I do. I got suspended for three days. But that happened *after* I received your note."

"I don't think so," she says.

"I got suspended the week after Thanksgiving. I got your note on November 12th."

Her mouth drops. "How the hell do you remember the date?"

I shrug. "The date was on the reverse side of the note. I still have it."

TWENTY-SIX

— PETE —

SOPHIE AND I are headed to my mom and dad's for Friday evening dinner. I haven't been there in three weeks. Sophie, closer to two months. During her turbulent separation, it was hard for her to focus on much. But things have changed now.

In our first couple of weeks of living together—or living in the same house, but not together in the classic sense—things have finally cooled off. For me at least. I have not been thinking of her in that way.

Not really.

Not all the time at least.

I park the car in the driveway and dread the decibel level we're about to step into.

When I'm asked if my family is like "that" Greek family in "that" movie, my answer of course is no. But the facts are considerably more depressing. My family is certifiable—no doubt about that. Don't get me wrong—I love them. But if evaluated, I am sure they would be diagnosed as clinically insane.

As Sophie and I approach the door, we hear voices that pound against the walls and windows, trying to break through the stucco and brick. It's hard to understand why everyone has to yell about everything.

I ring the doorbell. Then wait. Nothing.

Knock on the door and wait.

Ring it again. More waiting.

I'm about to knock again, when Sophie grabs my hand.

"Insanity is repeating the same thing over and over, expecting different results. Just turn the door handle. You know they never lock the door."

The explosion of noise nearly knocks me backward. I cringe, but Sophie laughs uncontrollably. She loves my batty family.

"Petros!" my mom yells.

"Sophia!" my dad yells.

After all these years, my family is still trying to change her name to sound more Greek.

A chorus of indecipherable words are hurled at us by everyone else. We are immediately assaulted by my parents.

"I love your hair, Sophia—"

"If we don't call, you never call—"

"You need to eat more—"

"My good-for-nothing son never comes. You should come without him—"

None of what they say requires a response. My parents have mastered the art of asking rapid-fire questions. And if you are silly enough to attempt an answer, your words will be left for dead on the kitchen floor.

"Come here, Petros. Come see me before I die!" Yiayia demands. Over the past year she has lost a lot of her mobility, but none of her wit and sharp tongue. She's perched on her throne, observing the family.

"You're not going to die," I say when we reach her. I hold her hand.

"You are idiot," she says, her accent unchanged even after fifty years in the States. "Of course I going to die. Your poor grandfather waiting for me. But how can I go if my job not finish here?"

It is a common fact that I am an idiot. And the 'job' she refers to is seeing me married. The reason why I'm an idiot is because I'm not married yet. A vicious circle? Maybe. But this is the circle of Greek life.

"How are you?" I ask, but she pays no attention.

Instead, she reaches for Sophie. "Sophia, is he eating?" she asks.

"Yes. He's—"

"Does he go to church?"

Sophie turns to me and grins. "I think so." I give her a thumb up for covering for me.

"He need to go," she says, then turns an angry eye to me. "You go and pray for wife."

"You're not supposed to ask for things like that. God will get—"

"Shut up. You want me to die knowing my grandson was left alone?"

And just like that I swear I see tears well in her eyes. She's talented. "No, of course not, Yiayia."

"Sophia, make sure he get married."

Sophie glances at me then winks. "I'll see what I can do."

DINNER, as always, is madness. The whole process, from the preparation, to the cooking, to the serving, is a mess.

Multiple voices yelling across the table...

"Where's the bread?"

...Food spilling just before it lands...

"The pilaf platter, hold it straight."

...The ever-shifting seating arrangement...

"Move over one, let Marcos sit there."

My parents' house is a zoo. I sometimes joke and call it organized chaos, but that's a lie. There's nothing organized about it. There are twenty people here, but you'd think it's a concert at the LA Coliseum. The noise, the laughter, the profane language.

Sophie sits next to me.

"How much pilaf, Sophie?" Mom asks.

"Just one scoop."

Scoop.

"Just one?"

Scoop.

"No more. Stop, stop."

Scoop.

"Okay fine, just one more."

Scoop.

Sophie's entire plate is rice pilaf. But to Sophie's credit she smiles and rolls with the punches. This is the family that accepted and loved her. She'll put up with things the rest of us won't.

My nephew burps.

"Hey, what are you doing?" Dad asks, in mock anger, then turns to Sophie, beaming. "This reminds me of a story."

A new story, or one of his recycled ones?

"When we lived in Chicago, I knew this guy Tito. One day, after lunch, he burped."

Nope, it's an old one we've all heard before. Including Sophie.

"So I said, hey what's the matter with you? Tito says, that means the food was good. So I said—"

I have to put a stop to this, "Dad, you've already—" but Sophie squeezes my thigh so hard I nearly jump.

"Go on," she says, urging Dad to tell his story.

"So I said, hey what's the matter with you? He said that means the food was good. So I said, maybe in the country of the pigs."

Dad laughs like he has never laughed before. The rest of the family shake their heads in exasperation, but Sophie... Well, she's Sophie. She laughs like he's the second coming of Eddie Murphy.

AFTER DINNER, Sophie, my brother Marcos, my sister Maria, and I go into the yard, Armenian coffee in hand. Yiayia prefers the Armenian blend over Greek. And don't ever mention Turkish coffee near her.

"Ten-year reunion," Maria says. "Hard to believe it was ten years ago you graduated. You know, I got married one year out of college. So did your brother."

Here we go. "Did you conveniently forget that Marcos got divorced six months later?" I ask, hoping to derail her train of thought.

"Bad luck," Marcos says. "That's all."

"Three times?" I ask. "That's not bad luck. That's a curse."

Marcos was indeed born with a curse: too good looking for his own good.

"You should've stayed with the first one," Maria says. "She was the best."

"You don't even remember her name," I say.

"Sure I do. It was Laura."

"Nope. Karine."

"Laura, Karine, it doesn't matter. She was the one."

"You're probably right," Marcos says. "But what can I tell you? I've never been good at holding on to 'em."

"At least he tried to have a family. You," Maria says, pointing at me, "I don't know what you're waiting on."

"He doesn't believe in love and marriage," Sophie says. "Right, Pete?"

"Where did we go wrong?" Maria says then crosses herself.

"Really, Soph?" Is she purposefully trying to get a rise out of them?

"It's the truth," she says.

"Fine. Yes, it's the truth. Have you considered that not everyone is destined to get married and have a family with kids who burp at the dinner table?"

"You mean making a commitment isn't your thing?" Marcos asks.

"That's rich. Especially coming from you, Marcos," I say. "What is this? Some sort of intervention?"

"Don't be an idiot," Maria says. "We have more important things to do than waste our time on your love life."

"Or lack thereof," Sophie says. My siblings high-five her.

Sophie may have to sleep in my parent's home tonight.

BACK INSIDE, Yiayia calls me.

"Come here," she says, urging me to kneel in front of her. The liberal consumption of wine has taken its toll on her.

"You know," she whispers, "Sophia looking very beautiful." I pull back and she smiles wickedly, then proceeds to pinch my arm hard.

"She's like a sister to me," I say with very little conviction.

"But..." she says, raising a trembling finger, "...she not your sister, eh?" Then she winks.

TWENTY-SEVEN

— SOPHIE —

I'M ABOUT TO return to the backyard to join Pete when I notice Yiayia sitting alone. Leaning forward, she is scrutinizing everyone. Her vision isn't what it used to be, but her need to be part of the conversation is as strong as ever.

"Hi, Yiayia," I say and sit next to her.

Yiayia brightens and takes my hand. "You are good girl. Better than my daughter and granddaughter."

"Shh," I say. "Someone will hear you."

"Bring them here. I tell them now." She then glances at me and grins, clearly feeling her wine. "Tell me, Sophia, is Petros almost married?"

"I don't think so."

She mumbles something in Greek. "Are you almost married?"

"I'm still in the middle of a divorce."

"It almost finish, so you have to think about the next one. Are you ready to be married?"

"No, Yiayia. I don't think I'll be doing that again."

"Why not? Are you sick?"

"Not that I know of."

"Then get married."

"I don't want to get married to another mistake."

"Then marry right person this time," Yiayia says. "Mistake was marrying because you felt sorry for that one. He was mistake. Love is never mistake."

Yiayia may be drunk, but her memory is intact and her ability to simplify everything to its core is downright empowering.

"No more mistake for you."

"No more," I agree. "There is someone. Who knows, maybe he's the one." I feel my cheeks turn red.

"Does he respect you?"

"Yes."

"Do you respect him?"

"Yes."

"Is he good kisser?"

I think of his lips.

"What are you guys talking about?" Pete asks.

My ears catch on fire. "Nothing," I say, then rise.

"We are talking about kissing," Yiayia says. "And love."

I grab Pete's arm and march out before Yiayia says anything else.

TWENTY-EIGHT

— SOPHIE —

"THAT LOOKS PERFECT," I say. I don't add, '*It better be for the amount your shop charged my car insurance.*'

"Let's hope whoever did it doesn't do it again," the body shop manager says.

"Yeah, well, I can't control crazy."

Linda clears her throat. I glance at her. She's not happy with what she thinks is my lackadaisical approach to safety. "You worry too much," I say, then lean down and look at the hood of my car again from multiple angles, wanting to make sure it still looks like a baby's ass. It does. No sign of Seth's love letter remains.

The manager hands me the invoice copy, then walks away. From the reflection off the car's window I see him ogling over Linda. When he turns his attention to my ass, I spin toward him.

"Thanks again," I say.

"Oh." He coughs. "Yeah, anytime." He picks up his pace and goes to the office.

I turn my attention to Linda. "Please change your mind about tonight. Follow me to Hollywood, I'll take a quick shower—"

"Thanks, but I'm going to skip it."

"It'll be fun. You'll meet my other friends, make new friends."

"Maybe next time," she offers, but I know she'll say no again. She never wants to go to restaurants or bars or night clubs. "Are you sure?"

"Positive. Have a good time."

Linda doesn't talk much about her past, but I do know she was engaged to her long-time boyfriend. I also know that he died unexpectedly. I also know she still wears the engagement ring on a chain that caresses her chest.

I slide into my car. It's so nice to have wheels again. I arrive home and grin when I open the garage door and see the space Pete has created for me so that I can park the car inside.

He's not home yet, so I run in to get ready for dinner with our friends. Pit has taken over my bed, his large head dug underneath my pillow.

While I'm bathing, my phone chimes. A change in plans, I bet. I wrap a towel around myself, grab my phone, and sneak a peek from the cracked door.

"Pete?" I call out.

No response. He's not home yet. I duck into my room then check the phone. There are two separate messages.

One from Pete. *I'm running late.* I relax. No concern that he'll see me prancing around with just a towel on, although truth be told, it is fun to see his reaction and how his little ears turn red.

There's another text from Jen, Raj's wife to me and Pam. *Change in plans. We're going to a place that's dinner and dancing.*

Awesome! Pam has already replied.

I haven't been this excited in months. I can't remember the last time I went dancing. No, that's not true.

It was at Raj and Jen's wedding. Me and Pete.

Heat scorches my face. I can still feel his damn lips on mine. I could have savored his lips for hours without stop. Although I had already asked Seth to move out, that night, I realized what I had not been getting from my husband: Passion.

Another realization stuns me. I am not looking at the past with sadness or disdain. It's almost like I'm glad it happened because what I have now is what I should have had all along.

Thankfully, the end is near. I should hear from my attorney next week. Since the threat of a restraining order, Seth has stopped putting up a fight and we have not seen him anywhere. No stalking, no craziness. My lawyer still thinks we should proceed with the permanent restraining order, but I'm not so sure. I hear Linda's voice in my head, chastising me for not being cautious.

I pray I'm making the right decision.

A sound from behind me makes me jump. I spin around, towel wrapped precariously around my body. It's Pit, snoring.

"Big oaf."

RAJ HONKS THE HORN. I step out, lock the door then practically run to their car.

"You look stunning," Jen says.

Coming from her, that's a real compliment. She's wearing a silk baby blue blouse and a tight black skirt. Her skin tone works beautifully with those colors.

"You look pretty hot yourself," I say and jump in the back seat.

"Pete just texted me," Raj says. "He's on his way."

My skirt runs up my thighs. I try to adjust it, but realize that's how high it's cut. For a moment I consider asking Raj to turn back so I can get something more reasonable. But only for a moment.

I remind myself that I'm free. I can wear anything I want. Or as little as I want.

TWENTY-NINE

— PETE —

I TAKE THE parking stub from the valet driver. Tall, square jaw. Must be an actor in waiting.

The music can be heard from the street. It's going to be loud in there with a bunch of horny "bros" hoping to identify their next conquest. I'm glad I've never had to resort to scavenger techniques.

"Raj, party of six," I tell the platinum blonde hostess.

She gives me the smile I've become accustomed to. It's what Sophie has been calling the result of my "Mediterranean" charm.

"I'd be happy to help you," she says. Her eyes search then land on my necklace, a white gold chain that glimmers against my chest. "That's a beautiful necklace," she says. She's found the in.

Any other time, I would bite. "Thank you. A gift from my girl-friend," I lie.

"She has great taste." She doesn't even miss a beat. Not a block. Just a challenge to overcome.

She's almost worth the game we're about to engage in. Almost.

"Is the party here already?" I ask.

She nods. "Right this way Mister..."

"Pete."

"Nice to meet you, Pete," she says and offers her hand. "I'm Grace."

Yes, she is. I shake her powder-white hand. Not sweaty. Not bone dry. Just right. She leaves her post to point out the table.

"Thank you, Grace."

"My pleasure," she says.

I walk away and head to where I see Raj and Frank, already at work on beers. The deeper I get, the louder the music, but at least it's good. The signs on the wall claim the DJ plays, "The best of the best." We'll see. Right now, he's playing one from before our time. *Brown Eyed Girl.* A great song for sure.

"Hey guys," I say and drop in the chair that I assume is the one across from Sophie.

Raj shakes my hand and Frank pounds my fist.

"Where are the girls?" I ask.

"The *ladies*," Raj corrects, "are on the dance floor."

"Alone?"

"Dude," Frank says, "look at that dance floor. It's packed. They're not alone."

I scan the floor but don't see them. "You guys let three women out there with all these single guys drooling all over them?"

"Don't worry," Frank says. "I have them in my sight. Also, Pam can knock out most of these guys."

He has a point. She may be the only paramedic who was also a Judo champion in her collegiate days. "Where are they?"

Frank points. I follow his finger.

Once I see Sophie, I'm sure I won't be able to unsee her.

Her silhouette is something out of an art book. She's wearing a red tight-fitting mini dress. Shoulders and thighs exposed. The dress hugs her body in all the right ways, and my mind thinks of all the wrong things.

The DJ mixes in the Shakira song she did with Wyclef Jean. The name is appropriately, *Hips Don't Lie*. Sophie and the girls cheer when the song starts, and leering men step closer to them. Sophie's body moves as if the music is coming from her.

"What makes Sophie's dancing particularly impressive," says Raj, "is that she maneuvers to a very complex percussive rhythm."

I glance at him for a second. But only for a second, because I don't want to stop watching her.

"Fascinating," Frank says, not sounding at all fascinated.

"You see, this song has a modified Reggaeton beat," Raj continues, "and Sophie's upper and lower body complement both the up beat and the down beat. She's like a percussive instrument in the way she moves and adapts to the music."

"Does NASA pay you to study music harmonics, or is this a hobby of yours?" Frank asks.

"No need to pay me. This is scientific observation that any rational mind would pick up."

"Meaning I'm not rational."

"No comment," Raj says.

They continue to talk, but all I can think of is how beautiful Sophie is. We used to go dancing all the time until Seth resurfaced. I lost my favorite partner until Raj's wedding night.

"Where are you going?" Frank asks, but I'm not listening nor in control. I want to dance with my best friend.

"Over there," I mumble. I slide my way through the others on the dance floor until I reach her.

Jen is the first to see me. She throws her hands out, like tentacles willing me to reach them.

Sophie glances in my direction and when she sees me, her eyes brighten. She turns to me and offers her hand. I take it and spin her once then bring her in.

My heart thumps with a unique cadence. A rhythm I feel only when I'm with her on the dance floor. She drapes her arms on my shoulders and clasps her hands behind my neck. She tightens into me. We're gliding to the music when the DJ changes it all up by playing a song that at first is not familiar.

"Elvis," Pam yells.

Surrender has been dubbed onto a club mix rhythm. We continue to dance, tight into each other.

Sophie closes her eyes and sings out loud for someone to surrender to her. I want to respond, but I can't. I do the best I can. I stay with her for the duration of the two-minute song until we're pulled off the floor by the others because the appetizers are on the table.

When we dance, things happen. Thoughts happen. I feel like a junkie, needing to spend more time with her on the dance floor. I don't want us to stop.

We're walking back to the table when Sophie bumps me with her shoulder. "She's got her eyes on you," she says.

"Who?" I ask, scanning.

"Two o'clock."

I focus in that direction. The platinum-blonde hostess. I give her a small smile. She returns it with a wave.

"When you dance," Sophie says, "all them girls notice."

We sit at the table, Sophie at my side. "You should get her number," she says, not bothering to conceal her voice.

"Who?" Jen asks. "What's going on?"

"The hostess is undressing Pete with her stare."

"Point that bitch out to me. No one is allowed to undress him unless I'm present."

"Jen!" Raj says and buries his face in his hand.

"In a sisterly way, of course."

I remain silent.

Sophie leans into my ear. "I can stay somewhere else if you want to—"

"Stop. Don't go there," I say, my voice a bit louder than I intended. "You and I are going home together."

Our friends suddenly pipe down, while Sophie's brows shoot up and a smile creeps on her lips.

A moment of silence.

"To be fair," I say, "for all we know she was undressing *you* with her eyes, Soph."

"He's got a point there," Pam says. "I was tempted to grab your ass a couple of times."

We all laugh. Sophie cringes. But for me, all I hear are Elvis's lyrics.

DURING THE ENTIRE drive back home, Sophie has been humming songs that we heard at the restaurant-slash-club. Her seat is slightly reclined and her eyes are closed. Her blessed dress is so short I have a hard time keeping my eyes on the road.

She giggles for no apparent reason. A permanent smile has been etched on her face. Every time I glance at her, I can't help but grin. This was a perfect night. It's been too long since we danced.

"We're home," I say after I shut the engine. I caress her cheek.

Her eyes flutter open. "Yay," she says. She's still a little tipsy. "I love home."

I open her door and help her out. She snakes her arm though mine and leans her head onto my shoulder. A faint breeze runs through her hair: the scent of it gives me a shot of energy.

We enter and when I flip on the light, Pit ambles toward us then nudges Sophie's calf. She blinks her eyes open.

"Pit!" She kneels down and grabs the dog's face and kisses him on his head. "We had such a good time," she reports. "We ate, we laughed." She rises then turns into me. "And we danced."

She slides into my arms and we dance slowly to the music of my heartbeat.

"We danced a lot," she says, smiling up at me.

"That we did."

"I love how we dance together," she says as she lays her head on my chest.

"Me too," I whisper. I could stay like this forever.

"My best partner. Ever," she says.

She pulls away and throws her hand behind her back. She grunts. Is she trying to reach the clasp on her dress? She changes tactics and tries to reach from below. Still no luck.

"Need help?" I ask.

Her arms drop to her sides and she sighs. "Yes, please. I... can't... even—"

"Turn around."

She does.

I run my hands through her hair, collecting it, then draping it around her neck, so I can see the clasp better. She lowers her head slightly, assuring her hair will not cover her back again.

I study her shoulders and neck—the smoothness. I am tempted to touch her, taste her skin.

I blink, then focus. I unclasp the dress hook then tug out the zipper's pull-tab. I pull down slowly. The sound of the zipper gliding on the teeth is low, rumbling. And as more and more of her skin is exposed, my heartbeat thrums louder. With one hand I pull the tab, while with the other, I take hold of one of the open flaps and peel the dress open. I am below her shoulder blades. I take in her spinal line, how it curves elegantly. A hint of her flanks come into view. A few more inches and the small of her back will be—

She takes a small step forward then turns. One arm is across her chest and the other hand is pinching the top of her dress, holding it in place so that it doesn't fall to the ground.

"Thank you," she says, sounding sober and fully aware. Her eyes are bright.

I stare at her. "You're welcome," I say, but my throat is dry.

A momentary hesitation. "Sweet dreams," she says as she steps into me and lays a warm kiss on my cheek.

My eyes go blurry. My heart wants to break through my ribs.

She steps backward, then turns. I stare at her bare skin and the hint of the dimple at the small of her back. She enters her room and closes the door.

I gaze at the door handle. I listen for the sound of the lock, but it never comes.

I shut my eyes, listening to the debate between my heart, my body, and mind.

THIRTY

— SOPHIE —

ONCE INSIDE MY ʀᴏᴏᴍ, I allow the dress to fall to the floor. I step out of it then kick the shoes off.

I sit on the edge of my bed and stare at the door handle, wondering. Hoping.

When I hear his door close, I realize I've been holding my breath.

The courage that I amassed leaves my body instantly and I fall backward on my bed.

This is not healthy.

This is torture.

THIRTY-ONE

— PETE —

I WON'T LIE. It's been rough. She's all I think about. But I can't act on it. That's not why she came. That's not what she wants. Last week when I nearly undressed her, she walked away from me. I need to be more mindful when I drink, or not drink at all, because if I slip up again, she'll leave.

I need to be smart and keep my feelings under control.

I drive to my parent's house to check in with them. In three weeks we head off to the reunion venue, The Resort at Pelican Hill in Newport Beach. Even the name of the place is awesome. But my mind keeps reminding me that I may be on a collision course with destiny.

"Mom? Dad?" I say as I shut the door behind me.

"They not here!" Yiayia yells.

I saunter to the kitchen and find her reading cards.

"How are you, Yiayia?"

"I'm dying," she says.

"Yiayia, one day, when you're as old as I am, you'll understand what I'm going through," I say and give her a wink.

She mumbles something in Greek and sips her tea. "You want tea?"

This is no ordinary tea. She brews the tea leaves in an old-world contraption that is probably the most unsanitary thing ever created. "Sure," I say, knowing any other answer would be deemed an act of war. I grab a glass cup and hand it to her. She has to do the honors.

On the kitchen table is a cheese dish of Greek Feta and a plate of precut pita bread.

"Eat something," she says.

I grab the bread, place some feta cheese, then fold the bread into a taco shape.

"How are you, Petros? Why you look sad."

"I'm okay." I take a bite and follow it with sweet tea. This is comfort food. The stuff that I lived on when I was home.

"Your mother tell me you going to big party."

"I'm going to see all my classmates from high school in three weeks. It's been ten years since I've seen most of them."

"Sophia going too?"

"Yes."

"Good. Make sure you dance. You dance the way I used to dance. You get this from me and your Papou."

"Okay, I'll dance for you and Papou."

Yiayia does the sign of the cross three times when I say Papou, then says, "Good. After you dance, you look for wife."

I don't have the heart—nor the stamina—to tell her I'm not interested in marriage.

"Let me read your cards," she says. She shuffles her tattered tarot cards before I have a chance to respond. She asks me to pull cards, then lays them side by side, as she chants.

She unfolds the cards one by one, explaining their meaning and significance. I'm listening, marveling at how for someone devoutly Christian, she plays around with things that could be considered— dare I say—witchcraft? Maybe I'll have her read my coffee cup, too.

I hear something that catches me off guard.

"What was that? Say it again," I ask.

Her eyes sparkle as she pulls her necklace closer and kisses the makeshift pendant. "You will find love. True love, Petros. Don't be idiot this time."

THIRTY-TWO

— PETE —

THE RUTH CHRIS bar is dimly lit to create ambiance, I suppose. But it also makes it nearly impossible for me to find the guys. Old Blue Eyes is crooning about a woman whose gotten under his skin and the boisterous happy hour crowd is loading up on appetizers and drinks. Most are dressed well, no doubt the business class from nearby Warner Center.

"Pete!" Raj calls out.

I slide my way between the tables and join him and Frank. "Sorry for being late," I say.

"No you're not," Frank says. "You're late, just not sorry."

I drop on the stool. "Yeah, you're right."

"I ordered filet sliders and a lager," Raj says. He's always planning, calculating. He's never late to anything. Even when he wants to be late, he's the first to arrive.

"So what's going on, Frank? What did you want to talk about?"

"Two things. Has Sophie told you about the restraining order?"

I squint. "What about it?"

"She doesn't want to move forward with it."

I shake my head. "I don't get it. Why? She hasn't told me anything about it."

"That's what I was worried about. She hasn't given me a reason but she's reversing course."

I want to call and ask her right now, but it's best that I ask her in person. I just hope she's not thinking of taking him back. "I'll find out what's going on."

"The other thing is that my friends from the LAPD tell me that the neighbor has reported seeing a red Audi driving by her home. So he's still searching for her but hasn't done anything out of line. Not even calls or texts."

"He probably doesn't want to leave a trail behind. Or the fear of the restraining order has kept him at bay. I'll try to convince her."

We're all silent for a little bit.

My food and drink arrive. I study the mini-burger that's actually not a burger at all but a thin cut of filet mignon in a sourdough bun. The meat melts in my mouth and the lightly toasted bun crackles with each bite.

"So," Frank says, then clears his throat. "You're both probably wondering why I asked you guys to come here tonight."

Raj and I stare at him. "Go on," Raj says.

"I'm going to propose to Pam."

Simultaneously, Raj and I yelp.

"That's awesome!"

"It's about time!"

When he became a sheriff, he said he would never get married because he didn't want to put anyone through that type of worry and heartache. Frank met Pam over the mangled body of a gang-banger from Panorama City, who had run in front of a bus while Frank chased him. Pam was the paramedic. Days later they started dating exclusively. That was two years ago.

"You're doing it..." I say.

"I am."

"Why? Why do you think you need to get married?"

"Don't you start," Raj says. "Just because you've written it off doesn't mean it's not the right thing for others."

"I don't begrudge anyone for doing what they want to do," I say. "I just think the concept is flawed."

"Flawed," Raj says.

"Yes. Think about it, the basic idea is find the person you love today and stay with them forever and love them forever and they'll love you back forever. Yet, most marriages are doomed because we see unhappiness, apathy, you name it. And the reason for all this is because today's love won't be the same as tomorrow's love, and that means staying together becomes torture which leaves only one option: divorce."

"Well, I sure feel better about my decision," Frank says.

"No, you should do it. Pam is awesome."

"Thanks for your blessing."

"Your problem," Raj says to me, "is that you haven't found the person that changes the way you see the world. The person who'll redefine love every day of your life."

I'm silent for a few moments. Is that even possible?

"Dude," Frank growls. "Stop overanalyzing things. It's not that complicated."

"But it is. The wrong person can ruin everything. How can you know you're picking well?"

Raj scratches his chin. "You don't know. You listen to your gut because your gut senses things. Deep down, you always know."

"I suppose," I say.

"Pete," Frank says, "don't sweat this crap. The right relationship will you when you least expect it."

THIRTY-THREE

— PETE —

I DROP RAJ off at his house. I'm about to leave when Jen stops me in the driveway.

"Come inside for a couple of minutes," she says.

Once inside, Raj squeezes my shoulder and walks me to the library. We sit on the plush sofas in the reading nook. Jen brings hot coffee for all of us. This has the look and feel of an intervention.

I study Jen. "So, what's new with you and Natalie?" she asks.

She knows we are no more. Why is she asking? "Nothing new. It's still over."

She takes a sip. "Good, good. Anyone new?"

She is so transparent. "Nope. No one."

Jen places her drink down and moves forward. "What about you and Sophie?"

I chuckle. "You know better than that."

"Do I? She's living with you, after all..." she smirks.

"Seriously, nothing?" Raj asks. "Nothing at all?"

"Of all people, you should know better. We're like siblings. I love her, but you know. That's not what we have." The room is suddenly warm.

"Do you remember a few months ago when we went bowling?" Jen asks.

"Hmm, sort of, not really."

It's a lie. Of course I remember. Both Sophie and I had one too many. We were flirting, giggling like school kids, and when we gave high fives, our hands lingered a little too long. But that had been the alcohol. That was not the real us. When we spoke the next day, all was back to normal. No indication of anything.

"Jen and I talked a lot that night," Raj says. "We thought we saw something we hadn't seen since our wedding."

Not the wedding. I don't want to open up that can of worms. "You saw two drunks acting silly," I say. "That's all."

Jen places her hand on my knee. "So... it appears that you do remember that night after all."

WHEN I GET HOME it's nearly eleven, but the TV is still on.

"Hi," Sophie says, but her eyes are glued on the screen. She's bundled in a blanket, watching mixed martial arts in the dark. Pit is asleep to her right.

I approach the TV and watch two women stare each other down.

"That's Ronda Rousey," she says. "Sit. I have popcorn." She opens up the blanket. "Slide in and get cozy."

I glance down at my clothes. Still in a suit. "Let me change first."

"Then change. But you better do it fast. I've seen this fight before. Ronda doesn't waste time."

"Okay," I say and sprint to my room.

"I could also pause it," she says, then cackles.

Nice. I change into sweats. "Beer?" I ask.

"Sure."

I grab two, pop them open and join her. She takes a bottle, clinks it against mine, then takes a big swallow. Pit opens one eye then dozes again. Sophie covers me in the blanket and squeezes tight into me.

"Look at her eyes," Sophie says with admiration. "She won't take crap from anyone."

I eye her. Is there a hint of anger in her tone?

"Here we go," she says, as the referee commands the athletes to fight.

"Oh!" I yell as Ronda grabs her opponent's head in a headlock then slams her onto the canvas.

"She's got her."

And in seconds, the opponent taps out.

"Well, that was anticlimactic," I say.

"Are you kidding? That was amazing."

"Yeah, but I changed, got us beer, you have popcorn. Now what?"

She shrugs. "Let's see what else is on."

After a few minutes, we find a movie we both love. *Love Actually*.

The movie has just started, the scene where people are at the airport waiting for loved ones, but that doesn't stop Sophie from sniffling.

"What's the matter?"

"Nothing, I guess. I've been like this all day."

"That's what happens when we get older. We become very emotional. Yiayia is the same way."

She glares at me then slips her arm through mine and leans her head on my shoulder.

"Why have you decided against a restraining order?" I ask.

"I don't want to do that to him."

"After all he put you through?"

"What he needs is help, not a piece of paper that'll keep us at a distance."

I try to pull away but she tightens her grip. "Don't go," she whispers.

I relax and she digs deeper into me. I won't go. I can't.

THIRTY-FOUR

— PETE —

IT'S THE QUINTESSENTIAL Los Angeles day. Sunny but not hot, thanks to the perpetual cool breeze. The kind of day that causes east-coasters to hate west-coasters. I take the canyons to the San Fernando Valley, top down, the rush of air invigorating. I challenge the curves, driving on the edge, feeling invincible. This is how I always feel when I'm about to spend a day with my closest friends.

Raj and Jen are the foundation of our group. Always going out of their way to bring us all together.

They picked up Sophie earlier because she wanted to help set things up. The girls don't know but Frank will propose to Pam today.

I'm the last to arrive. Quietly, I open the side gate and slide in. Sophie has her back to me, looking like spring in her orange-yellow sundress. She turns slightly, revealing her profile. She's smiling ear-to-ear, listening to something Frank and Pam are saying.

Raj is fussing over the barbecue. No sign of Jen. Every time I see them together, I still remember how he told us about her. He had gone home to England for an extended summer holiday and returned to L.A. to shock everyone.

"By the way, I'm engaged," Raj had said.

"What do you mean?"

"Engaged to be married."

"How's that possible?"

"You ask the girl, she says yes, you get married. It's a simple process, really."

"But who?"

"Jen, of course," he said.

No one had heard of Jen-of-course. Three months later, Raj and I were at the airport to pick her up and meet her. She turned out to be a knockout Indian girl with a sultry British accent and a passion for life that made me feel old and washed up.

Time for my grand entrance. I slam the gate closed. "The festivities may commence," I declare in a deep booming voice. Faces turn.

Frank gives me the eye. "Who invited him?"

"Hey you," Sophie says, then lays a peck on my cheek.

"Drinks are in the fridge," Raj says, his back to us, barbecuing fish that will show up in his famous spicy salmon tacos. His skinny, hairy legs are on full display. Shorts never look right on him. Nor those sandals.

Jen steps out of the kitchen and hands vegetables to Raj, then turns to me. "You're late," she says. A baby-blue sundress drapes her naturally tanned body while she stares me down with her Bambi eyes.

"I had to get this for you," I say, and produce a small crystal pomegranate that she can add to her ever-expanding collection.

She marches up to me, one eyebrow lifted. "Let's have a look," she says, still frowning. She plucks it out of my palm and studies it, nodding. "Good. This'll do. You're forgiven." She evaluates the gift some more. "It's a beauty. Frank, you should acquire some manners from your friend."

Frank gives me a dirty look then saunters over. "Must you make me look inadequate in front of Jen?" he asks.

"Hate to say this, but it doesn't take much." I duck from his bear hug.

"Oh good," Jen says. "I absolutely adore Greco-Roman wrestling. Can you lads apply oil before you start?"

"Jen," Raj says, his back still to us, "must you start so early in the day?"

"I haven't done anything inappropriate, Raj. It's not like I asked them to undress completely. Not yet, at least."

AFTER LUNCH some are chatting about the reunion when Pam taps Sophie's wrist. "You always wear this," she says touching Sophie's leather wrap-around bracelet. "What's the story?"

"I know this one," Jen interrupts. "Rather dull, if you ask me. At her eighteenth birthday party, Pete gave it to her."

"You have good taste, Pete," Pam says. "You need to learn from your friend." She nudges Frank playfully.

Frank's eyes narrow as he looks at me in disgust. *Suck up,* he mouths.

"Has it been surgically implanted on your wrist?" Jen asks. "Do you ever take it off?"

Sophie spins it around her wrist. "Well, I would take it off, but I can't."

"Do tell," Pam says, grinning. "Did you promise Pete you wouldn't?"

They all chuckle, but Sophie glances at Pam and a smile creeps on her face. She then glances at me. I know that look—it's dangerous. "Do you want to tell them, or shall I?" she asks.

"I guess you should," I say since I don't have the slightest clue what she's talking about.

"It's time this group was told the whole story," Sophie says, rising.

What the hell is she doing?

"When Pete gave it to me on my birthday, he made me promise that I would not take it off until a specific day in the future."

She's behind me now. Everyone is silent.

"What day?" Jen asks, in a near trance.

The only sound I hear is from the water fountain that feeds the crystal blue pool. Everyone's eyes are panning from her to me and back.

Sophie inches closer, her thighs touch my back. Electricity runs through my scalp. She places her hands on my shoulders, then gently squeezes. "He said that one day, he would take it off and replace it with an engagement ring."

The group's voices collapse all over themselves. They're clamoring to understand, repeat, articulate. Frank and Raj look stunned. Like Wile-E-Coyote, their jaws splayed on the floor.

That's when Sophie breaks into a belly laugh and slaps my head. "You guys are funny," she says and sits back down.

Sudden silence, as if a giant remote control has put them all on mute. They all stare at her.

"Was that a bloody joke?"

Sophie nods.

"You bitch," Jen says. They hiss and boo.

"Truth is, each time I take it off, it's difficult to put it back on because the clasp is super tiny. I can't latch it with one hand. So it stays on."

They all sigh, someone throws a balled up napkin at Sophie.

"Hold on!" I say. "Of all people, you guys believed that I would have talked about marriage?"

"Sure," Raj says. "Back then you were normal. You became this jaded version of yourself later."

"I still have hope for you," Jen says.

"Amen to that," Pam says.

Frank stands up. "Well, if we're going to tell tall tales, I've got one."

We all rotate in his direction.

"This ought to be good," Pam says. "Try to minimize the blood and guts. You know how Raj gets."

"Do I need to leave the room?" Raj asks.

"No, this is very PG-13," Frank says. "Like all good stories, it has a beginning, a middle, and an end."

"A purist," Sophie says.

"In the beginning, there was me," he says.

Suddenly all the smartass comments drop. I'm studying Pam, whose eyebrows stitch together for a sec. A smile is still on her face, but she seems confused.

"Sinatra said it best, 'I did it my way.' I thought I had it figured out. It turned out, I was clueless."

"Do tell," Jen says.

"In the middle came Pam."

"Ahh," Sophie says, and instantly both she and Jen glance at Pam. They can sense what's coming.

"And I realized my middle would have been a muddle without her. I also realized, we are designed for companionship."

A tear trails down Sophie's cheek. She doesn't bother to wipe it. I don't even think she knows she's crying. Sophie holds my hand and squeezes it. I squeeze back.

"In the end... well it turns out this end is just a new beginning," Frank says then extends his hand to Pam. He raises her to her feet. "It's too much of a cliché to get down on my knee. And I know you hate clichés, so instead, I'll simply ask, will you be my 'till death do us part?" He produces a small purple velvet box.

Pam does not break eye contact. She's not even aware of the box. Instead she throws her hands around his neck and slams her lips into his. They kiss, lost in each other.

We all leap to our feet and cheer. We slap them on their backs and then converge into a team hug. Their lips part and all they do is smile at each other.

"Bloody hell," Jen says. "Who would have known he's a romantic?" She glares at me. "Pete, you need to take lessons from your friend."

I pay Jen no attention. Instead, I glance at Sophie, who's loving every minute of it. She has not let go of my hand. "That's how it should be," she says. "Respect and love intertwined. You can't get better than that."

Respect and love. Is that the equation that I've been missing all along? If so, I may be very close to having it now.

THIRTY-FIVE

— SOPHIE —

WE'RE HAVING BREAKFAST when I place my hand on Pete's. "I have a huge favor to ask," I say. "I need a stand-in boyfriend for tonight."

"They have services for that type of stuff."

I squint. "I'll let that one slide because I need your help. Company party with one of our customers. The head cheese, this old guy, has been getting a little too cozy with me."

"Is he rich?"

"I'm serious. Will you pretend to be my boyfriend?"

I love testing his limits.

"Yeah, fine, but don't you get fresh with me, missy!"

I grin. If he only knew.

I pour coffee for both of us then decide to test him. "She's still living in New York. Hasn't moved to L.A. yet," I say.

It takes him a few seconds to register my words. "Who are you talking about?"

"Claire. I think she'll be at the reunion next week."

"Whatever."

"So hearing this doesn't impact you in any way? You've let go of Claire? Completely?"

"Yes."

"Glad to hear that," I say, but I know he's full of it. "Years back, you told me that if you had a chance to talk to her, you'd want to know why she left. Why is that important? What happens once you know? What changes?"

"Generally speaking, I don't like open threads in my life."

"Or is it because you're hoping for a chance at rekindling what you almost had all those years ago? Isn't that what you really want to know?"

"No, that's the last thing I want. My entire identity is built around the guy who lost his chance at true love. It's a good soap opera. What if the truth is nowhere close to that? What happens when that's gone?"

"You're not serious."

"Damn serious."

"Pete, if I had a chance to know once and for all that the love of my life was interested in me, or ever had been, I'd kick the living crap out of caution and jump into that wild fire. I would not waste one more minute."

We're quiet for a few moments. "Why did you marry Seth?" A question he has never asked.

I touch my bracelet.

"I thought he would fill an emptiness in my life. I wanted to be loved." I look up at him. "The way you talked about Claire made me wish someone would think of me the same way. I thought Seth could be that person."

"Was he ever close?"

"No. You can't replace love with a substitute."

"ARE YOU ALMOST READY?" I call out from my room. He'd come home late and has been changing in a hurry while I apply the finishing touches.

"Yeah, all done. I'm going to pull out the car."

I grab my purse then quickly study my outfit in the full-length mirror Pete installed on the back of my door. The tight black skirt, cut a few inches above my knees, complements my body well, and the three-inch heels accent my toned calves. I shift this way and that, observing how the ivory blouse shines with my movement. Classy, yet sexy. Just the look I was hoping to achieve for our date.

Date? I grin at my reflection. Sure, why not?

Pete is on his cell, rubbing his face when I slide into his car. His black denim pants, white buttondown shirt, and gray jacket give him a decent hipster look. Appropriate for an industry event. I catch a glimpse of his chest through the open buttons of his shirt. The workouts have been helping him. His pecs are full again, like plates. I stare for a little too long.

"I'll call you later, okay?" he says. "I have to go." Pete runs his hand down his face then hangs up.

"Is everything okay?" I ask.

"Yeah, it's—" he turns to face me and freezes. "Wow, Soph, you look fantastic."

Heat spreads across my face. "What? This old thing?"

WE MINGLE WITH THE OTHERS, but my eyes dart across the converted sound stage, scanning for the person I hope to once and for all turn down without having to actually turn down. True to industry lingo, I plan on *showing* him I'm not interested, not just *telling* him. Even a wedding ring hasn't dissuaded him in the past. Maybe a physical presence will do the job.

"Is the dude here?" Pete asks.

"No, not yet."

He glances at his watch again.

"Are you okay? Do you have to leave or something?" I ask.

"I'm fine. Trying to connect with Sandy's contact. For whatever reason, the client's always busy or leaving town."

"Sure, go take care of it."

I watch him stroll through the soundstage, then step outside. I hope this client can be the difference in his career. He can do so much if he breaks free from his employer.

"Lady Perez," a booming voice says from behind me.

Crap.

I find a smile and turn to face the leering man. "Hello, Donald. How have you been?"

"Like hell, until I saw you. As improbable as it may seem, you've become more beautiful than the last time I saw you."

His mane of silver hair seems more made up than in past encounters. The tailored coat looks nice on him and white scarf adds a classic touch. If I had been suffering from missing-father-figure syndrome, this man, who is just north of twice my age, could have been a great catch. As it were, I feel embarrassed.

"Thank you, Donald. You're too kind." *Where is Pete?*

"Trust me, I'm not," he says then grins. "Let's get drinks and catch up."

"Maybe just one drink. We'll be leaving soon," I say and hope he heard the "we" part of my statement.

"Don't go yet," he says, clearly missing the key word. "The party just started. If you're worried about drinking too much, I can have you driven back to your place afterward."

"That won't be necessary," Pete says and slides his arm around my shoulder, immediately releasing all my tension. My date is back. "She's in good hands." Pete turns to me, his obsidian eyes latch onto mine. He winks. "Sorry about that. Had to take care of business."

"No problem," I say. "Pete, I don't think you've met Donald."

Pete shakes hands with Donald, who at first stammers but regains his balance soon enough. In no time, the Hollywood executive finds his rhythm and slides into neutral. It does not go unnoticed that the same eyes that lusted over me now hold me in distaste.

"Picture time," one of my co-workers says as she moves in front of us.

I am sandwiched between Donald and Pete.

"Give me a big smile, guys," she says then aims her phone's camera.

Pete pulls me closer and I nestle in. This feels right. Finally.

Blinding flash.

"Beautiful," the friend says.

Donald seems to get the message because as soon as the picture is taken he waves goodbye and joins the crowd of young women who have been eyeing him.

We spend another hour at the event, munching on finger foods and loading up on California red. By 10:00 p.m. we head for the exit, my mission accomplished. Donald is lusting over a couple of new women now. They look like they're ready to oblige.

"Hi Sophie," I hear a familiar voice call out. My boss.

"Oh hi, Genie. I didn't see you."

Her focus turns to Pete. "And you are?"

Pete introduces himself, his charm on full display. He's heard her name before. He knows she's my boss.

"Sophie," Genie turns to me, "have you made your decision? We need to know by the end of next week."

I feel my face burn. Pete doesn't know about this. "I'll let you know soon," I say and hope she drops the subject.

"It's an amazing opportunity. I encourage you to take it," Genie says.

"What opportunity?" Pete asks.

Genie is about to explain, but realizes she's said something she shouldn't have. She's as sharp as they come. "I'll let Sophie fill you in. I need to say hi to someone."

She escapes. *Well played, Genie.*

Pete is looking at me with expectant eyes. "Are you getting a promotion?"

"Not exactly," I say then break eye contact. "Let's talk on the way home. It's loud in here."

He studies me for a moment, then takes my arm and walks me out.

My phone chimes just as we get to his car. I slide in then sink into the bucket seat before I check the message. A text message from my co-worker who had taken the picture earlier. It's the picture of the three of us, me in the middle, leaning toward Pete whose smile shines, and his solid chest is partially visible. We appear very cozy in the shot.

"What do you think?" I show Pete the picture.

"Nice. I look very handsome."

I grin. "Yes, Pete you're beautiful."

"And you're okay too."

"I try."

In a moment of inspiration, I open the image in a photo editing tool and crop Donald out. Much better. A few more adjustments and then I'm on Facebook. I upload it and consider what caption to give it. Fun at work? We have good teeth? No. Those won't do. I type, "My date," and post it.

There. It's done. Harmless, yet accurate.

The two-mile drive through Melrose to his house takes more than twenty minutes. Traffic in this stretch of town always seems tight as the glamorati drive slowly, hoping to be seen. Various forms of the paparazzi, from the professional to the weekday wannabes, stroll the streets in hope of snapping a shot of a drunk celebrity.

My phone chimes a few times. Friends have seen our picture on Facebook. Everyone loves it. I study the image again. We look right together. Like a real couple. A message from Linda pops up. *Hot!*

I smirk. She's right about that.

"Are you going to tell me about the 'opportunity' your boss mentioned?"

I return to the real world. His voice is dry. He has waited as long as he can.

"I've been given the opportunity to move to the UK arm of the studio."

The car swerves a bit. He glances at me. "London?"

"Yeah."

"And...?"

"And I haven't decided yet."

"But you're considering it."

I nod. "It seems like the cleanest way to create distance from Seth."

Pete says nothing for a while until he pulls into the driveway.

"When would you leave if you said yes?" He's studying my eyes.

"Probably mid-May."

"In three weeks."

I nod. "Maybe late May, if I pushed a little."

We're silent for what seems an eternity.

"Why didn't you—?" he starts, but his phone rings. Both his phone and his car's computer display shows an international caller I.D.

"It's the client," he says. He blinks heavily. "I better get this. We'll chat later."

I don't argue. I slide out and run up to the front door. I'd hoped to delay this conversation until after the reunion. There goes that plan.

I'M in a white tank top, cotton PJ pants, and fuzzy slippers, scanning through pictures I've been asked to prepare for the reunion. I study the faces from the past. From those who were friends, to those I loved at one time or another, and those whose place in my life are still to be determined.

I find a bunch of great pictures of Pete, Raj, and the rest of the gang.

I come across nice pictures of Claire and Robby. They seemed so perfect for each other ten years ago. I open the digital album named "Him." I study the pictures of another couple who at the time also seemed perfect. How did things change so badly? I had always imagined a different turn of events. As usual, I was wrong.

I return to Facebook and find our picture from earlier. This is how we should always be. Together.

A slew of new comments has appeared. Including a "Like" from Robby. For a brief moment, I consider messaging him when another comment shows up from Jen. "I *want* details! Fast!"

They're all too funny. A simple line like, "My date," and everyone clamors for clarity.

I take a deep breath and scan around my room. I'm in a safe place, with the person who'll do anything for me. When I looked into a relocation option, it was because I was afraid of being alone. But I'm not alone. I'm with Pete, safe. How can I leave especially when something's happening with Pete? What, I don't know. But I feel it. I want to know if it'll go anywhere or if it'll be another misread on my part.

I open my bedroom door. The light from the office splashes across the hardwood floor. He's on the computer.

He needs to know that I won't go to the UK. I want him to know my place is here, with him.

THIRTY-SIX

— PETE —

I HANG UP the phone and take a deep breath. A good call, no doubt. The client's assistant seemed very eager to get the ball rolling. Maybe Sandy *has* landed us with a great opportunity after all. I'll have to wait a few weeks before I can meet with the actual client, but from what the assistant told me, they've already looked through my portfolio—which Sandy conveniently sent them—and they love what they've seen.

I run up the steps, ready to share the good news with Sophie and I am immediately reminded of the conversation we were having before the client's call.

UK.

I open the door and step in. Although I don't know for sure, it seems obvious that Sophie has already decided. I could see it on her face and the way she fidgeted when her boss mentioned the opportunity. Off to London for a fresh start. I shake my head, hardly able to believe that she'll be gone in a few weeks. I thought something was happening between us.

Once again, I misread and misinterpreted the feelings of others. To think I actually believed Yiayia's prophecy. Maybe I wanted to believe. Maybe I want to have a real relationship after all. But maybes don't count in real life. I can't believe she didn't even discuss it with me.

I laugh at my own stupidity. Of course she'd leave. Because life doesn't work that way. There are no happily ever afters in real life. Life kicks you in the balls and leaves you high and dry right before prom. Or puts the girl you love in the arms of another when you're traveling. Or sends her off to the UK just when you think maybe... *Seriously, fate can suck balls!*

Thanks, Yiayia. So much for finding my true love at the reunion.

I press my fingers into my eyes. I'm getting a headache. I'm feeling sick.

Sophie's door is closed. Clearly she's trying to avoid the conversation. I grab a beer then go to the office. I turn to my computer and visit Facebook. The abandoned notifications stare at me.

Pit ambles into the office and nudges my leg with his gigantic head, causing my chair to swivel.

"Hey you," I say. With one hand, I rub his head, while with the other I go to work on the computer. I start with the friend requests. I see names I recognize from HPA. I accept them quickly, clicking away on "Accept."

Then I land on a name that gives me pause. No, not a name. An acronym.

C.M. The same "name" who sent Erik the flowers?

I check C.M.'s profile. No pictures. No information. As private a profile as you can get. Could it be her?

My finger hovers over the "Accept" button for a second. Then drops.

Fate?

At that instant, a Facebook message flashes.

A message from C.M.

It says, *"Are you there?"*

My heart bounces into my throat. I was right! It must be Claire.

I type, *"Yes."*

"Hi Pete."

I don't hesitate. *"Claire?"*

Nothing happens for at least thirty seconds. *"Yes,"* she finally types. *"Claire, your long-lost friend."*

Friend? We were much more than that. My enthusiasm wanes. Another message pops up.

"So much for being incognito. I thought I was being all clever. There goes my career aspirations with the CIA."

I laugh, then scratch my head. She has a sense of humor about it. I don't know if I should be annoyed or intrigued.

I write the first thing that comes to mind. *"How are you? How have you been?"*

"I'm fine, thanks," she writes. *"This is really awkward."*

Understatement of the decade... literally. But I decide to give her a pass. *"Not awkward at all (okay, just a little). It's good to hear from you. It's been too long."* Political and accurate.

"Way too long." A pause. *"I'd love to catch up. Talk about things."*

Still being incognito, I guess. After all this time she could be more forthright.

"Will you be attending the reunion?" she asks.

As my fingers rest on the keyboard, I hear Sophie's voice in my head. *"If Claire shows up right now, what happens to Natalie? What happens to anyone?"*

I don't know the answer. But why does she care? Sophie has made up her mind. A plan she never even shared or discussed with me. Maybe the real question is how will she handle it?

I write, *"I'll be there,"* and hit send.

Truth is I want to see Claire and find out what happened. Not that it'll make a difference... but maybe it will.

"What about you?" I ask.

"I want to, but honestly, I feel like I don't belong. Like I should just stay away."

"You should come," I say. *"You still have friends here. You still belong."*

The seconds tick by.

"I appreciate that. Since you're forcing me, I guess I'll be there."

I cross my arms and lean back. Answers. Finally. We'll see what comes of this. An uneasy feeling moves in my gut. I hope I know what I'm getting myself into.

"Love the picture that you guys just posted," she says.

What picture? Who's "you guys?" I notice a slew of new red indicators. I check quickly. They're all comments about the picture of Sophie and me at the work event. That is a great picture. I read the caption. "My date." Is that how she saw it? A date who was left in the dark? After all these years, how could she make a decision that big without telling me—including me?

Another message pops up from Claire.

"So are you and Sophie a thing?"

How I wish I had a different answer. But there is only one answer. *"No, we're not."*

THIRTY-SEVEN

— SOPHIE —

I APPROACH HIS office. He's on Facebook. Can't be anything important.

"Hey," I say.

He jumps, then swivels his chair to face me, his hands are on his heart, his cheeks a bit red. "You scared me."

"Sorry," I say. "Everything went well with the client?"

"Who? Oh yeah. Solid potential." He rises.

I step closer. "That's great news." I need to tell him. "Pete—"

"Claire just contacted me. Can you believe it?"

My mouth opens slightly and my brows rise. "Is that right?"

He nods knowingly. "I think she's ready to tell me everything." His eyes bore into mine. "What if what Yiayia said about finding true love at the reunion is related to this?"

My mouth goes dry. "You thought Yiayia was losing it when you first told me. Now it's a prophecy?"

"Maybe," he says.

Here we go. I shake my head. It's happening again. When it comes to Claire, he's willing to believe anything. Do anything. I was right all along. So be it.

My brain sends dozens of insults I can throw his way, but at that instant, my phone chimes with a text. But this chime is specific. It's a text from Seth.

"What's wrong?" Pete asks.

"Seth." I pull the phone out of my PJ pocket and drop on Pete's office chair before I read his message.

You've moved on already? Going on dates and you're even staying with him? We're still married!!!

I read it a few times. I set the phone on Pete's desk then notice his Facebook Messenger chat screen. I read the last two lines.

C.M.: "Are you and Sophie a thing?"

Pete: "No, we're not."

I drag my eyes away, certain those words have etched a mark in my sight.

No, we're not.

"What does he want?" Pete asks.

Stupid silly girl. I hand him my phone. When he's done I snatch it back. "I have to call Linda."

"I'm getting a drink," he says as I dial.

"Hey, *chica.* What's up?" she asks.

I tell her.

"You're separated and finalizing the divorce," she says. "You're allowed to have a life."

"But I didn't want this. I didn't want to open up a whole new batch of stupidity and emotional turmoil. I came here to distance myself from him." I think of that night when I decided to accept Pete's invitation. I had hoped we could grow closer. Now she's back and he's gone. I ball my hand into a fist. "A stupid decision. I should've never moved in with Pete. One more dumb mistake to add to my greatest hits list."

I hear a bottle cap snap open. I turn and Pete is a few feet away from me. He's staring at me. His eyes are drawn and his smile is all gone. *Did he hear what I said?*

He raises the beer in toast. "To us," he says, then takes a few swallows. He turns then goes to the den.

Crap.

After I hang up, I steady my breathing then join him in the den. I sit next to him. We're both silent for a few minutes.

"Are you okay?" I ask.

"Are you?" he replies.

I shrug. "I suppose." I find the courage to ask the question that I don't want to ask. "So with Claire... are you going to the reunion with her? Is she your date?"

He glances at me. "We're going together, remember? You and me."

He uses the right words, but there's no conviction behind them. "Don't worry about what we said. I'll go with Robby."

He sits up. "Did he ask you?"

"Yeah," I lie. "Like I said, don't worry about me."

"Sort of like a do-over of the prom," he says, his voice distant.

I study his eyes. "Sure. Let's call it that."

I WAIT PATIENTLY for his response. It is past midnight so he may be asleep.

There! He's typing.

I reread my question to Robby. *"Are you going to the reunion with anyone?"*

His reply pops up. *"No. Are you?"*

I smile. *"You want us to go together?"* I type. *"As friends,"* I add.

"That's an awesome idea. I'll arrive at the resort a day early, can you be there early, too?"

"I think I can manage."

I lean back and smile. And in that instant I feel guilty. I'm trying to get back at Pete. I'm being stupid and petulant. Just like prom.

"I've missed you," Robby writes.

What I'm doing with Robby is not about Pete. It's about me. My attraction is purely physical, I admit. Maybe that's just what I need. Allow myself to be irresponsible for once before I leave for the UK.

Oh, and thanks for chatting about UK, Pete. It seems like when Claire is in the picture, no one else need apply.

I switch to email and reread the draft email I've composed for my boss. "I'm going to take the offer." I stare at the 'Send' icon for a while.

Instead, I hit "Save Draft."

Part III

Partners

THIRTY-EIGHT

— SOPHIE —

"DOES HE KNOW?" Linda asks. We're standing around her kitchen island, drinks in hand.

"He knows the offer's on the table."

"But he doesn't know that you're a click away from accepting the role."

I shake my head. "He hasn't even asked since first hearing about it."

Linda puts her hand on mine, squeezing it. "Don't you think you should say something?"

"I'll tell him. Eventually."

Linda stops me. "No, I don't mean just about the job. I mean about how you feel. About him."

I stroll around the island to the butcher block. "Our story is the same one, over and over again." I take a slice of cheese and Prosciutto ham. "There can be no us, because he will never be over her." I slide the finger food in my mouth and promise myself to run an extra mile. "And I will forever be relegated to the back seat. Claire always wins. Then you add his negative attitude about relationships, and it just equates to a beautiful mess."

"I think I understand," Linda says then also rises and walks over to the dinner table. The wine bottle is empty so she grabs a bottle of *Quilmes* beer.

I glance at Pit. He's already asleep on his favorite babysitter's couch.

"Something interesting happened this past week with one of my students."

I welcome the change in topic.

"There's this tenth grader, smart girl, but shy—sort of the odd duck out. Just doesn't fit in." She saunters over to the sofa and sinks in. She taps the space next to her. I sit. "I noticed this thing she does where she wants to answer the question but hesitates. I can see it in her body language. Her arm fidgets like it's trying to shoot up to answer, but she holds back. So other kids get ahead of her. If the kid gets it right, the dejection on her face is heartbreaking. And if they get it wrong, her eyes go wide, again, waiting for her courage to break through. But it doesn't happen. Ever."

"Did you talk to her? Have you coached her?"

"I've spoken to her privately. And have also approached the topic with her mom."

"And?"

Linda shrugs. "And nothing. She's stuck. Until she decides to be courageous and take the chance to speak up, she'll remain stuck."

"Do you call on her? You know, to force her out?"

"I've done that too. She freezes up."

"How sad. I wish she'd see how that will follow her forever."

Linda raises the beer bottle in a salute. "I wish you would see how much you're just like her."

I grin. "Well played, Linda. Should've seen that one coming."

"You told your boss you'd tell her next week, right?"

I nod.

"Then see how things play out this weekend during the reunion. But be open."

That was my request to Pete when he asked me to move in with him. And he ran with it until Claire showed up. Always Claire.

THIRTY-NINE

— PETE —

IT'S THE DAY before the reunion. We've decided to check in a day early, enjoy the resort before the big day. But before we head out to Newport for our pre-reunion getaway, Sophie and I agree to have breakfast at BeefStro. I step inside and realize Sophie is still outdoors reading something on the window.

I yank the door open and pop my head out. "Coming in?"

Her face is blank. "I can't believe it," she says.

"What?" I step out and read the handwritten sign.

"*After nearly twenty years, BeefStro will be closing its doors on June 1st.*"

They've written more things, but I stop reading. I can't imagine not having BeefStro around. I glance at Sophie.

"Our place is shutting down," she says. "What will we do?"

I take her hand. "We'll enjoy the last few weeks as much as we can. No regrets."

Minutes later, as I drink the expertly prepared double espresso, I realize nothing lasts. Not even those things that have always been a part of my life.

SOPHIE'S nearly done with her egg-white omelet with spinach and feta cheese. What remains are trace amounts of the hot sauce she dumped on her meal. She's leaning forward, arms crossed on the table, her eyes frozen on the bread basket.

We've been silent throughout. Distant. This is not us.

I eat the last piece of the bacon then wave down the waitress.

"What can I get you, Pete?" she asks.

"Two lattes, but instead of sugar, bring us a small jar of Nutella."

The waitress's eyes widen. "Nutella?" she asks, wondering if I've lost my mind.

"You should try it," I say. "A heaping spoon or two, mixed gently into the hot brew adds texture and hazelnut goodness to the experience."

Her eyes trained on mine, she swallows. "That sounds like food porn."

"You have no idea, I say." I glance at Sophie. Her expression has softened.

"We haven't had that since..." Her eyes dart around, searching her memory.

"Since you left for law school," I say.

Her eyes freeze on mine and she nods. "Has it been that long?"

"That was our drink," I say. "Time to bring it back out of retirement."

She smiles. "When we get back home, I'll make us Nutella pancakes."

There's always home. "Sophie, when you talk like that... a lot of things happen to my heart."

She places her hand on mine. "That's my job," she says.

THE RESORT at Pelican Hill in Newport Beach is the resort for resort lovers. The reunion committee picked well.

As I drive up the manicured path to the porter's station, I notice the cars parked there. Half a dozen Maseratis, Ferraris, and Porsches. It feels like we're going to an exotic car dealership, not a resort.

"Perfect weather," Sophie says as we step out and head toward the front desk. I wonder if Claire is here yet. She also planned to arrive the day before.

I glance around as Sophie checks us into our individual rooms.

"How many keys?" the receptionist asks Sophie.

"Two," Sophie says.

I don't want to react, I just have to remain passive. But why two?

"And you, Mr. Nicos?"

"Two," I say. There.

As I get mine, Sophie takes one card key from me and gives one of hers.

"Oh," I breathe.

"You have adjoining rooms," the receptionist says and points to the location on the resort map.

"Adjoining rooms?" I ask.

"Just like home," Sophie says.

We drive up to our bungalows. She strolls to hers, and I walk up to mine.

"Give me ten minutes," she says, then steps in.

The bungalow is beautiful—the rooms are pristine and the attention to detail unmatched. I drop my bags and change into full-relaxation mode. I hang up my nice stuff for the reunion party and throw my daily stuff into the drawers. I step out and find Sophie taking pictures of the flowerbeds. We stroll down the paved stone pathways to the spa. Sophie wants a massage. I, on the other hand, want to go to the pool and veg.

"You should get a massage too," she says.

"No, I'm good."

"You look like a tense coil, ready to snap."

"It's a new look."

Sophie takes more pictures as we walk. The incessant chirping from her camera is a sound I've gotten used to over the years. She wanders away, leaving me stranded. I take a deep breath and close my eyes. I can hear the ocean and the birds, even the gentle rustling of the wind through the trees. It's a beautiful day.

After a few minutes of relaxing, I start getting anxious. I'm convinced she's walked off and forgotten me. Then I hear the *chirp-chirp-chirp* of her camera, and she reappears from somewhere else.

"You're not taking pictures at the reunion, are you?"

"I thought about it, but then I'd have to share my work with everyone."

"Heaven forbid. Other mortals looking at your work."

She backhands my shoulder.

We part ways and agree to catch up at the pool when she's done. I rent a cabana that overlooks the Coliseum Pool—a reverse-infinity pool that's 136 feet in diameter. It's a spectacular site. Beyond the resort lies the Pacific Ocean. A beautiful, clear day that looks like it could be the front of a California postcard.

I drop on the lounge chair and scan the sunbathers. I don't see Claire. Even though this place is large, I bet I can spot her a mile away. I have her mobile number, but I won't call. She can call me when she's ready. She's the one who sought me out. I'm not going to chase her. Not anymore.

My eyelids are heavy and my neck muscles suddenly give. I can only think of sleep. I slide the lounge chair forward so that the sun's rays scorch my skin. I silently thank Sophie for getting me in better shape for the reunion, then peel off my t-shirt, apply suntan lotion, and lay back for a bit. Just a minute or two.

Or three...

FORTY

— SOPHIE —

I ALMOST WISH I hadn't told Pete that I'd meet him at the pool. That massage was heavenly. I want to go to the sauna, sweat it out to the point that all thoughts vanish, then sleep in the Jacuzzi.

But I promised Pete.

Has she shown up yet? If the past is an indicator, the moment Claire resurfaces is the moment he forgets about me. As annoying as that is, this had to happen for him. That doesn't mean that I just walk away completely either. I want to keep tabs on how things evolve between those two.

I check my phone, expecting Robby to contact me any minute now. As excited as I am to see him after all these years, I need to play it safe. I'll need to be careful that I don't lead him on.

I take a quick shower, change, then head toward the pool. The brisk pace of my walk pumps blood into my limbs again. I feel the transition from relaxed to ready—the athlete in me needs more.

I head toward the Coliseum Pool's restaurant which leads to the pool. The breezeway separates the restaurant from the bar. The change from bright sun to a dark passage clouds my vision momentarily. In that instant, from the corner of my eye I feel someone reaching for me. My training with Linda kicks in: I extend my left arm, fingers open, to keep the person at an arm's length, I step back, crouch slightly and cock my right fist.

"Whoa, whoa!" he says as he backs off.

Seth. Fucking Seth! I can't believe he came.

I don't relax, my eyes dart around. I eye a waitress from the restaurant who immediately takes steps toward us. He must have been at the bar.

"What are you doing?" I ask. My jaw is tight, my words come out clipped.

"Nothing. Nothing, I swear. I just came to talk," he says. His arms are up, in the universal language of surrender.

I lower my hands, but I'm still ready.

"Is everything okay, ma'am?" the waitress asks.

I relax then turn my attention from Seth to the her.

"Everything's fine," Seth says, but I don't pay him any attention.

I nod to her. "I think so."

She studies me carefully. "I'll be right over there," she says.

"Thanks," I say, then turn to Seth. I want to remind him that he has a restraining order, but he doesn't. I allowed it to lapse. "What are you doing here?"

He gives me his smile. "Hey, it's my reunion, too."

My eyes narrow. "Seriously? You're going to play games now?"

He puts up a hand. "Okay, look I'm sorry. You're right." His voice is soft. "I just want to talk to you, to explain what's going on."

"Do you mean before or after you vandalized my car and broke into my house?"

His face reddens. "I started therapy again... and my meds. Two weeks ago."

"Good."

He takes out a piece of paper. "This is from my therapist. He says I've made great progress in these two weeks." He holds out the paper, but I don't take it.

"I'm very happy to hear that." *Why is he doing this?*

He waits for me to take the paper, but I don't need to see it. I don't want to care anymore. "Sophie, I'm trying," he says.

I break eye contact and search the sky for answers. I can't go through this again. I focus on him. "What are you trying, Seth? Are you in therapy because you realize you need it? Or is this your way of getting me back and then it's back to the same crap all over again?"

"Don't give up on me."

"I can't do this."

"We had something great," he says.

"Had. I tried. I asked. I begged. For nearly three years of our marriage. And now you wake up."

"Not having you with me has brought me to my knees. I understand now."

"I understand also. We are better apart."

"I need you," he says and he sounds genuine, but I can't let him do this to me.

"Seth, sign the divorce papers. Make this process easy on both of us."

"We can't just give up. We need to try to work it out."

I take a step back. "I'm leaving the country. If you want the attorneys to drain both our accounts, fine. Otherwise, just sign it. Please."

I spin and walk away from him. I had not planned on seeing him here. I don't need him here. I don't need him in my life. I don't want to feel guilty for doing the right thing.

And I definitely don't want to change my mind. I don't.

FORTY-ONE

— PETE —

I JERK UP, confused and disoriented. Recognition sets in once I see the oasis that lays in front of me. I study my watch. I've been out for more than an hour. It's hot and my throat is dry. Thankfully, the waitress brought a pitcher of ice cold water while I slept.

I guzzle a cup, then look to the pool. The crowd is larger now. The kids in the water are laughing and loud, and the faint sounds of the crashing waves add an ambiance that is all Southern California. I take a peek at my phone. Nothing.

I glance around. Where's Sophie? Probably passed out on the massage table, drooling. I touch my cheeks just to make sure there are no trails of my own.

A handful of guys in their late twenties is huddled around one guy. Either a wedding party or a bachelor party. It reminds me of a similar scene three years ago at the Mandalay Bay in Las Vegas for Seth's bachelor party.

I should've known it then. Something was already happening with him. The fight he instigated at the casino, and the propositions to the strippers. If I hadn't been there, who knows what else he would've done. He laughed it off and said it was a big joke. I gave him a pass and didn't tell Sophie because leading up to the wedding we had all detected some erratic behaviors, but when we asked Sophie about it, she dismissed it, attributing everything to the stress of wedding planning. We all wanted to believe, I suppose.

I finish off another cup of water then step into the pool. The water is warm, soothing. I swim around the enormous 360-degree pool, keeping an eye on the sunbathers around the perimeter. Like a predator in the water, I keep as close to the surface as possible so that others don't see me. I don't want to bump into anyone else. I only want to see Claire. That's all.

As I dip in and out, I wonder why now. Why does she want to tell me the truth? Does she still—?

I stop the thought. "Who cares?" I say out loud at the same instant I submerge. The salt water quickly fills my throat, and even though I shouldn't worry, I panic. I jump up, inadvertently forcing the water deeper into my lungs. I cough uncontrollably while at the same time I attempt to make my way out of the pool. I reach back, hoping to slap my own back to dislodge the water.

"He's choking," someone yells.

What? I spin around. *Is she talking about me?*

The lady screams louder for help. Before I know it, complete strangers jump in the water. This is a scene out of a bad movie. I'm trying to explain but the words don't come out. I'm still coughing.

From behind, someone grabs me by my chest and pulls me onto the pool's ledge. The stranger slaps my back, causing me to cough out a portion of my lung. That slap does it though. I put my hands up in surrender.

"Okay. I'm okay."

"You all right, buddy?" That voice.

I turn. Robby.

"Pete? Holy shit, Pete! How are you?" Robby grabs me and brings me to my feet. He hugs me so hard I start to cough again. "I thought you were gonna die," Robby says.

Die? He's become a bit melodramatic. "I wasn't drowning."

The crowd dissipates, reassured that I'm not dying.

That's when I notice that his once patented blond streaks are all gone. His brown hair is darker now, and his chiseled face has a five o'clock shadow. Robby's physique is startling. He's built like a Greek statue. The same kind of statue my dad wanted to install in the front yard but didn't when the neighbors threatened him. And the amount of ink on his skin is staggering.

"When did you get here?" Robby asks.

"Pete, over here," someone calls out. Another familiar voice —Sophie.

Robby turns to the voice. "Sophie? Oh my freakin' God!" He marches off, nearly jogging toward her.

My head drops. Our reunion has officially started. I follow Robby a few steps behind. As we near Sophie, her eyes light up.

"Robby! You look awesome!" She runs into his arms. He lifts her off her feet, spins her then lands her down.

Sophie turns to me. "Did you guys just bump into each other?"

"Yes—" I start to say, but Robby interrupts.

"Did we ever. He was about to drown."

"Pete?" she asks, suddenly concerned.

"I was not drowning."

"Oh, that's good," she says then turns back to Robby. Her eyes are bright, her smile like sunshine. Maybe I should've played up the whole drowning thing after all.

UNDER OUR CABANA, I study Robby's physique. Sonofabitch doesn't have an ounce of fat on him. He probably exercises all the time, living off his parents' wealth.

"So tell me," Sophie says.

"What do you want to know?"

"Everything. What you've been up to, what you're doing now...

Everything." Her interest in him is all too obvious. I should've exercised more.

"Things are better now. Learning to take things one day at a time," he says.

"What do you mean?" she asks.

He hesitates. "The war... it took a heavy toll."

"War?" she asks, taking the words right out of my mouth. "I saw something on your Facebook profile about the Marines," she says, "but didn't realize you had been deployed."

"Marines are always deployed," he says.

"Didn't you have an athletic scholarship?" I ask. "I thought that's what you were going to do. Claire had said—" I stop myself. Both he and Sophie stare at me. Sometimes my mouth...

"I did," he says, releasing me of my stupidity. "But things changed. Going to college and playing basketball lost its appeal. I wanted to belong to something bigger, I guess. Do good."

"How long did you serve?" Sophie asks, studying him intently.

"Eight. Long. Years," he says. "I spoke to a couple of people from our class a bit earlier and they talked about how the ten years went away in a beat. On some level, I agree. But for me there were months that felt like decades. There are minutes that stretched on forever."

She leans forward and lays a hand on his arm. My eyes remain fixed on her hand touching his skin.

"I'm sorry," she says. He glances up and their eyes lock. "But you're here now. With us. I'm glad you're here."

The corners of his lips turn up slightly. He breaks eye contact with her then drops his hand on my shoulder. That arm must weigh a few hundred pounds.

"I wouldn't have missed it for the world. And Pete," he says and squeezes my shoulder, nearly snapping my tendons, "I need to buy you a drink and chat about something that's been on my mind for years."

It has to be about Claire. As much as I'd like to avoid that topic,

I'm not going to be a coward either. "I will never say no to drinks and a talk," I say. "Whenever you want."

"Cool." His eyes dart to Sophie instantaneously. "Later," he adds.

Whatever is on his mind, he clearly doesn't want to discuss it with Sophie here.

He turns to her, his voice suddenly firm. "Not sure if you heard, but I think you should know. Seth is here."

My eyes snap around.

"Yeah, he's here," she confirms. "He already ran into me."

"When?" I ask. "What happened?"

"Everything okay?" Robby asks.

She produces a half smile. "Everything's fine, but it's nice to know I have two bodyguards. Don't worry about it. I can handle this."

I want to remind her to stay away from him, to not lose sight of the goal. But those are empty words when the threat still exists. This is exactly why she may be leaving for the UK. Because he's still around.

Robby shifts in his seat, stares at something by the pool then turns to me. "Claire's coming, too." I see something in his face. A flinch. A moment of weakness.

"Yeah, we know," Sophie says.

"She said she needs to talk to me," Robby says. "After all these years, I'm not sure I want to hear whatever it is she wants to say."

Something primal tugs at me. Why? I don't like that feeling. So, she reached out to both of us. She has to clean things up. But why with him? She and Robby had already split up. Why should she call on him? Unless she never got over him.

FORTY-TWO

— PETE —

WHEN ROBBY RISES TO LEAVE, Sophie agrees to catch up with him a bit later. We don't speak after he's gone, we just lounge. As I begin to fade, I gaze at Sophie who has her camera in hand, zooming in and out at things that only her finely-tuned eyes can pick out. I study her profile, blinking with heavy, tired eyelids. I let go under the Pacific sun and drift.

The world is a muffled, dark place for a good while. The blurred faces of friends and teachers visit me in my dreams. Claire in my car. Sophie on the dance floor. Then something hovers over me. I jolt awake and scan my surroundings. Sophie is leaning over her lounge chair, adjusting her towel.

Inadvertently, my eyes remain glued to her butt. She has the curves to kill for, but it's how they connect into her rounded hamstrings, which are full and muscular—no waif, starved body here—that make her stunning. She is powerful. She is beautiful.

She spins to face me. "Dude, are you checking me out?"

I feel the rush of blood. "Don't be silly. I was just observing. Sort of like studying you."

She glares. "Oh, I see. The way a farmer observes or studies a cow?"

"Not at all. You're far prettier than a cow." I lean back and close my eyes. "With a much firmer rump."

Shock explodes across my chest. I shoot up. Ice water all over me. I turn to her as she places the empty glass on the table.

"I'm sorry. Did I accidentally pour water on you?"

"Soph, you're about end up in the pool!"

"You may be bigger, but I can still take you down."

She's right. "You're lucky I'm a lover, not a fighter."

"Ugh, please. Get up. Let's get coffee," she says.

In truth, after drooling over her body the way I had been, cold water was probably the best thing that could've happened to me.

We stroll toward the Caffè which is a short walk from the cabanas.

"Can you believe how handsome Robby looks?"

I glance at her. She's way too taken by him. "Whatever."

"You don't have to be an ass about it. He looks great. He looks a little like Chris Hemsworth with dark hair, don't you think?"

"Thor? No, I don't think." Maybe a little but I'm not going to just concede that easily. "Who do I look like?" I ask.

Sophie considers my question. "I don't know. You look like Pete."

"Great."

As I take the corner into the hall, someone walks directly in front of me. "Hey," is the last thing I hear, but I can't react fast enough.

The collision is immediate. She bounces off and falls to the floor then slides.

"Oh crap!" I say. "I'm so sorry. Let me help you—"

"Pete," the woman sprawled on the floor says. "Of course it would be you."

It's Diana. My prom date. The demented one. "I'm sorry, Diana. Let me help you up."

She studies my hand for a second then lets me help her up.

Sophie jumps in. "Di, are you okay?"

"Do I look okay? Your BFF knocked me down."

199

"It was an accident," I say.

"For your sake, I hope my husband saw it the same way," she says.

"You're married?"

"What's that supposed to mean? Like I'm some leper no one would marry?"

"No, I mean—" I stammer.

"There he is now. Come here, honey."

Her honey is hunched over, dragging five pieces of luggage. He isn't thirty yet, but looks eighty. He is pale, panting, and perspiring.

"This is the 'date' I told you about," she tells her husband, signaling air quotes. "My prom date who ended up making out with another girl."

"You weren't my date," I immediately interject, but it's no use. My shoulders sag. "We weren't together, remember? Sophie, say something."

Diana glares at Sophie, eyes tight. "Yes, Sophie. Something you want to say?"

Sophie's mouth remains partially open.

"Never mind. Let's go," Diana says and yanks her husband by the elbow. "Soph, I'll see you later."

I drag my hand through my hair and stare at the floor.

"Pete, you're a walking lighting rod," Sophie says. "Let's go before it gets worse." She tugs at my arm. We barely make five feet when this time, she stops.

I look at her. She's focused on something in the distance. I follow her gaze. Not something. Someone.

Seth is in a serious conversation with two other ex-classmates. He's flapping his gums and they're listening intently. My generation of reality TV addicts are sucked into real drama. At least his version of it.

"Come on," I whisper, but she doesn't budge.

Seth catches sight of us and stops in mid-sentence. The others turn slightly and see us. Their brows shoot up and they quickly turn. They say something to Seth and walk away.

But Seth continues to stare at us. No expression on his face. Just observing us.

I glare at him and take a step in his direction.

Sophie grabs my arm. "No," she says. "Don't do anything. Let it go."

Her words show more strength than her body language. Her eyes waver between pity and anger. I can't let her change her mind about him. She needs to remember that he's bad for her.

"Come on, Sophie," I say, squeezing her arm.

She doesn't speak as we walk out. I can only imagine what's going through her mind and the debates she's having internally. I take her to her bungalow and open the door.

"Let's have dinner tonight."

She eyes me. "Thanks, but I can't. I promised Robby I'd meet up with him."

I want her to be with me. Not Robby. And certainly not alone on a date with him. "Then let's all hang out together."

She's about to say something when my phone chimes. A text message. I read the name and my heartbeat bounces all over the place.

I glance at Sophie, who grins. "Let me guess. Claire?"

I nod.

"Always Claire," she says. "I think it's best you do what you came here for and I'll do what I came here for." She turns to leave.

"Hold on," I say.

She turns.

"What did we come here for?"

"Come on, Pete. We came here for second chances. We came here to get what we think should have been ours back in high school. Tell me I'm wrong."

I hesitate.

"You see. You just told me without having to say a word."

She steps in and closes the door.

FORTY-THREE

— SOPHIE —

I AM SPENT. Drained. Seeing Seth here is everything I didn't want. What is he telling the others? These are people that know me. People I like. But I never discussed my marriage with others. Now he's here saying God knows what. I don't even know what I'm doing here. And now, Pete will see Claire.

As much as I wanted him to have closure, I know what'll happen next. Either I'll lose him forever (the worst type of closure), or he'll come back with a broken heart, even more jaded than before (not closure at all but a death nail).

My best bet is to hang out with Robby and stay out of Pete's way during the weekend. Let him do what he has to, and I'll move on with my life.

When I first decided to meet up with Robby, I thought maybe something would come of it. But now that I've seen him, all I feel is a deep care for him and his state of mind. Yes, he's beautiful to look at and ogle over, but never to act on. I don't feel what I have to feel. And I can't do what Pete does. That's not me. It seems that London may be my path after all. Break away from all this. Create the separation from all my heartbreaks and start over.

My phone rings.

Robby.

"Hey," I answer.

"This will sound so cliché but... do you want to work out?"

I laugh. Cliché or not, I love the idea.

"What did you have in mind?"

"JUST LIKE THE OLD DAYS," Robby says, as we jog around the resort on their perfectly maintained hiking path. "Cross country, track and field, basketball," he continues, never losing his breath.

I glance at his body again, for the hundredth time. He has kept himself in fine shape. He's wearing a tank top with wide, deep cut holes exposing his sides. As he pumps his arms back and forth, I catch a glimpse of the flexing and striated muscles on his flanks. His legs look rock hard. And holy crap, he has a lot of ink on him. I never cared for tats, but on him they work. They work real well.

"I guess people like us need this," I say as I refocus on the path. "It keeps us sane."

"It's the only thing," he says. "Drowns out the voices in my head."

I turn to him. "Voices?"

Our pace slows. "Sometimes it's so bad, Sophie. I hear the cries as if I'm still there. The explosions. The rattle of gunfire. This," he sweeps his arm around our surroundings, "This helps." He slows down once we reach the end of the track. "I had a feeling that talking to you would help, too."

I don't know what to say, so I just snake my hand through the crook of his elbow. We both have a mist of perspiration. Nothing we weren't used to during our scholastic days. Now, his arms are made of stone. "Talk to me."

We stroll toward the gym.

"I talk about it all the time with my therapist. But it doesn't make a difference. So I thought of friends or family that were always there for me. Those I could speak to comfortably. And I thought of you. We always had such good talks."

I recall at least half a dozen talks we had. All deep and honest. "We had great talks."

"The problem now is that talking doesn't seem to help. I just end up reliving it and then bam! It's in my dreams. I see the faces. All of them. You're surrounded by your brothers and sisters and that's great but it's those quiet moments that are the worst. When your mind goes to that shit hole." We sit on a bench. "Soldiers were dropping all around me. We lost amazing warriors all for a patch of sand in the middle of fuckin' nowhere. The only reason we kept on going was for each other. To help each other, make sure we didn't lose another one of us."

"You made it, Robby. You're here now."

"I didn't have a choice. Not really. I couldn't stay anymore in the shape I was in—I was a liability. I was a mess."

"What happened to you? Was it just the insanity of it? Or—"

"We were there to train the locals and protect them. To give them a fighting chance. That was our job. It was not our job to be ambushed by the same people we tried to help."

My mouth opens slightly. I am aware of all my actions because I just want to be a sounding board. I don't want to add to the emotion, but I can feel my heart tearing at the seams.

"Two brothers served in my team. We hear a distant blast. Turn and the older brother is on the ground. More blasts from far away, and bullets spray us. A sniper. The little brother eats some bullets too as he tries to move his brother out of harm's way. We eventually got the sniper. And you know what? He was someone we trained. *We* taught him how to kill. And he did."

I have no words to offer him. I know all he wants is an ear. Not someone who will try to fix him or tell him it'll be all right. Just an ear to bend without judgment.

"That was the end for me. Watching that Marine, blood pouring out, yelling at his brother to not give up." A tear escapes and he immediately rubs it. "That's some fucked up shit, Sophie. So that was it. I couldn't do that anymore. I had run my course. I needed to leave."

"You're home now," I say.

He glances at me.

"T.S. Elliot said, 'Home is where one starts from.' So start from here. With friends."

He's silent for while, just studying my face. "This is home?" he asks.

"What better place to start?" I rise. "And since this is your new start, we should do something different, completely new. Something you would not do."

"Eat poorly and get drunk?"

"No. This is a new start. A good start. We don't want to kill you." I snap my fingers. "I got it. Yoga."

"Yoga?"

"It's awesome, c'mon!"

He shakes his head. "I don't know. I was expecting a new drug or an organic brew. Yoga really isn't for me." He studies his large frame. "I don't even think I can bend like that."

"Trust me. This will be cathartic for you. The crap I went through with Seth, only Yoga and beating up a heavy bag gave me peace."

"Let's beat up a bag."

"You've done that before. We want something new!"

"Yoga?"

I nod.

He rubs his face. "Then let's go do yoga. I gotta admit, I saw your pictures on Facebook doing that stuff. You look... really, really good doing it."

I chuckle and offer him a hand. "Come on big boy. Let's see how flexible you really are."

FORTY-FOUR

— PETE —

I RE-READ CLAIRE'S TEXT. *I'm at the resort. Text me when you can meet.*

It's time to get answers. Once and for all. *Give me thirty minutes and I'll meet you wherever*, I reply.

I take a quick shower to cool off and get my thoughts straight. What am I hoping to accomplish here? Is Sophie right?

On my cell is a message from Claire. *I'm at the Caffè.*

I'm ready. Back then we had something, or so I thought, yet she never once tried to call or write me. Not even a carrier pigeon. To think she has something special in mind with me now is dumb. My goal is to hear it from her—why she left. That's it.

I knock on Sophie's door to let her know but she doesn't answer. Did she leave already? Knowing Seth is here concerns me. I text her.

As I stroll through the grounds, Sophie replies. *At the gym with Robby.* Some fifty feet away is the gym. I walk by slowly and hover outside the glass walls, stealing a few glances. Yoga. Sophie's so good at it. Frankly, she looks damn hot. Whether she's doing it correctly is for someone else to judge.

For an instant, I have a flashback to how she looked in my living room a few weeks ago. She's solid, grounded to gravity. She doesn't trip or jostle. Robby's keeping up, but he is clearly too muscular for some of the moves. When Robby falters, Sophie breaks her formation and helps him with the posture. Their hands linger on each other's shoulders and backs.

Sophie catches my eye and waves. Robby turns and when he sees me, he signals me to go in. Others also turn to the window. The instructor is waving me in now.

"No, no," I mouth and inch backward. I'm such a dork.

I turn to run and come face to face with Diana.

"Twice already," she says. She spies through the window then gives me a dirty look. "Are you stalking them?"

"No," I say. I don't want to be her enemy. I actually liked her—before she went psycho on me. Ten years and she still holds a grudge over nothing. "We weren't dating. It was all a fake set up remember? We walked into the reception together. That's all. Why does it bother you that at the after party, Shannon and I got a little close? That's exactly what you were going to do with your boyfriend."

She considers me. "Pete, do you seriously not know why I'm upset with you?"

I grimace. "I'm not sure."

She shakes her head. "That's the problem. I don't know if this is a male genetic defect or what, but the fact that you are clueless as to what you did is almost more disappointing than what you did. Almost."

"What did I do?" I look deep into her eyes. "And whatever it is, I'm sorry."

"You can't be sorry for what you don't even know you did. It doesn't work that way."

"Then help me be sorry for whatever I don't know I did. Wow, that sounded weird."

She considers it. "You're right, it is. I would love to tell you, but it's not for me to tell." She leans in. "I have to leave. I have an appointment at the spa. Here's a hint: think about prom night. Think about what happened that night. Come up with a theory, then let's talk. Tomorrow is the reunion. If you get remotely close—within the same zip code—I may let you buy me a drink."

"Deal," I say, almost excited that I can put this stupidity behind us, but just as quickly I frown. Where do I start? At least she's not ready to gut me.

As she leaves, I realize there are a lot of mysteries in this world. I've found the more I study mysteries, and the more information I collect, the more confusing they become. That's why I like puzzles. Information gets you closer to solving the puzzle. Women are a mystery. I need to drink to this revelation.

"Pete, what's up?" Sophie asks. She has stepped outside.

"Nothing. Just wanted to see...um...make sure Seth hadn't confronted you again."

"No, I'm in good hands," she says which gives me a momentary pause. Is that her way of saying she and Robby are getting close? "Have you seen Claire yet?" she asks.

"Going to meet her now." Two can play this game, although I'm not sure it's a game for her.

She gives me a wink. "Good luck."

I traipse away, my mind preoccupied with the mess that's developing in my life. Is Sophie seriously interested in Robby? I pick up my pace. I can't worry about that. Not right now. I have a ten-year-old conversation waiting for me.

I see the Caffè in the distance. A small crowd of people are ordering drinks and pastries. Some move, creating an opening. Among them stands the person I came for.

I'm back in school again. Familiar butterflies invade my gut. A tightness, a loosening, a constriction, a freedom all at once.

What's going on with me?

Claire leans against the glass and marble counter, laughing about something with the young all-American barista.

I move toward her. Less than thirty feet separates us. A date that was ten years in the making.

My pace quickens. Claire is wearing a black bikini top and tan shorts—very short shorts. I stare at her. I know I shouldn't. I don't want to think of her curves, and her skin, and how her lips stretch when she smiles. I don't want to remember what it felt like to touch her body.

Just like that, the same insecurity and excitement of a decade ago takes over body and mind.

Sophie was right. I still feel something for Claire. But what is it? It can't be love. Not after all these years.

She turns, sees me, then does a double take.

She smiles a heavenly smile, then runs toward me and embraces me. I hold her and breathe her in. Her scent brings back memories of years past and how I could smell her in my car, on my clothing, on me.

"Oh Pete."

I don't want to do this, but my arms wrap around her tighter. She is warm, soft, real. This is wrong. I should let go, but we're frozen. Time has stopped.

She pulls back. "Look at you," she says. "Holy Greek Gods, you look amazing."

"It's a curse," I say, and she laughs.

"You've become hotter than your brother!"

I make a mental note to text Marcos.

"Do you want to take a walk?" she asks. "Do you have time?"

"I have plenty of time."

We step outside and the late afternoon sun caresses us.

"Thank you," she says, her voice low.

"For what?"

She shrugs. "You know. For being nice. And not giving me the cold shoulder. For still being the same you."

I chortle.

"I'm serious, Pete. You don't know how many times I thought of contacting you, but lacked the courage."

Somehow I struggle with the idea that Claire, the girl that

everyone wanted to be associated with, lacked courage. But I decide to give her a pass. "You see, it's not so bad. Not yet at least."

She smiles, but she's still tight.

"Are you okay?" I ask.

She shakes her head. "Nervous, I guess." She glances up at me.

"You're nervous to talk to me?"

A sheepish smile. "A little, sure, because you could've totally gone off on me. With good reason, too."

She's as cute as ever. That sheepish smile still gets me. "I still may," I say.

She gives me a playful shoulder bump then takes my hand and squeezes. "Thank you for being a friend."

Friend? There it is again. Downplaying our relationship. Or was it me that made it a bigger deal than it was. I don't like it, but I say the right thing. "Always have been a friend."

"Thank you," she says. We're silent for a few moments. "Full disclosure: I stalked you on Facebook a bit and noticed that you're still with the same group of friends from school."

"Yup. Raj, Frank and Sophie. I'm considering a restraining order."

She laughs. "Dispel a rumor for me, please. I heard that Sophie and Seth started dating a couple of years after high school. Did I hear right?"

"You heard right. They actually got married."

She stops, her mouth frozen for a few moments. "You're kidding. But on her Facebook I don't see anything... I mean, not that I was spying or anything."

"Not that you were, no. She's in the tail end of the divorce. She's taken down the pictures. They stayed married for just a bit over three years."

"I don't get it. She didn't love him. Why marry him?"

"I think she did love him."

"No way, she didn't." Claire shows no hesitation.

"How can you be so sure? You weren't even here."

She shrugs. "Women's intuition."

Women's intuition, also known as wild-ass guess. But if Claire is right... then why?

We stroll in the silence of ten lost years.

"Are you involved?" she asks.

"No."

She eyes me. "Why not?"

"Haven't found the one," I say, and silently laugh at the use of Sophie's line.

Like an aberration, I see Sophie's face, and just as quickly I see Robby holding her hand, kissing her. I shut my eyes for a moment then glance at my intertwined fingers with Claire's.

"I was certain you'd be married by now," she says.

I come to. "I'm the eternal bachelor. When I'm fifty, I'll be 'that guy' who wears shades at a nightclub, the buttons of my shirt open, exposing gray chest hairs that poke out like barbwire. I've got it all planned out. What about you? Are you involved or married?"

"No. There was someone early on, but things didn't work out for many reasons."

What does that mean, I wonder? Was she married? Just serious? I decide to let it go for now. "Have you seen anyone else from school?"

Her eyes brighten. "Yes, I saw Diana just a bit earlier."

"Oh yes... my prom date from hell."

She cringes. "Yeah... she mentioned something about that."

"I'm sure she did. Come to think of it, I seem to recall a conversation you and I had about going to the prom together. Does that ring a bell?"

She closes her eyes. "I am so so sorry for doing that to you," she says, the agony in her voice unmistakable. Claire takes a seat on a bench, unable to make eye contact with me. She's the one who wanted this. Then why the agony? She studies the horizon. She's silent for a few moments, then glances at me. "You didn't deserve that."

"Hey, I should've known better." I sit next to her.

She swivels to me. "Why do you say that?"

"Some things just aren't meant to be. It was silly to even think about going to prom when so much was going on around us."

"Maybe you're right. But in the process, I hurt you." She eyes me, then smirks. "But I hear on good authority that in order to get over the pain, you managed to set up two dates for prom?" A sly grin slides over her face.

"For one, that's a vicious baseless lie. And two, Diana is certifiable in thirty-seven states and greater Canada."

"I see. Blame the victim."

"She's no victim. That I guarantee."

"I'm open minded. Speak."

"After you vanished," I eye her, "and it became clear you weren't coming back, Sophie fixed me up with Diana on a fake date for the banquet portion of the prom. Diana already had a boyfriend, but her parents didn't know about him. So in order for her to experience prom, and because Sophie really wanted me to go to prom—something about it being a rite of passage—we decided to 'enter' the reception together. That was it. After the banquet, at the real party, Diana's boyfriend would arrive, and I could get drunk."

"I don't see how this equates to having two dates. You're holding out."

"I'm getting there. What happened was that Shannon happened."

"Who's Shannon?"

"A junior who was on the prom committee. She and I got a bit close leading up to the dance. I would've taken her, but I had this whole bizarre thing set up with Diana, so we agreed to hook up once we were there." I remember how easy it was with Shannon. I spoke to her with courage. It was a new me talking to her. My time with Claire had caused a change in me. A new level of confidence, a level of certainty that I never had before.

"So I entered the banquet with Diana then I spent the rest of the night with Shannon dancing and stuff, which pissed off Diana to no end."

"Why?"

"Who knows? Even after her boyfriend showed up at the after party, she was still disgusted with me. Of course, I was too drunk to care that night, but after that, I was certain that if not for Sophie, Diana would have dismembered me. To this day, she's pissed."

"I can't believe that."

"Believe me. Right here, at the resort, she's still pissed at me."

"Very odd."

"I never figured out what I did wrong."

"All this because I flaked on you."

It's time I get a clear answer from her. "Why did you leave? What happened on that last day at school?"

She hesitates for a few moments then zeroes in on my eyes.

"On that last day, my mom picked me up to take me to an unplanned doctor's visit." Her voice is dry.

"Why? For what?"

"To get an abortion. I was pregnant."

FORTY-FIVE

— SOPHIE —

WE STROLL TO THE ROTUNDA. It's silent and peaceful. No one here to bother us. I sit on the floor and lean against the wall. He sits next to me.

"How the hell did you end up with Seth anyway?" he asks.

I slide a hair band off my wrist and tie my hair in a ponytail, eyeing him. "Don't hold back, Robby. Just ask whatever is on your mind."

He chuckles. "I don't want to sound mean, but..."

"But why not." I throw my hands up in the air. "It's simple really. I was alone. He promised to fill the gap."

His mouth drops open. "Alone? How could you be alone? Bright, beautiful, good to the core—"

I put up my hand to stop him. "Your words are kind and I appreciate them. But none of them resolved my lifelong issue. I was alone. I had lost both my parents in a span of three years. It's true, Pete's family took me in, but they weren't my family. And then Pete... oh, Pete."

"What about him?"

I look away, unsure if I should even bother. But the moment I turn to him the words come out. "He was too busy running after one college bunny or another. So when he went away for a couple of weeks for a school project and Seth showed up..." My voice catches momentarily. "The thing is that Seth was so kind and loving that I thought my luck had finally shifted. It was finally my turn."

He takes my hand. "Don't cry," he says.

I pull back, upset at my weakness. I wipe it quickly.

"You wanted to believe," he whispers. "I get it."

"I did. And then when the true Seth came back, I refused to believe what was right in front of me. I believed that he could go back to the other Seth again. If he could do it to get me, then why not do it again to hold on to me? If I really mattered, he would've done it."

He leans back against the wall. "You got lucky." I eye him. "What if you had a kid together? That ball game would've been a whole lot different."

I shiver. I would've been one of *those* statistics. The spouses who stay married for their children.

"And on balance, you seem to be handling the whole situation real well. He's here, he confronts you, and you seem to be going with the flow. You have an inner power that most would kill for."

"I suppose," I say with a shrug. "What about you? Are you ready to see Claire again?"

He flinches, but recovers quickly. "I think so. I hope so. I'll admit, I was surprised when she contacted me. I was sure I'd never see her again. After being so close for so long to no communication whatsoever, I felt like a ghost from my past was calling on me."

Not me. She was always there even when she wasn't. Maybe it's because I could see how Pete was forever altered after she left. Her presence always surrounded us. "You'll do fine."

His eyes betray him. He can't lie even if he wanted to. He still cares for her. "I guess I'll find out soon enough."

"She's with Pete as we speak. Maybe we'll get some insight from him."

Unexpectedly, he chuckles as if he remembers an internal joke.

"What?" I ask.

"It's silly," he says then leans forward stretching his hamstrings. "Back during school, if I ticked her off, she'd say, 'Keep this up and I'll go and hang out with Pete.' It was a joke, but there was always some level of understanding that maybe it was real."

So she did like Pete. That'll do wonders to his ego.

"Once—only once—I bit back. I told her I'd go hang out with you, Sophie."

"Me? That's an empty threat." Then his words register. "Why only once? Was I that improbable?"

His face straightens. "Just the opposite. I only said it once because that made her cry."

"What?"

He shrugs. "She was always threatened by you. She knew that you and I were connected on a different level. We had a lot in common."

"We were friends. We were athletes. That's all."

"I know that. You know that. But she was convinced I would one day betray her."

I cringe. I always knew there was nothing between us, but hearing it directly from Robby has a finality to it that stings a little. I guess I was never the right one for him. Just a buddy. The same way Pete sees me. A sister, one of the guys.

Ugh. I am such an idiot.

I jump to my feet. "Come on, Robby. I need a drink."

"Already?"

"Yup, no better time than the present."

"The bartender at the pool bar seems to like me. She'll add a little somethin' somethin' if I smile."

"Practice that smile of yours. We all could use a little somethin' somethin'."

FORTY-SIX

— PETE —

PREGNANT? SWEAT BREAKS out on the nape of my neck. *It can't be.*

My eyes burn and my head spins. A warmth pushes onto my lungs, making it hard to breath or think. What is she saying?

"Claire," I stammer. I almost ask how, but catch myself. Of course I know how, but who? Me? No, it had to be Robby. Or had she been with someone else? Was that why she and Robby broke up? Either way, it couldn't have been me. We had been safe... most of the time. The first time. Did that do it? Is that why she wanted to meet with me first?

"The night before my mom got me from school for the last time, I took a home pregnancy test. The next morning, while I was in class, my mom found it. She rushed to school to get me. That's when I was with you. She was... hysterical might be an understatement. We were going to handle the situation."

I hear the words but I'm listening for the key word. *Who!*

"They wanted the termination to be done quietly, discreetly."

I'm trying to recall when we were together. Do the dates line up? I'm sweating now.

She glances at me for a moment then takes my hand. "Did I stun you into silence?" she asks.

"A bit."

"Come with me," she says.

I stumble on legs that don't feel like they're mine. We come to a stop by the pool.

"Back already?" an older woman asks Claire.

"Just for a bit," Claire says. "Emma, this is my friend Pete. Emma is my guardian angel."

I shake her hand. Who is this woman?

"Pleasure," she says.

"Mommy! Check this out," I hear a boy yell. *Mommy?*

I scan for the voice until I see the kid. A good-looking boy with dark, wavy hair swims toward us. He looks nothing like Claire. She's a mom, but she said she was going to have an abortion? Did she change her mind?

"Come here, Nick," she says.

The boy reaches the pool's edge.

"Nick, this is Pete. He is my friend from high school."

The boy studies me then pulls his hand out of the water and offers it to me. "Nice to meet you, sir," he says.

I kneel down and shake his hand. He has a firm grip for little guy. "You can call me Pete," I say.

"Mommy says that when adults say that, they're just being polite."

"What were you going to show me, sweetie?" Claire asks.

Nick creates some distance from the pool's edge then completes a reverse flip, executes a handstand and disappears under the water. He pops out of the water, his eyes expectant.

"Awesome," she says.

He swims away, content.

I take her hand and walk her away from earshot. Even from here, I can hear the crashing waves crash. The wind carries the cold ocean air and slams it into us. The breeze lifts her hair.

She stares into my eyes. "What's wrong, Pete? Your eyes are blood shot."

"Is Nick...? Did you not get an abortion?"

She shakes her head. "I didn't go through with the abortion. I kept him. That's why my parents moved me to New York. To raise him away from everyone."

"Who's Nick's father?" I blurt.

She recoils. "Oh, no, no. I'm sorry Pete." She touches my cheek. "You're not the father."

I almost collapse from the relief. But I have to make sure. "Are you sure?"

She breaks eye contact momentarily. Then stares deep into my eyes. "I was already pregnant by then." The words sink in. "I'm sorry."

Emotions are slamming into my chest. Why did she sleep with me if she was already pregnant? What was she thinking? Was she even thinking? And the father... it must be Robby. He told us she wants to talk to him too. Is this how she's going to tell him? This is sick. "Robby?" I ask

But she doesn't reply. Instead her hand drops from my face and her gaze focuses behind me. I turn. Sophie and Robby are behind us, mere feet away.

Did they hear our conversation?

Sophie's eyes are snapping from Claire to me. Robby's eyes land on Claire. Words aren't exchanged.

Claire tries to keep a straight face, but I see what's trying to break-through. In that instant, she smiles. "Hi, Rob," she whispers.

He returns her smile and engages in a silent conversation that only they could understand. A momentary hesitation, then they hug. Initially they look awkward, as if unsure what is appropriate. But then they melt into each other. Claire fits into him and he holds her tight, with care. They remain connected for what seems an eternity. In that moment, my jaw spasms because I've been clenching my teeth.

I glance at Sophie. Her cheeks are red.

Robby eventually steps back. "It's good to see you again," he whispers.

"Mom!" I hear from behind us. "Can I get ice cream?" I step aside and a dripping wet Nick, with Emma in tow, reaches Claire. Claire's eyes are latched on to Robby's face.

His eyes are wide.

Sophie is slack-jawed.

Claire forces a smile then places her hand on Nick's head. "Yes, of course," she says. But I don't think she knows what she's agreeing to. She's trembling. "Nick, these are more of my friends. From school. This is Sophie," Claire says. "An amazing athlete and an even better person."

"Hi dude," Sophie says.

Nick puts out his hand and they shake.

"And this is Rob," Claire says. "He was...he is mom's dear friend."

"Hello, sir," Nick says and they shake hands.

"Hi, Nick. It's a pleasure to meet you, buddy." Robby must be stunned, but he's not showing Nick anything.

Nick analyzes Robby's face, then body. "Those are some real cool tattoos, sir."

"Thank you. Do you have any?" Robby asks, an eyebrow arched.

Nick laughs. "No," he says. "Mom won't let me. Not yet."

"Sweetie," Claire says to Nick. "Go with Emma and get the ice cream."

Nick shrugs then runs back to the nanny.

I look at Claire. Her hands are squeezed together, her eyes red, and her lips tremble a little.

I'm numb. I shouldn't feel hurt, yet I do. She slept with me, multiple times, knowing she was pregnant. But if Robby is Nick's father, then Claire should have told him years ago. Why do it like this?

"Claire," Robby says. "What's going on?" Blotches of redness appear on his neck and cheeks.

"This is not how I wanted to tell you," she croaks out.

"Am I...?"

She nods.

I can see the rushing blood attack his face. "Why did you wait?" He runs a hand through his hair. "Why not tell me for all these years?"

"You had a scholarship, you had your entire life ahead of you. I didn't want to ruin your life."

Robby releases a pained laugh. "Ruin it? You really don't know me. Not at all."

Sophie pulls me away. "Let's go. They need privacy," she whispers.

She doesn't know about me and Claire. I never told her. So she can't understand why I'm hesitant. But one look into Sophie's fiery eyes and I know there is only one response she'll accept.

FORTY-SEVEN

— SOPHIE —

"IS THAT WHAT you were asking her when we showed up?" I ask Pete when we're out of sight. "I heard you mention Robby's name."

He nods. He seems badly shaken. Did his perfect image of Claire suddenly get thrashed? I hope he isn't resentful of Robby; he's done nothing wrong. I look over my shoulder, but I can't see them anymore. I can't imagine how he's taking it. Maybe I shouldn't have left him like that.

"Poor guy," I say.

"Poor guy? How about her?"

I stop and glare at him. "Pete, you're letting your filtered view of her blind you."

"What filtered view? I'm being objective. She's the one who had to raise a child on her own."

"Yes, that sucks. It's hard. Probably harder than anything I've ever dealt with. But put yourself in his shoes," I say. "She never reached out to him. She had ten years but didn't tell him. Just like that, he's a dad. That's a shitty thing to do. She should have been way more responsible."

"Sophie, she was barely eighteen. She didn't make the decision to leave. She was handed a deck of cards and missing from the deck were a bunch of options. She had to figure it out. Alone."

"I'm not blaming her. But I can't overlook the fact that there's a guy over there who thought he was about to start a new life—get a fresh start. She decides to drop it on him like this. At the reunion no less. What if he was involved with someone? Now what? She needs to do the right thing here."

"And what does that mean?"

I drop my head, exasperated. He still wants her. After all this time, it's still the same crap. "I'm sorry, Pete," I say, then look up. "You can't be objective because you have clearly made this whole thing about you. This is not about you. Imagine what he's going through right now. Just put yourself in his shoes."

He rubs his face. "I get it," he says. "I really do. For a few minutes, I thought... I was so sure. He even looked like..."

I'm about to add more fire when I notice fear in his eyes. Something is not right. "What are you talking about?"

He drops his gaze. "I thought... that maybe... he was mine."

I'm searching his face, trying to understand. "What are you saying, Pete?" My voice catches. "Did you sleep with her?"

He lifts his eyes until they land on mine. "Yes."

I take a step back, searching for the words, but nothing clear is formulating. "When, Pete? When did this happen?"

He slumps against a wall. "After she broke up with Robby. On the night of..."

"Speak up!"

He faces me. "The night of your birthday party."

I feel my face go numb. "And you decided that my birthday was a perfect time to screw her? Real classy!"

His eyes are red, his face flush. The pain on his face burns into my retinas.

"She asked me to—"

"And you jumped all over it, right?" I feel betrayed. Why, I don't know. He was not my boyfriend. But he was my best friend. I search my memories and something else dawns on me.

"After that, you were always exhausted and sleepy. You were with her, weren't you?" I was such a fool, thinking he and I had a chance even at that stage. "You kept on seeing her."

He nods. "Every night. Every single night until Erik passed away."

"Why would you keep this away from me?"

He chuckles. A sarcastic laugh. "Because I didn't think you'd understand. I thought you'd hate me and judge me."

I don't know what to say. I don't know where to go from here. "Seems you were right," I say. I can't do this. I spin and walk away.

FORTY-EIGHT

— PETE —

I HEAD UP a path only to realize I have no idea where I am. I scan the surroundings, find something that appears somewhat familiar, and continue walking again. Every few minutes I pause, trying to find my way back, hoping somehow I'll find my room.

Nothing feels right when Sophie's not around. What kills me is not that she's mad at me. Because she's not. She's disappointed. She expects more from me.

I swipe my room key. It doesn't work. I try again. No luck. I stare at the card then realize it's her room's card I've been using.

I recall Yiayia's prediction. *You will find love. True love.* She was dead wrong. It's all falling apart. I need to fix this.

I pull out the right card and swipe.

I walk into my room and send Sophie a text.

FORTY-NINE

— SOPHIE —

I RUN. MY arms pump up and down and my knees kick high as I create as much distance as I can between me and the cesspool that's behind me. I was so naive and trusting. Meanwhile at my own birthday party, the night I thought Pete and I would finally breach our friendship borders, he turned around and slept with her. I visualize them, naked. Where? In my room? In the storage shed in the back yard?

I'm spent, but I won't stop. I breathe with precision and timing. I command my legs to work harder, to catapult further. Then I see me, stupid, young, me preparing for my birthday, waiting around, hoping that maybe he'd fall for me.

Stupid little Sophie.

I slow down to a brisk walk. My lungs are laboring and my chest is slamming into my ribs. I moderate my breathing, trying to control my heart rate when I get a text. I check my phone. A message from Robby. *Can we talk? I need advice. And help.*

Poor guy is suffering from some form of PTSD. He's trying to get a handle on his life and now Claire dumps this on him. No tact, no finesse. I clench my fists. How many lives is she going to throw into chaos?

I want to focus on Robby, but all I can think of is Pete and Claire. *Every night*, he said. For how long? A couple of weeks? Suddenly, his attitude about sex and relationships is starting to become clearer. He slept with the girl of his dreams multiple times. They were a couple for all intents and purposes and then she left him without warning. This is the reason why he's been so hung up on her.

Why am I really angry at her? Is it what she's done to Robby, or what she did with Pete? Or how she made a of fool out of me?

In senior year, Pete confessed that he was still a virgin. And so was I. But he gained experience in a hurry with the hottest girl in class. Of course no one else had a chance. I was so stupid to even think we had a chance back in school. To think we would be each other's first.

No wonder he never got serious with anyone after that. It was all about the sex. Did he break up with all the others because to him, relationships became about the physical attraction? Did the women he slept with not measure up to Claire?

I'm feeling ill. I need to talk to him. As hurt as I feel, as angry as I am, I can't leave things like this. If he had told me then maybe... Maybe what? What could I have done but feel thrashed? As much as it would have killed me to know, I still would have preferred knowing over finding out like this. Christ, what if he had gotten Claire pregnant? Careless and reckless.

My phone chirps. A text from Pete. *I'm sorry.*

Foolish Pete. How can I judge you for your failures from ten years ago? *Let's talk later,* I reply.

I'm back at the room. Please stop by.

I pick up my pace.

I'll try. On my way.

I can help both Pete and Robby. I can be there for both of them. They want my friendship, that's all. I guess I should be thankful for that. A friendship is all I'll get from Pete. I should never have expected more.

I practically run up the hill toward our bungalows. I don't want to be mad at him. Even so, I feel hurt, betrayed.

"Sophie!"

I spin. It's Seth, waiting near my room.

"What are you doing here, Seth?"

He steps up to me. "We're still married, Sophie."

I smell the alcohol on his breath. I take a tentative step to the left. "Don't do this, Seth. Please go back to your room."

He rubs his face, his jaw clenched. "But we're still married. You took a vow in church."

"We got married in Vegas. That was not a church."

His eyes go wide. "You supposedly believe in God, but look at you. I have pictures, Sophie. Evidence!" He takes a step forward.

What is he talking about? I shift slightly just in case. He's been drinking. That'll be a problem.

"I tried for years," I say. "We were over a long time ago. You know that."

"Till death do us part, Sophie. And now you spread your legs for both Robby and Pete. At the same time!"

"Fuck you, Seth!"

He lunges toward me, arm raised.

I clench my fists. I'm ready this time.

From my left Pete suddenly appears, slams into Seth and takes him down.

"Don't do this, man," Pete cries. He rolls off Seth then gains his feet.

Seth shambles up then jumps Pete and tackles him back to the ground. Pete grabs hold of Seth's shirt and shoves him to the side. They both roll away from each other.

"Are you okay?" Pete asks me, his focus diverted from Seth, who charges.

Given the opportunity, Seth charges. He jumps on Pete and grabs a hold of his neck. He's maneuvering, trying to land a punch.

I charge, grab Seth's shoulders and yank him to the ground, on his back. He reaches to grab my hair. My training takes over.

Armbar!

I grab his arm, twisting it while I simultaneously throw my legs across his body. He's resisting hard. I pull his arm to my chest then kick my feet toward the sky while wrenching down his arm.

"Ahh!" he yells.

I have him.

I drop my legs over his chest, one on each side of his arm while drawing his wrist toward me. I use his body as fulcrum, and pull his wrist to my chest.

"Stop!" he yells a guttural cry.

I heave harder, arching my back. I can feel his elbow bending in the wrong direction.

"Sophie, stop it," I hear Pete.

"Aghh!" screams Seth.

I want to snap his arm, the same arm with which he hurt me just weeks ago.

Pete drops to his knees, next to me. "Please, Soph. Don't do it."

I glance at him for a moment, then release my hold.

Seth rolls away, pulls his limp arm toward his body, and cowers away. His face is covered with tears, perspiration, and grass clippings.

I jump to my feet.

"Don't you ever touch me again!" I yell.

He stumbles away.

"I didn't stop you before. But never again."

He nearly falls as he marches down the hill.

Pete wraps his arms around my shoulders and walks with me. I try to keep my eyes on Seth, but Pete rushes me up the incline to his room.

"Are you okay?" he asks as he closes and locks the door. He's brushing my hair out of my face, studying my cheek, my forehead.

"I'm fine," I say, but he doesn't stop inspecting. "Stop, Pete. Just stop."

He does.

"We have to get an immediate restraining order. Let's go to the police and make this happen."

He's right, but I want to talk to my lawyer first and get Frank's guidance. "Frank will be here tomorrow. I'll get his help."

He takes a deep breath. "What happened?" he asks, his glassy eyes trained on mine.

"He thinks I've been sleeping with you," I choke out. A tear rolls down my cheek.

He embraces me. "It doesn't matter what that idiot says."

I push away. "He'll say I was cheating on him with you," I say. "He'll show evidence of us living together, dancing together. He'll embarrass me by posting pictures, spreading lies."

"No one will believe him. He has no credibility. It doesn't matter."

"It matters to me."

FIFTY

— PETE —

I'M TRYING TO read Sophie's face. But she's stoic, at best. I want her to forget about Seth's empty threats. I want to say something about what she did to Seth, about how damn scary and sexy she looked. But more important than anything else, I want to know what she meant when she yelled at him. Did he hit her?

I receive a text message.

Can you meet me in an hour by the Rotunda?

"Is it Claire?" she asks.

I nod.

She maneuvers around me and opens the connecting door to her room. Apparently, she left her side open. She goes to her room and I follow her to the door. She pops both sneakers off. Barefoot, she hoists one of her bags on her bed, then pulls out a bottle of *Patron*.

"Join me in a couple of shots." Her voice is dry, almost disconnected. She snaps the bottle open. "I don't have lemons or salt. It'll have to be straight shots."

I grab two glass cups and set them on her dresser. She splashes the equivalent of three shots in each.

She lifts a glass. "*Amigos*," she says. I raise my glass to hers. She taps it, we hold eye contact for a moment, then tip the glasses to the heavens.

"Ahh!" I say, and feel the warmth in my chest.

Sophie says nothing. She plucks my cup out of my hand, sets it next to hers and splashes some more.

"Another?" I ask.

She doesn't respond. Instead, she picks up both cups and hands one to me.

"*Amor*," she says, then toasts mine again.

We tip the glass up.

I set mine down, my eyes focused on hers. She walks to her bathroom and turns on the shower, then marches back to me.

"What did you mean when you told Seth never again? Did he...?" I can't even utter the words.

She pulls her top off and stares at me. She's in her sports bra.

"Did he?" I ask again.

She rolls up the material of her bra slightly to show the top of her ribs, just underneath her right breast. I step up and see a faint scar. I reach to touch the raised skin, but the moment my fingertip makes contact, she steps back.

"How?" is all I'm able to say.

"We had been married for a year," she says, no emotion in her voice. "Frank's birthday."

I remember that day.

"You and I danced. When we got home, he went crazy. He was convinced you and I were seeing each other. That we had been seeing each other ever since I lived in your parent's home. I laughed at the absurdity. He didn't like that. He threw a crystal glass at me. Cut me."

She releases the fabric then turns to show her left side. She points to her ribs. "Bruised ribs. A week before I filed the divorce papers. He wanted to punch the wall behind me. He missed."

I realize I'm crying. I touch her face. "Oh, Soph. Why didn't you tell me?"

"I guess we all have secrets." She steps away from my touch. "Robby is waiting for me," she says. "And Claire is waiting for you."

"It's not what you think," I say.

"Nothing ever is." She undoes the strands of her shorts and drops them to the floor. She steps out of them. She's in her underwear, looking alluring, vulnerable, powerful, and unreachable.

"We both have things to take care of tonight," she says.

She turns. Her back to me, she peels off her top, then crosses her arms, covering her breasts with her hands. She faces me. "Leave. We're both a bit tipsy now. We're both hurt and exhausted. Never a good mixture. We don't want to make mistakes we can't take back."

She would not be a mistake. I slowly reach out to touch her, but she steps back. "Don't," she whispers. "Just don't." There is anger in her eyes.

She turns, drops her hands, and with her bare back to me, she marches toward the bathroom and enters. From the open door, her barely-there underwear flies out and lands inches away from my feet.

"It's best that you leave, Pete," she says then shuts the door.

I stay planted for a few more moments.

I am bombarded with thoughts.

I am devastated with emotions.

I don't want her to be with Robby tonight. Or ever. She should be with me.

I SHOWER AND CHANGE, all along replaying what Sophie said.

She didn't want me.

She didn't want me to touch her.

What is she going to do with Robby? She wouldn't. That's not her.

I approach the connecting door, listening for any sounds from her side. But there's nothing. She's already on her way. I study my watch. Almost time I met up with Claire. Why, I don't know. Maybe she needs a shoulder to cry on. Maybe Robby has told her off and she needs someone who will come to her emotional rescue again. Not me. I'm done.

I leave my room and call Frank.

"What do you need now?" he asks.

I tell him about Seth and the attack and what he's done in the past to Sophie.

"I'll leave in an hour or so to keep an eye on the asshole. Is she safe now?"

I begrudgingly admit the truth. "Yeah, she's with Robby."

A beat. "Oh." A longer beat. "Okay." There's silence on the line. "Text over her room number."

We hang up just as I find my way to the Rotunda, framed by rolling grass hills and the ocean in the background. She's the only one there. This feels like our high school rendezvous. She'd text me and I'd show up, ready to do whatever she wanted.

"Can I join you?" I ask.

Claire's face shifts to mine. She rises. "I need help," she says, her voice hoarse.

FIFTY-ONE

— SOPHIE —

THE DISADVANTAGE OF low body fat is that alcohol has a free pass to the liver. I'm feeling the Tequila—both the shots with Pete and those I had with Robby after dinner. Dinner was good, I think, but I'm not sure. I was too busy hoping I wouldn't throw up all over Robby.

We're lounging outdoors around the fire pit. The heat is nice—perfect in fact. So is the hot coffee. We're seated on comfortable, plush sofa chairs next to each other. Our bare feet are up on the wide brim of the fire pit, feeling all toasty. The flames are enchanting, dancing with the wind—an orchestration of give and take that only nature could conduct. For an instant I catch sight of two figures, intertwined, dancing. Like me and Pete.

I tap Robby's foot with mine.

He glances at me. "Sup'?"

"Are you going to eventually tell me what happened with Claire? I've been patient, drinking all the shots you ordered, stuffed my face with all those appetizers you wanted, and even sat through your analysis of next year's NFL draft. You're killing me. If you don't open up, I'm going to hunt Claire down and force her to tell me."

He frowns. "I thought you, of all people, would appreciate my football analysis."

I get to my feet. "Yes, invigorating. Get up. Let's walk off this intoxication as I guide you to your room."

I try to help him, but he's too big for me to make a dent. Thankfully he still has some control over his movement.

He throws his arm around my shoulder as we walk.

"I don't deserve to have a friend like you."

"I am everyone's best friend," I say and try to control the snarky tone.

"Until you become one lucky bastard's girlfriend."

"I'm bound to stumble onto a bastard here or there."

He chuckles then goes silent. "I have a son, Soph. Can you believe it?"

I grin. "You are a dad. The question is, do you want to be a father?"

He stops, covers his face with his free hand. I think he's about to cry but when he removes his hand he has a Cheshire-cat smile. "A father. What a trip."

"I'm sorry we abandoned you like that."

He shakes his head. "I'm glad you did. That was not my finest moment."

I peer at him. "Tell me you didn't act like a jerk."

"No, no. Just a petulant idiot."

We negotiate up the stairs toward his row of bungalows. "Petulance is forgivable given the circumstances. What does she want from you?"

"I didn't really give her a chance to say much unfortunately. But I recall her saying that she has no expectations. She just wanted to come clean with me and that she wants to tell Nick."

"I have to ask this, because I'm a lawyer. So forgive me, but—"

"She said she'll give a paternity test whenever I want it."

I decide to drop the subject. This can be a very touchy subject. We get to his bungalow. Still in my hold, he swipes the door open.

"Come inside," he says.

I frown. "I don't know..."

"Can we talk?"

He loves Claire so much that even if I wanted him to seduce me, he wouldn't. That's how my world spins. "Okay. Let's talk."

We step in and I close the door. He stumbles into the room and flops on the couch. "I can't believe this is my life. For all these years I had a son and had no clue."

I grab a bottled water from his mini-fridge and prepare tea. "Can you tell me once and for all why the hell you guys broke up?"

He sits forward. "Simple. Because I'm an asshole."

That doesn't even compute. Robby shifts uncomfortably.

"Just speak," I say. "What happened?"

"You is what happened."

"Shut the front door! What are you talking about?"

He takes a deep breath. "Remember when coach told you that your jersey was going to get retired?"

"Sure."

"Do you remember crying on my shoulder because you wished your dad had been alive to see it?" I nod. "Well, some busybody went and told Claire that they saw me with you."

I straighten. I recall wondering if the rumors were about me. "Go on."

"Claire had been snapping at me for a couple of weeks. That day, when she accused me of not being faithful, I got pissed and reminded her that it was *she* who lost her virginity at fifteen during summer camp."

I drop onto the chair. First I have to digest the revelation that she had sex at such a young age. She couldn't have known what she was doing. Then I wrestle with Robby's low blow. "You basically called her a whore."

"Which is precisely why I'm an asshole."

"She's thinking the boy she loves is being unfaithful and you go after something that she probably regretted."

"Not only regretted, but went to therapy over."

My hands go to my face. "You're killing me, Robby! What happened to the poor girl?"

"During summer camp, a seventeen-year-old kid took advantage of her."

I straighten. "Was she raped?"

"No, she never called it that. She was willing because she wanted him to like her and she thought he'd be her boyfriend, but the next day he didn't want to talk to her or be near her. Then the word spread that he had done it on a twenty dollar dare."

I picture a young Claire, the summer before she started dating Robby. She thought she was in love. Emotionally and physically unprepared. Gives herself up only to be betrayed. She must have felt dirty and cheap. I notice my clenched fists. I want to find this bastard and beat him.

"She shared this with me after two years of being together. I turned around and threw it in her face at the first chance."

"What did she say?"

"The look on her face," he says. "I wanted to apologize, to tell her I didn't mean it."

"But you didn't."

"My pride. My stupid pride. During my years with her, I could have been with other girls. So many chances, but not once did I even think of being unfaithful to Claire. So when she accused me of being with you—the one person I respected and valued—I held my ground. I was tired of her paranoia and continual accusations. I can only assume that she must have interpreted my reaction as admission."

My mouth is open. "So she thought you and I were trying to hook up?"

"I suppose," Robby says. "In the past, I would have found her within minutes. A text, email, call. Something. Not this time. She had to come after to me. Next thing I know, after your birthday party, she's with Pete."

My birthday party. I run my hands through my hair. "She must have thought that you were trying to break up with her to start something new with me. That must be why she came to my birthday party even though she hadn't RSVP'd. She was expecting to catch you in the act with me. Meanwhile with all this going on, she knew she was pregnant, but she couldn't talk to you about it."

"Which also explains why she was so off during those days. She was pregnant, probably hormonal, and she had a dick of a boyfriend. But I bet Erik knew. She told him everything. At least, I hope she spoke to him about it."

Suddenly, I recall the argument Pete and I witnessed between them after school. Is that what she told him?

That poor woman went through hell and back during those years. And from our viewpoint, she looked like the perfect girl. The homecoming queen to a bereft kingdom.

FIFTY-TWO

— PETE —

WE'VE BEEN WALKING AIMLESSLY for some time. It's cold and a bit humid. The thick coastal layer from the Pacific has made the air heavy.

I study her for a moment. She's focused on the ground, kicking little rocks out of the way. She's as beautiful as ever, maybe even more so. But something has shifted between us. We both know it.

Before Claire disappeared from high school, each time I saw her at night meant sex. Raw, and sometimes sloppy. To my inexperienced heart, each time was better than the last. Then again, I didn't have anything to compare to. Even when we bumped knees or when our elbows slammed into the car's door, or when we accidentally hurt the other person by yanking on the hair, it was all part of the passion we had for each other. It was all beautiful and timeless. And messy. Sometimes when we were drenched in sweat and the windows were steamed to the point that there were streaks from the built-up condensation, we'd joke about running away so that we could do this all the time.

We were wild... and stupid. Even though we had only bypassed the condom the first time, so much could have gone wrong in my life with that one act of carelessness. Ironic that her preexisting pregnancy might have saved my future.

A lesser person could have pinned this on me. Told me the child was mine. I was so in love with her, I wouldn't have questioned anything. My life, every aspect of it, would have been a shadow of what it is today.

"My life is such a mess," Claire says.

I snap out of it. Something dawns on me. I am alone with the person I suffered over when she left me. The person who arguably continued to have a hold on me with every relationship I got into. But I'm mentally checked out. It's almost hilarious because I'm behaving like I behaved when I was with Natalie—and all the others. Physically present, mentally absent. But it's supposed to be different with Claire. She's the one. Isn't that what I always said? She was the prize that would have finally proven to everyone else that I mattered.

Prize?

Did I just say prize? Is that what she was to me? Is that why I wanted to tell everyone that she was going to be my prom date? Suddenly I'm sick with myself.

"Are you okay?" she asks.

I shut out the voices in my head and focus on her.

"Yeah, I'm fine. I'm just lost in the past, it seems."

She chuckles. "Yeah, me too."

We walk onto another street of bungalows. I have no idea where we are. I hope she has a better sense of direction.

"Why didn't you tell him?" I ask. "Why did you keep it away from Robby?"

"Truth is, I didn't want to force him to be with me or marry me. But in fact, I really did want him to be with me and marry me. Maybe I have a martyr complex. Maybe I hoped he'd fight for me. But when he didn't... well, at that point it didn't make sense to tell him anymore. He clearly didn't love me enough to even come after me, much less be a father and parent."

"Not to be mean, but... overanalyze much?"

She chuckles. "Poor Erik felt the same way. He wanted me to tell Robby immediately. He wanted the two of us to decide together. And when he found out that you and I were seeing each other, he thought I lost my mind."

I frown. "I thought he liked me."

She eyes me. "He liked you, but he wanted me to do the right thing with Robby and frankly, he called me out for being a coward."

Poor guy was trying to help her avoid making a ten-year mistake. I study her. She looks like breathing is a new concept for her.

"Claire, what do you want? Ideally, what do you hope will happen?"

She glances at me. "I want Robby in Nick's life."

Just like that, I feel release. Not because I'm glad that I have no responsibility or part in all this. I feel release because for once I do not feel tied to her. I am not jealous, or possessive. Not at all. I am done. Because I know what I want to do. What I have to do.

From less than thirty feet away, we hear voices and we both turn. Standing by a bungalow door are a couple. A powerfully built guy with short hair, his arm draped around a short redhead. They are standing in front of the open door.

"That's..." Claire starts but never finishes the sentence.

They go into his room and close the door.

Part IV

Dancers

FIFTY-THREE

— PETE —

I WAS UP, wide awake until 3:00 am, waiting for her. It was at 5:00 a.m. when I heard Sophie stumble in, then close the connecting door.

Today is the day of the reunion. The day of second-chances. And everything sucks.

I have to talk to Sophie. To tell her I no longer feel anything for Claire, and hope and pray nothing happened with Robby. But we saw them go into his room together... His arm, draped across her shoulder. A pinch in my chest turns, bores deeper. That's not Sophie. I just don't understand. Is this some form of payback for what I did ten years ago?

I was tempted to call her. To drag her away from whatever she was doing. Instead, I tried to sleep. But no matter what I did, I couldn't find comfort. I tossed, turned right-side up, lay out on the couch, went under the sheets, went over the sheets. I tried to sleep with my head under the pillow, over the pillow, on the side of the pillow. Nothing seemed to work.

My mind was hijacked with all the revelations of the day before and what may have been happening with her and Robby. I can't pretend any longer. The idea that Sophie may be with Robby kills me.

She didn't want me to touch her last night. She doesn't want me. She wants him.

I shower and change. I need to take a walk. Do something.

I quietly open the connecting door to Sophie's and peek in. She's in bed. I step in and observe her.

Her face has sunk into the pillow and her hair is plastered all over the place. All she has on is a white tank top and black panties. Her shirt has crawled up her back and only one leg is under the covers. I am planted, studying her, when a snore jolts me.

"The twe ith there," she mumbles, followed by something even more indistinguishable.

I sit on her bed. "Hey, bum. Wake up. It's late already." I check my watch. It's not even seven yet. I ruffle her hair and pick up the scent of Robby's cologne.

Crap.

She lifts her head, barely opens one eye, then turns the other way and sinks back into the pillow. She looks wasted. I stand up, cover her fully, then leave.

I don't know what to do, or where to go, so I leave the bungalow and walk aimlessly until I reach the club house. I rent golf clubs and a bucket of balls and head to the driving range.

By the time I empty one bucket of balls on the range, my everything hurts, but I don't think it's from hitting balls. Nothing feels right without Sophie. Like the rising and setting of the sun, I have come to depend on her. The voice of reason. The calm and the fire.

What now?

Even though it's early, the sun is searing me—I'm sure I'm burnt. But maybe I deserve it. Maybe I deserve more pain. I can feel the tightening of skin around my neck and forehead. I should find shade. Instead, I get another bucket.

I can barely grip the club at this point. I must be damaging ligaments. But I keep at it. This is my penance. I am nearly done with the second bucket, just a handful left, when I see a few guys returning from a round.

Seth and a few classmates. The same ones he was talking to yesterday.

Seth yaps loudly and laughs. The other guys are not making eye contact with him. They're looking down. What is that idiot talking about?

That's when I hear him say, "That bitch..." but I don't catch the rest of it.

They stroll around the club house to the Pelican Grill. I drop my club and follow them.

They can't see me, but I can hear him clearly now. I am around a post, not more than five feet away.

He has that disgusting smile on his face. The one that would be used in a dictionary to show the definition of leering. Did he not learn anything from last night's whooping? With each passing moment, I hate him a bit more. The way he walks, the way he points, the way he laughs. I hear Seth say, "Yeah, she's a piece of ass."

My jaw clenches. I don't know whom they're talking about, but the topic, the person discussing it, turns up the heat in my lungs.

"Is the divorce almost final?" one of the guys ask.

"Do you think that'll stop me from getting me some?" He laughs and puts out his fist, expecting a pound but the other guy's face goes slack, as he takes a step back.

"I'm staying away from that one," the other guy says.

The world has gone a bit cloudy.

"The things I've done to Sophie. It's a good thing she's an athlete. I could have broken her."

The things he did to Sophie.

My Sophie.

My world goes silent. All I can see is Seth's face, laughing, talking, jostling.

I walk, then run, and in the last few steps I growl as I charge, gang-tackling Seth, lifting him off the floor.

"What the—" Seth yells.

"Holy shit!" someone yells.

I drive Seth over a table. Glass pitchers of drinks spill all over us, then shatter when they hit the ground. We both slam into the chairs and tables and stumble. I grab him and throw him to the grass, then land on top of him. I clench Seth's collar, lift him then slam his head into the turf.

"Stop—" he yells.

I want to strangle him.

He wriggles around, trying to get me off of him. I slam his head into the ground again. I'm about to punch him when someone grabs me and pulls me off that bastard.

"Let me go," I yell.

"Pete, he's not worth it," the person says.

I turn and come face to face with Frank. He must have been trailing him all along.

"Big mistake!" Seth staggers up. "I'm going to sue the living crap out of you!"

Frank pushes me back. "Seth, you may want to reconsider anything you do."

Seth gets in his face. "Are you fucking my wife too?" he whispers. But I hear it.

I see Frank's fists clench so I immediately pull him back and smash my fist into Seth's temple. Dammit, I missed. But I hit hard. Hard enough for him to fall on his ass.

A few people cheer, including two of the three guys he was playing golf with.

"Why'd you do that?" Frank asks as if I've taken away his toy.

"Because you were about to punch him," I say. "You're a cop. You can't get into brawls."

He grabs me and walks me away when one of the guys approaches us. "If he sues, let me know. I'll testify that he attacked you first."

"But he didn't," I say.

"That's not how I saw it."

WE SWEET-TALK the receptionist into giving Frank his room keys early.

"Make sure either you or Robby are with her. If one of you can't, then text me so I can stay with her. After I shower I'll go track that idiot again."

I march off, wet from the spilt drinks. There are dark stains and grass skid marks, also. Some of my clothing is sticky and both my hand and side hurt. I hope I haven't fractured anything.

All I hear is the deep, heavy thudding of my heart, nearly canceling all other sounds. With each breath, the fire in my lungs expands. But one thing is for sure, I am happy, fulfilled. Getting the best of Seth, even if he sues, has made the whole trip worthwhile.

When I enter my room, Sophie steps in from her side. Her hair is slightly wet and smells like shampoo. She stops dead and takes in my condition.

"What happened to you?" she asks.

"I... had an accident"

She studies me for a second. "Are you drunk?"

"Never more lucid."

"Then change, for cryin' out loud." She focuses on my shirt. "Is that blood?"

I look down, noticing the red blotch for the first time. "I don't know."

She lifts my shirt. I have a small cut just above my waist line, below my ribs—similar to hers. It's not a deep one, but it's bleeding. "Take your shirt off," she says.

I do.

She runs outside with my car keys, then comes back with the first aid kit from the Beamer. She makes me sit on the edge of the chair while she tears into the kit. "This'll sting," she says as she kneels on the floor and starts cleaning the wound.

It does sting, but I'm staring at her. She's perfect. But she doesn't want me.

Don't, she said last night.

She looks up. "What?"

"Nothing."

She frowns then snips pieces of tape. She applies a gauze pad then tapes it in place.

"There, good as new." She stands up, looking down at me.

"You seem very energetic," I say. I don't add, for someone who was busy until five in the morning. Someone who spent all that time with someone who is a father now. Someone who you thought should have a chance at being with his newly-discovered family.

She seems to consider my words. "I suppose I am. I'm going out to have breakfast with Robby. You want to come with?"

Why would I want to watch them eat and get all cute and cuddly? "Nah. I need to clean up," I say and rise.

"Be sure to keep this dry," she says, touching my hip.

The electricity reverberates through me, causing me to catch my breath. I waver momentarily. She realizes what just happened, but doesn't say anything nor move her hand. Her cheeks turn red and her eyes become glassy.

After a long pause, she peels her hand away. "I better go."

"Why Seth?" I ask.

She steps back. "I'm going to be late," she whispers.

I hold her hand. "Why Seth?" I ask again. What I should really ask is *Why not me?*

I feel her resistance, but she doesn't break free. "Because for the first time in my life, someone wanted me. He pursued me. He asked me. Imagine that. After all those years of hoping for 'the one,' my prince charming had to be the toad. I didn't have the big breasts and short skirt and the sexual appetite of a porn star, so I got who I got." Her last words come at me like a punch.

"That's not fair," I say.

"Fair or not, those are the facts. Seth was the only one."

"You were like a sister," I say, answering an implied accusation.

She blinks and tears form in her eyes but don't drop. "I still am, Pete. Always your sister." She pulls her hand. "I have to go," she says and turns to leave.

"How could you be with Robby?" I say, my voice rough. "He's a dad now. He should be trying to reconcile with Claire. But you go and spend the night with him. How could you do that?"

She stare at me, her eyes glassy and her features soft.

"You are better than that," I add.

She steps up to me, barely a foot separates us.

"Give me your hand," she says.

I frown but I reach out. She takes it, opens my palm then presses it on the swell of her breast. She lays both of her hands on mine and squeezes harder.

"Can you feel it?" she asks.

I don't answer.

"Can you feel the beat of my heart?"

I nod.

"Do you really think this heart that you've known for most of your life beats for *that*? When did I become so cheap in your eyes that you think I'd become that type of person? All my heart wanted was to be loved. That's all."

She releases my hand then marches out.

FIFTY-FOUR

— PETE —

I STROLL THE grounds with no direction in mind. I know I showered and changed because my clothes are different. But I don't remember any of it. I am operating in comatose mode.

Her words replay over and over again in my head. I don't think I will ever forget them.

I somehow land in the coffee shop, but don't order anything. Then I go to the restaurant overlooking the pool. Sophie is eating breakfast with Robby, laughing about something. I turn away before they see me. I think of Sophie and Robby and what it is that's happening between them, but most of all, I think of Sophie. So many opportunities in the past...all blown.

I find a spot, pull out my phone, and text Frank to let him know that she's safe. What now?

"Pete! How are you, buddy?"

I turn to find Robby, but without Sophie. She must still be at the restaurant.

I study his eyes, his face, his smile. Does he look like he slept with Sophie? I know what she said, and I believe her. But I know what I saw. And I know what I feel. Broken. "Okay, I guess," I say. "Sorry for bailing on you yesterday when the whole thing with Claire happened."

"Don't worry about it. I would've done the same."

I try to keep my tone casual. "So what happened with Claire? What's going on with you two?"

He drops his eyes to his hands, inspecting something that isn't there.

"With the two of us, nothing. But with Nick... maybe everything." He studies his palm for a few moments then meets my eyes. "He's my son," he says, and a smile emerges.

I squeeze his shoulder. "Given your reaction, I'd say congrats are in order."

"Thanks. This whole thing... it's wild, awesome, and crazy as shit."

I chuckle at his sincerity. "I can imagine." In fact, for a few minutes I thought he was mine, but I don't tell him that part. "So, what's going to happen? Are you two... you know."

"No. I don't see it," he says. Not the answer I had hoped for. He studies me. "Are you still—?"

I raise my hands. "No, no. Nothing like that. I'm not chasing that ghost anymore. I just thought that if you're going to get involved in Nick's life then maybe..."

He runs his hand over his face. "I need to talk to her. And I mean talk, not the temper tantrum I had yesterday. I need to clean it up with her. That's not the tone I want to start with," he grimaces, "but I was such a royal dick."

"Just do it. She probably gets why you snapped. She may have even been expecting it. She's had ten years to visualize the various reactions you could've had. I am sure what you did was not the worst-case scenario." I scratch my head. "You want me to talk to her?"

His eyes go bright. "You'd do that?"

"Between you and me, if I don't keep myself busy, I may go back home and skip the reunion."

He laughs, but I'm serious. I turn to head to the pool, but Robby holds me back. "Pete, thank you. This is the second time you've come to my rescue."

"What are you talking about, Robby? I don't remember ever coming to your rescue." Quite the contrary, I think, but I don't point out that when he and Claire broke up that was the happiest day of my life.

Robby looks deep into my eyes. "Prom night, after party. You found me in the bathroom, lying on the floor."

I think back. I was pretty messed up myself that night. But I remember something.

"You forced me into the shower, clothing and all."

It's coming back.

"You poured cold water all over me, then slapped me. You said—"

"Don't give up. Nothing's impossible. Nothing," I say.

Robby nods. "Those words saved me. I wasn't there just because I was drunk. I had sleeping pills with me. But your words gave me something to hold onto."

"Christ."

"When I was in Afghanistan, I told my troops that same thing." He turns and points to his calf. A tattoo, in gothic letters proclaims, *Nothing's impossible. Nothing.*

"Amazing."

He faces me. "Thanks for everything," he says, then gives me a bear hug.

"Maybe you guys should get a room?"

We both spin. It's Sophie.

"Please don't misunderstand," Robby says. "This is strictly sexual."

We all laugh, and the tension of the moment is lifted.

"What's with the lovefest?" she asks Robby. She's avoiding eye contact with me. I've really messed up.

Robby, to his credit, is an open book—an honest man who is good to a fault. He explains.

Sophie's eyes snap to mine. I know the question she wants to ask.

What if I lose Claire by helping Robby? She doesn't know that I'm no longer interested. I don't care. None of that matters now.

"I get it now," I say, and hope she believes me.

Claire is not the one. Never was.

She's searching my face. I don't offer more.

I want to ask her to come with me, so we can talk. But I don't say anything. I turn my attention to Robby. "Let's do this."

"One more thing," she says, her eyes penetrate mine. "I just heard." Her jaw muscles clench.

"Heard what?"

"Oh, that," Robby says. "I better excuse myself." He takes a few steps away. If he's running away, this can't be good for me. "I'm headed to the boy's room."

She waits until Robby is gone then glares at me. "You and Seth. Why did you do that? Which part of that stupid act sounded like a good plan to you?"

I stare into her eyes. "You assume I actually thought before I acted."

"For the love of God, Pete. Do I have to worry about you?"

"No, I'm done. I got it out of my system. But it needed doing."

"Seth is who he is. I can't change that. You can't change that either. It's entirely up to him. If this is your caveman way of showing you care for me, then please stop."

I grab her hand.

"You're wrong about me. I'm not a good friend."

"What are you talking about—?"

"I should have done more when I had the chance, but didn't. I should've done the right thing, but didn't because I'm a coward. I should've forced you to be honest with me. Ask the questions that would have given you the opening to tell me what you were going through with that asshat. Instead, I was chasing... chasing the wrong things. But today, when Seth talked about..." I can't even bring myself to say it.

"What?"

"About you. He was saying such horrible things that all I could do was wrap my fingers around that bastard's neck."

She offers me a pained smile. "Forget it. I don't care anymore. What I care about is now and the future I create. If something happened to you because of me—because of your old-world Greek chivalry—I would never forgive myself. You are not a mindless brute. You are my friend. Got it?"

Friend? Just friend? Not best friend? I wink. I definitely get it. Finally. But I'm afraid it may be too late.

I am about to add something when I notice her wrist.

"Where's the bracelet?" I ask.

She looks down at her wrist and rubs a finger over a couple of scratch marks.

"It broke, I think. When I fought with Seth." She glances into my eyes. "The leather was threadbare already. Barely holding on. I guess it was time." She drops her eyes. "At least I got ten good years out of it. I'll just have to hold on to the memories."

FIFTY-FIVE

— PETE —

I FIND CLAIRE at her usual spot, watching Nick like an eagle.

"Top o' the mornin'," I say.

Claire grins then turns to me. "My favorite Irish Greek."

I plop on the lounge chair next to her then look around, but don't see Emma. Claire may put up a fight if her nanny's not here. Even if she wants to talk to Robby, without Emma, this plan may be dead on arrival.

"Where's Emma?"

"Gave her the afternoon off. She'll have her hands full tonight and tomorrow morning."

A bit of panic sets in.

"Can I join?" We both spin. It's Sophie.

Claire focuses on her. She and I both saw what happened last night. We saw Soph and Robby enter his room. For an instant, I think Claire is about to launch an insult, but doesn't. "Sophie, I'm sorry. I didn't properly say hi yesterday," she says.

She gets to her feet to hug Sophie, but then studies her face, almost in a trance. "You are more beautiful than ever."

Sophie blushes as they hug. They were not close during school. They were always nice and mutually respectful, but never close.

When they separate, Sophie moves a strand of hair out of Claire's face. "So, can I meet your handsome little man?"

"Of course," Claire says and introduces Nick to Sophie.

"Nick," Sophie says, "you want to play some football?"

"Yes!"

Sophie jumps in and I follow. The salt water momentarily stings my side. The three of us toss a Nerf football to each other. I keep a close eye on the stairs. And when I see Robby stepping down, I attempt to climb out of the water, but Sophie holds me back. Her touch is my medicine.

"Let me," she says.

Sophie sits next to Claire and they talk, but I can't hear them. Claire shoots a glance toward Robby, the frown unmistakable. She turns to Sophie and continues to listen. A few moments later, a smile threatens her lips. Then a nod of agreement.

Sophie rises, so does Claire. "Go," Sophie says, "Nick's in good hands."

Robby is still ambling toward Claire when she strolls up to him. He says something that makes her laugh, and they walk away, side by side. A scene I used to see all the time during our school days. I take a deep breath and exhale years of pain and loss.

Sophie jumps back in. "Okay, kids. Let's have some fun."

WE ENTER a pottery painting class already in progress. Nick and I team up against Sophie. Nick thinks this is fair because girls are better at everything than boys. He may be onto something there. The rules are easy: who can build the coolest clay something-or-other.

I study Sophie. I will use these opportunities to repair all I've messed up with her. I can still fix this.

Nick chooses a coffee mug and we agree that it will be given to

Claire. I mix the colors and suggest the possible design. We agree on a multi-colored cow pattern, because, "Duh, you use milk in coffee."

Sophie's next to us. She has paint all over her fingers. Without hesitation, she grabs my shirt and cleans her hands.

"Hey! That's an expensive t-shirt," I say, but I love how she's messing with me.

"No it's not. I bought it for you."

I glance at it. She's right. "Okay then."

She gives me her awesome double-dimple smile. But just as quickly, it fades.

All is not lost. It starts here and by the time we're in L.A., I'll fix this. Robby lives in San Diego. I will have time and... what about the UK? Has she committed already?

"What do you think?" Nick asks, bringing me back to the present.

"Perfect."

"Yeah, not so much," he says, "but it's something, right?"

At the end, we unanimously agree that my shirt should win first place, but since we can't give my shirt to Claire, the rainbow-cow-coffee-cup wins.

We move to the next event. An outdoor "chefs in training" exhibit. Cooking stations are set up for people to learn from the resident chefs.

"What do you think Mr. Robby would like?" Nick asks.

Nick must suspect something. "I don't know, do you think he likes chocolate or candy?" I ask.

"No. He wouldn't eat that stuff. He's a war hero, you know."

"Is that right?"

"Yup, Mom told me that he's a hero and that I should be very respectful when I speak to him."

"Good advice. Okay, let's make something healthy for Mr. Robby."

Sophie chops up whatever Nick requests.

"Pete," she calls out.

When I turn to her she slips a julienned red bell pepper in my mouth. "Thankth," I say as I chew.

"Say it don't spray it, son," Sophie says, causing Nick to laugh.

I'm about to join in, throw more comments, but again, Sophie checks herself. Almost like a veil of sadness envelops her each time she considers returning to the way we used to be with each other.

We head back to the pool. No sign of Claire yet, which may be good news for Robby. We jump in the water again. Nick, Sophie, and I play more football.

We launch the ball straight up and wrestle for it when it storms down. Sophie and I make fools of ourselves, allowing Nick to catch most of the balls. When I try to jump, Sophie tugs on my shorts, enough to stop me from jumping. I return the favor by tripping her just as she's about to leap.

Nick is a good athlete. Like his father.

"Throw it high," Nick says.

I launch it up high and like a bomb it descends to earth.

"I got it," Sophie yells.

"Dream on!" I say.

"It's mine!" Nick yells as he performs some tribal dance. He leaps backward and after he catches the ball he collides into Sophie. Both sink.

They emerge out of the water.

"Ouch, I hurt my ox," Nick says.

Sophie looks at me. I shake my head.

"What's an ox, sweetie?" Sophie asks.

"You know..." Nick says, blushing. "Butt—ox."

We are drained. Even Sophie, athlete-extraordinaire may be a bit winded. We agree to call the game on the grounds that Nick is killing us. The three of us huddle together. She has her arm across my back. I collect myself and say, "On the count of three, team. One, two—"

"Team!" we cheer.

We break formation, but Sophie still has her arm draped across my shoulder.

"Excuse me," says an older woman who is on a water cushion floating toward us. Sophie and I turn to her. "Just had to say," she continues, "I haven't seen parents as involved as you two in a long, long time. Look around here. The parents are reading their books or checking their phones, while the kids are running around aimlessly with no parental involvement. I loved watching you two with your son."

"He's—" I start, but am interrupted by Sophie.

"Thank you," she says. "That's very kind of you."

The lady floats away and I tap Sophie's shoulder. "So, we have an illegitimate son now?"

"We felt like a family, didn't we? Having fun, laughing, creating new memories. Isn't that what families do? He was ours for the afternoon."

Ours.

She removes her hand from my shoulder and stares at me momentarily. "Maybe an afternoon of family life is all I'll ever get. Maybe that's all I deserve." She's lost in thought. "Anyway," she mumbles more to herself than to me. She swims to the edge of the pool and climbs out.

FIFTY-SIX

— PETE —

NEARLY TWO HOURS after Claire left with Robby, she reappears. Her eyes are focused on the placement of her feet. One foot in front of the other. She seems lost in thought. No Robby in sight.

Once she reaches us, we all wait for her to wake up from her slumber. But she doesn't. Not really. She sits on the open lounge chair, while we watch her in wonder.

I eventually move in. "Hey, you okay?"

She wakes up, her eyes wide open. "Oh! Sorry. Yes, I'm fine." She turns to Sophie and produces a tired grin. "I'm sorry. Lost in thought." She turns her gaze to Nick. "So, did you guys have fun?"

"I had a blast, Mom." He grabs the rainbow-cow mug and hands it to her. "This is for you."

She takes it and nods in approval. "This is a fine piece of work."

"And this is for Mr. Robby," Nick says and gives her a plastic to-go container with an array of colorful vegetables and fruits.

"For Rob?" she asks.

"Yeah. Healthy stuff, because he's healthy."

She reaches for Nick, who immediately steps into her arms and is engulfed by her embrace. They are like that for a few moments. We don't belong here. I wink at Sophie, who nods in agreement.

We attempt to leave, when Claire takes notice. "Wait," she says. "Nick, Mommy has to talk to her friends for a second."

Claire turns to Sophie and holds her hand. "I didn't know I had access to so many babysitters. More importantly, I didn't realize I had so many good friends."

"Always," I say.

Sophie glances at me, but there is no warmth in her eyes. She studies me then turns her head.

"All good?" Sophie asks Claire.

"All hopeful," Claire responds then glances at Nick. "Definitely hopeful."

Minutes later, when Sophie and I leave, I find that I can't speak. Not yet. I don't know how this will end, but it feels like the end. Not quite how I had expected it to happen. But there it is. I know Claire wasn't for me. But what will I be left with? More regrets?

Sophie's also lost in her thoughts. Her shoulder grazes mine and instead of cracking a joke, or bumping my shoulder harder, or sliding her arm through mine, she corrects herself and creates a space between us.

Something has changed between us. My heart rate quickens and my breathing is strained.

We reach our bungalows. I need to say something. "So are we back on?" I ask.

She peers at me. "On what?"

"The reunion. Going together. Are we back on?" I give her my best smile, the one that always makes her buckle.

But she doesn't smile back. She just studies me. "No, Pete. We're not. I think it's best we keep things as is. I don't want there to be any confusion."

"Oh..." is what comes out of my mouth.

She breaks eye contact. After a pause, she gazes into my eyes. "Also, I'll be moving out when we go back."

I stare at her. "Why?"

She forces smile. "London is calling. I've got an ocean ahead of me. Maybe my luck will turn once I'm there."

I come to a stop next to her bungalow door. "Sophie, I don't want you to leave."

She shrugs. "But I have to." She opens her door. "It's the only choice I have." She slides in and shuts the door behind her.

FIFTY-SEVEN

— SOPHIE —

I SHUT THE door and lean against it for a few moments. Time to move on.

I undress, peeling off my bikini, but my lungs don't seem to want to take in air. My heart doesn't seem to want to beat. And my knees have forgotten how to balance the rest of my body.

I stumble toward the shower. I spin the dial to high heat and stand there, my hand under the water testing the temperature. I remember the shower in his home; he was on the other side of the wall. Always an impenetrable wall between us. My throat constricts and a moan escapes, but I quickly cover my mouth.

I can't do this.

Slowly, I lower myself to the ground and slide my legs to my chest. I hug my legs and cry. I force it out. I want to cry it all out, get it out of my system because I don't want to hurt anymore. I don't want to feel like the person who everyone claims is perfect, but the truth is, I am not perfect enough. I am not enough.

FIFTY-EIGHT

— PETE —

I ENTER MY room and collapse on my bed. I don't know what to do, where to go, how to think, and what to feel anymore. I am incomplete. And exhausted. I need rest and sleep.

I rummage through the mini bar and open a small bottle of vodka. I finish it off in seconds flat. I can hear the shower running from Sophie's room. I can practically see her naked body in my mind's eye. But she doesn't want me. She didn't want me to touch her, to be with her. She wants to leave me.

I need to close my eyes and rest. I eye the bed. I flop down and the sheets engulf me.

I wake to the sound of my cell phone. I grab it off the dresser and study the time. I was out for less than twenty minutes.

The cell rings again. My eyes readjust and I read the screen. It's Mom.

"Is everything all right?" I ask as I open the call.

"I don't want you to get worried."

"What is it? What happened?"

"It's Yiayia."

266

FIFTY-NINE

— PETE —

AS SOON AS I hang up, I squeeze on shoes and rummage for my wallet and keys, then check the connecting door. Her side is open. I run into Sophie's room and knock on the bathroom door. No answer. I try one more time. Harder this time.

"Coming," she yells. "I'm coming. What is it?"

She opens the door slightly, enough for me to see her wet hair. She's covering her body with an oversized towel.

"Pete, are you okay? Your eyes..." She opens the door a bit more and steam rushes out.

"They think Yiayia had a heart attack—she seems to be doing okay now, but I have to go."

Her face goes slack, then her lips part slightly as she pulls the door open. "I'll come with you."

"No, it's okay."

"I'm not asking for your permission. If something happens to Yiayia and I'm not there, I'll never forgive myself. Just give me a second to change."

"Mom said they just pulled her out of intensive care. If there's any risk, I promise to call you. Hell, I'll come and get you. I just have to go right now. I don't know when—if—I'll be back."

The space between us disappears in a blink and she hugs me. Her wet body clings to mine, her wet hair caresses my face. I find the strength to hold her, to smell her hair. I close my eyes. I don't want to let go.

"I don't want to lose her," I say. "I don't want to be alone."

"You're not alone. You'll always have me," she whispers.

But you *are* leaving me. London is calling.

I can't do this. I brace myself and pull away. "I have to go," I whisper.

"Please, call me."

I stagger out of the bungalow to my car and collapse behind the steering wheel. I don't dare look back as I punch through the streets, onto the freeway.

This is what it comes down to. On this day when everything is supposed to come together, my world is shattering at its seams. Everything has changed.

SIXTY

— PETE —

IT'S NEARLY FIVE when I reach Cedars Sinai. I run through the corridors, fumes are the only source of fuel I have left. I'm up against time in all areas of my life. And losing gloriously at the same time.

The nurse's station confirms that Yiayia is doing well. I send Sophie a text. When I approach Yiayia's room, the first thing I notice is the volume. Then I notice the number of people there. Nearly a dozen talking at extreme volumes.

"Pete!" yell out a chorus of family members.

"What he doing here?" Yiayia asks, her voice frail but determined.

"I called him, Yiayia," my mother says.

Yiayia puts on a disgusted face. "He was going to find wife at party."

Neither an oxygen mask nor tubes in her arms have altered her sense of humor. I sit on the bed next to her and hold her fragile hand.

"You are good boy," she says, her voice cracks. "But also stupid."

I nearly laugh. If she only knew.

"Leave me alone with Petros," she says.

Most move. "I'm your grandson, too," my brother says.

"Out," she says.

Once they all leave, I lean in. "You have to take it easy."

"I take easy when I die."

"That's not funny."

"You don't think so? Old age not funny. It not easy. Everyday something hurt, something ache, something fall off."

I chuckle, then kiss her matted hair.

"But you know what kept me alive all this time? You kids—my grandchildren. We could not teach our children the most important things—they too smart to listen. Now you kids need to hear the truth. Truth about life." Her tears well. No acting this time. A tear reaches the oxygen mask and slides underneath the plastic cover. I grab a tissue and dab at it.

I'm ready to cry with her. "Please relax. This is not good for you."

"I will say what I have to say, the way I want to say." She's back. Yiayia's fire has returned. "Dying alone is hard. Living alone is hard. We need people we love to surround us. We need large family and many, many kids. We need people to talk to, who will talk to us, listen and laugh at our stupid jokes. Old people die when there is nothing to live for."

I blink and a tear escapes.

"You are alone, Petros. You need to love and allow yourself to be loved. We live when we have people in our life. Memories are all we create and leave behind. You need new memories. Don't waste time. You can have that now. Work, money, all those things are stupid. God, love, and health. That's it. Do you understand?"

"Yes, I think I do."

"Stop thinking. Always thinking. This is problem with young people. Either do, or don't. Do you understand?"

"I do."

"Good." She reaches up and caresses my face. "Now, get out. Go back to your friend. And don't lose Sophia."

My heart drops. "Sophie's my frien—," I say, then just as quickly I stop myself. That's been the line I've used for years. I know better now. She's the one I've always loved.

270

"You so smart, but so stupid. Look with your heart, not your eyes. She is the one. Where my necklace?" she asks. "Your mother put in my purse."

I dig in and find a paper towel. Wrapped in it is her necklace and makeshift pendant. "Here you go."

She takes it from my hand, studies it, then kisses it. "Take with you for good luck. It yours now."

"I can't take this. It's your—"

"I know it my," she snaps, grabs my hand, and shoves it in my palm. "You take. It always give me luck. Now it your turn. There is reason why God put her in your life. Don't take what you have for granted. Do not lose her."

I study the pendant that hangs from the chain then slip the necklace into my pocket.

"Good," she says. "Call your mother."

They all stream in.

"Tell your son to get out of here. He need to go to party and come back with wife. I can't hold on forever."

An explosion of laughter fills the room. I kiss her, but she's shoving me out.

I jog, then sprint out of the hospital, jump into my car then peel out of the parking lot.

SIXTY-ONE

— PETE —

IT'S JUST PAST six now. Another hour to go. Maybe more. Traffic tightens up and I watch the minutes tick away. The reunion begins at 7:00 p.m. I won't make it for the opening.

My mom rings me. I immediately assume the worse.

"How's Yiayia?"

"She's fine. Don't worry. Will you make it in time?"

"Hopefully. Is Yiayia awake?"

"No, she's sleeping, thank God. She told me about the conversation she had with you."

I cringe. I don't want to talk about these things with Mom. Yiayia is different—she's cool. Mom, on the other hand, is... Mom. A BMW shoves itself in front of me. I honk at the idiot.

"Don't let Yiayia get to you," she continues. "She means well."

"I know."

"She doesn't understand what you guys have. I must admit, I always found it odd for you two to be so close, yet not as close as I would have expected. In the early days, we used to joke about it with her parents."

I rub my face. Now a Mercedes glides in front of me. No blinker. No nothing.

"But it happens, I guess," she continues. "Your father and I were sure that something would happen with you two. But we're not like Yiayia—old fashioned. We realized that you guys are different—the generations are different nowadays. And unlike Yiayia, we sort of gave up hoping."

"Hoping?"

"Sure. You know we love her like our own. In fact, I think your dad loves her more than you, but that's neither here nor there."

"Gee, thanks Mom."

"Not me. I love you both equally."

"Equally? I'm your son. You should love me more."

"Well... that's your fault, isn't it? You made her a part of our lives and we can't imagine life without her."

"Me neither."

We hang up. I lean back and my entire body sinks into the bucket seat. I need to do something. She has to change her mind. Even if she doesn't feel anything romantic for me, she needs to know how I feel and what she means to me. I close my eyes and drop my head. Will I be able to convince her? Will she believe me?

A horn blares behind me. The traffic has opened up. I punch the gas pedal.

At 7:09 p.m., I run into my room. I can still smell Sophie's perfume. After a quick shower, I study the clothing I'm going to wear. I remember her words when we picked out my outfit. *You look incredible.*

Does Sophie think of me romantically? Has she ever? God, because no one else will do.

I head out of the bungalow but stop. Yiayia's necklace. I go back in, find the chain, kiss the pendant, and clasp it around my neck. I can use all the help I can get.

I walk-run to the hall. I glance at my watch. It's nearly 7:30 p.m. What had they said? When was I supposed to deliver the speech? At the start, or a little bit into the event. As I approach the hall, I hear amplified sounds coming from the far room. I reach the door and hear someone making announcements. My shoulders sag.

I open the door and see Robby. He's giving the welcome speech. Robby has taken my place. That should be me.

SIXTY-TWO

— PETE —

THE HALL LOOKS PERFECT. Classy, not ostentatious. Light dances on each table from the floating candle centerpieces, casting a cloud over the room. The sconces accent the perimeter. Ten tables intimately encircle the dance floor and small stage.

On the stage, Robby delivers the speech. He's good. Maybe too good. We all thought of him as the athlete, not the hero or public speaker. Then there were the school icons, like Claire, whose every move was recorded in the annals, often inaccurately.

I listen to Robby and understand why Sophie would like him. He's funny. What if she's fallen for him? Earlier today she made it clear that she hasn't been with him, but that doesn't mean she doesn't *want* to be with him. If that were the case, how would he like it if he knew she was living in my home? He wouldn't. He'd ask her to leave. I take in a gulp of air and release it.

A new thought crosses my mind. If she was interested in Robby, then why is she leaving L.A.? Maybe it's not too late.

Next to Robby stands Pat, our class president, smiling, hooting, and cheering along. I formed unfair opinions about some of my classmates and in this one weekend I realize I've been wrong about so many things.

I scan the room and catch sight of Claire. I stretch up, hoping to get a better view of her. Her chair faces the stage. She's listening, grinning, and clapping along. She looks pretty. No surprise but there's something else. She appears lighter, maybe even free.

I always thought I loved Claire. But I now know. Compared with true love, what I felt for Claire was infatuation. Maybe even lust. She was my first, and the one who all my other lovers were measured against. But love, it was not.

I scan the room for Sophie, ready to truly see her.

I amble over, on feet that aren't very stable or sure, then I lean into the bar.

"What'll it be?"

"Your most potent beer," I say.

The bartender makes a move then stops. "Sir, I think all beers have approximately the same amount of alcohol."

"In that case, pour some extra." The bartender chuckles and pours a nice lager. I toast him and take a sip then turn to face the group.

I think of Yiayia. *Nobody wants to be alone.* I gaze at the stage where Robby's reeling it in. Sophie steps up to the stage to join him and Pat.

She is stunning.

Breathtaking.

My vocabulary is limited. I need more words. Newly invented words that can appropriately describe how beautiful Sophie is to me.

I move slightly so I can see her from head to toe. Spaghetti straps hold the tight-fitting black dress to her toned body. Sequins sparkle every time she moves. Her dress and her manner remind me of the days when women wore simple, elegant dresses that accentuated their beauty, not exposed it. Much like the homes I design, she's a classic.

She whispers something to Robby and he covers the microphone to listen then nods.

"We just got word that Pete's grandmother is doing better and that he's on his way back."

Cheers erupt. My fellow classmates and their spouses clap and hoot. This is akin to hearing speeches at your own funeral. My classmates don't know I'm here. There's no reason for them to be nice. Yet they are.

All, except for one person. Seth leans back in his chair, his tie loose. His eyes are dark, locked on Sophie. Why is he still here? Has Frank been keeping an eye on him? I scan the room and find him. He's staring at Seth like a sniper following his target. I love that big oaf.

I study Sophie, who appears worried, but continues to force a smile. But then her eyes land on mine. We hold each other's gaze and I nearly die from the buried longing I feel for her. I lift my glass in toast to her. Her eyes soften and a genuine smile washes over her face.

She steps down and slinks toward me. When she gets closer she practically runs into my arms. Air escapes my lungs when she presses into me and I breathe her in. I need her. She is everything. And for now, in this moment, I can hold her without having to worry that she may not see me the same way.

She steps back and places her hand behind my neck. My skin tingles as she lowers my head close to hers and whispers, "I'm so glad you made it back."

I lean back and beam. "Me too."

"Tonight would not have been the same without you."

I look deep into her amber eyes and recall her saying the same thing about our prom. But I never got what she meant exactly. We weren't together that night. We barely even spent any time together. She was too busy dealing with a drunk Seth and I was with Shannon.

We're still looking into each other's eyes when Robby finishes the speech. The applause coupled with the start of the evening's music is cue for everyone to start the party. Conversations commence across the tables.

"Come with me," Sophie says and takes my hand. "The guys have a seat for us."

SIXTY-THREE

— PETE —

AT OUR TABLE sit our closest friends: Frank and Pam, Raj and Jen, Sophie and Robby. Sophie and Robby still came to the reunion together? So much for my theory. Robby seems distracted, stealing glances at Claire, who is at another table. Am I being hopeful or am I seeing something in his eyes?

I need to come up with a plan to show Sophie I'm serious. And soon, because I can't watch Sophie with Robby all night. Otherwise, I may have to make friends with the bartender.

I glance toward Claire. She is surrounded by classmates. They gush over her, hug her, kiss her. She is at the center again. And I'm alone. Some things never change.

I turn my attention to Raj and Jen. They're studying me like they can see through me. I can't pretend any longer. This time, I smile at them, flick my eyes to Sophie, and shrug.

"Tell me, love, how's your gran m'ma?" Jen asks. How I love her Brit accent.

"She's well. She no longer has her knickers in a twist."

"That was a pitiful attempt at speaking the Queen's English."

"I so want to speak like you. I would have instant credibility and sound hot at the same time."

"Sorry, love. You need more than a proper accent to sound hot. It's a package deal."

They all laugh. Frank throws a sugar packet at me.

Jen is still studying me. I know this look. She's up to something. She sips her Cosmo and smiles, nearly biting the rim of the glass.

"You know what I just recalled?" she says. "At our wedding, the way you and Sophie danced that sexy swing dance. That was hot."

"Amen to that, sister," Pam says.

"You were always an amazing dancer," Robby says.

"She's still brilliant. You should have seen how these two torched the dance floor when we got married."

Robby looks at Sophie then me. "I bet."

"I guess we did all right, huh Soph?" I say.

"As Jen put it, we were brilliant, love."

"Her accent is better than yours," Jen says. "Why don't you give us an encore performance? For old time's sake."

An encore performance? What a night that had turned out to be.

Does Sophie remember what happened that night? Does she remember how our lips found momentary bliss?

I look into Jen's eyes—the perpetual marketing strategist, she's setting up the chess pieces.

"Jen, I recall a lot of tequila that night. So I guess it depends on how drunk you get me," I say.

"Oh, I can take care of that bit," she says.

"I hope I can still pull it off. I haven't practiced in forever," I say.

"Don't worry," Sophie says, "it's in you. You can't lose it—even if you wanted to."

SIXTY-FOUR

— PETE —

I LEAVE THE hall and head toward the restroom. The double doors leading to the yard opens. Seth steps directly in front of me. No one else is around.

"What do you want?" I ask.

His nose is red and his eyes are bloodshot. He must be on something.

"I want to take a closer look at you, stare you in the eye and see if you have any guilt or remorse for stealing another man's wife."

I step into him, forcing him to tilt his neck to keep eye contact.

"Seth, I don't hate you. I feel sorry for you. Not because I think you're ill or mentally challenged. I feel bad that you had her and you didn't know how to keep her. If you are reborn a thousand times you'll never find another person like her."

His eyes narrow.

"You had the best, but you pushed her away," I continue. "No one else would've stayed with you, or given you so many chances. Only her."

"She cheated on me!"

"Bullshit. I call bullshit with confidence. We have never, ever been intimate."

He chuckles then reaches inside his coat. I hesitate. What is he about to do? He wouldn't... He pulls out crumpled sheets of paper.

He pushes them into my chest. "Give these to her." He takes two steps back, starts to turn away, but hesitates. "Do you think the only way to cheat on someone is by sleeping with them? Is it through sex only?"

I blink.

"You feel sorry for you me, Pete? Get this: when your heart is with someone, then you are closed off to anyone else."

He walks away.

I track him as he disappears into the darkness of the outdoors. I try to digest his words, but I don't think I can do it properly.

I stare at the papers in my hand. The signed and notarized divorce papers.

I stumble toward the hall when Robby steps out of the restroom. I grab him. "Come with me," I say.

We step outdoors and I breathe in the cool ocean air. "Talk to me," I say. "What did you and Claire agree on?"

"Had a great talk. She asked me what I wanted. So I told her all I wanted was a chance to be a source of support to Nick. And her, if she needs it."

Robby rubs his hands together. Is it cold? Maybe. I don't feel anything anymore.

"And? Did she agree?"

"She did. She's moving back to L.A.—her parent's old home. I'm still in San Diego but also plan to move up. We'll see each other more often at that point. Sophie told me she can help me find a place somewhere nearby."

She's trying to bring him as close to her as possible. But if she's going to London, then why is she trying to bring Robby closer to her? I wonder if she's told him about the UK. Maybe she's not going to London after all, or maybe she doesn't feel close enough to Robby yet. Either way, this gives me hope. I hate doing this to Robby, but I have to set things right and that means there can be no Robby in the picture.

"I'll spend the whole day with Nick and Claire tomorrow," he continues. "We may tell him then."

I study his eyes. He has more on his mind but he's not verbalizing it. "Maybe she should join our table. It's a new start, right?"

His eyes light up. "I was thinking about that, but I didn't feel comfortable mentioning it."

"I'll do it. Plus, it's time she started hanging out with the cool people in class."

He grins. "How are you holding up?"

"I don't know what to say. My life sort of sucks right now. But at least I have these." I hold up Sophie's divorce papers.

His eyes go wide. "She's free. She's officially free."

Free to choose, I think.

THE PARTY HAS MOVED into the slow dance segment of the evening. Claire's eyes search for Robby, but Robby doesn't notice. He walks up to Sophie, says something and they both walk to the dance floor.

Something deep within snaps. Dancing is our thing. She shouldn't dance with anyone else but me.

Claire studies them intently. I plod over to the bar again. Even though I'm not looking at them, I can still see her with him. The image is burnt into my brain. It's not like they're officially a couple. Claire has to step up if she wants him to be in her life.

"The usual?" the bartender asks.

"No. Tequila. The best one you have. Double."

"What is this about Sophie leaving in two weeks?" an angry British voice hisses in my ear.

I turn to find Jen behind me. "What?"

"That's what she told me. She's leaving!"

SIXTY-FIVE

— PETE —

"ARE YOU SURE? Did she say she's leaving *for sure?*"

"No, I'm not sure. I like to get hysterical because it's my favorite pastime. Don't be an arse. That's what she told me."

I stumble toward our table. Jen drops into her seat and Raj joins us.

"How are you, Pete?" Raj asks.

"Shitty."

"Yeah, you look it."

"Thanks, man. You're awesome."

Jen elbows Raj. "What? He said it. I just agreed."

"Pete, you really need to stop this," Jen says.

I look up. "Stop what? I didn't do anything."

"Precisely. You didn't do anything. Nothing. Stand up, march over there, tell her you fancy her, then kiss the woman."

"Holy shit! You're right." I rise. "Why didn't I think of that?" I slump back down.

"You are an imbecile. You think you understand everything? Mister 'I'm a bloody architect' and therefore an artist and understand people's inner motives. What she needs is *you*. But you're not doing anything about it."

When the possibility was there, Sophie told me to leave. Yet, everyone thinks they know. I eye her. What if she knows something? Is it possible that Sophie told her how she really feels? "Jen, I love you. You know that. But what makes you think she wants me?"

"Women's intuition," Jen says.

"Oh, for fuck's sake."

Intuition my ass. She doesn't know anything. I step away from the table, heading for the bar when someone snakes an arm through my elbow. I turn. It's Claire.

"Come on, let's dance and talk," she says.

As we stroll to the dance floor, eyeballs track us. I don't want anyone to jump to conclusions—particularly Sophie. I create a pocket of space.

"I feel like I'm dancing with my dad," she says, then pulls me in. "The least you can do is act like you're enjoying it."

I crack a smile. "I'll do my best." We dance for a few moments.

"Let's pretend it's ninth grade. Let's pretend you asked me to the Winter Formal and I said yes."

"Would you have?"

"In a heartbeat. I even opened the door for you in history class."

"Social Studies," I correct.

"That's right!" She glares at me. "Are you saying you realized what I was trying to say and you still didn't ask."

"Oh no, that's not what I'm saying. I wasn't that smart. It was Sophie who decoded your question into woman-speak."

She smiles. "Fun memories," she says. "Let's pretend it's thirteen years ago and life has not taken the twists yet. We haven't gone through the pain, the love, the fear, and the bliss called life. Let's pretend that I didn't notice how Sophie gazed at you. Let's pretend I didn't wonder what it was about this boy that attracted a beautiful, smart, and genuinely good girl like Sophie."

I blink cautiously. My eyes are weathered crystal, ready to disintegrate. I notice tears pooling in her eyes as well.

"Let's pretend I wanted to know you better and see what made you the apple of her eye. I'll even pretend I wasn't envious of her. I'll pretend I didn't marvel at how she was always good and decent with everyone. I'll pretend she wasn't the one person I wished I could emulate."

A tear rolls down her cheek and catches the light. "All this pretending is very depressing," I say. "I'm glad it's just pretend."

"I'm sorry, Pete. I shouldn't have done that to you, or to her. But I had a crush on you for the longest time. From the first time you got your bell rung when Seth threw that basketball at you, to how you always made me laugh when you impersonated the principal, to how you danced at parties. So when the stars aligned, as reckless as it was, the opportunity was too good to pass up. The crush became something else for a little while until that decision crushed us both again."

"We were a mistake."

"No, I wouldn't say that. It meant something back then. And even if that's not true, then you were my favorite mistake."

I chuckle.

We're silent for some time.

"Are you upset?" she asks.

"No, of course not. The past is the past. We've made it. More or less."

She laughs. "Hopefully more than less."

"Back then, I was afraid I'd be among the lost and forgotten. I didn't want to be a nobody. I wanted to matter. I wanted to be that one guy who showed them that the wimp can actually become the super hero. In all of high school only one, maybe two, will stand out. The rest of us are not third, or fourth. We are last."

"Oh, Pete, don't say that."

"It's true. Let's be honest. We're all looking for the beautiful girl, the beautiful degree, job, home, car, children. The madness goes on and we eventually hope to have a beautiful retirement plan. In the end, all we have that's ours is our memories and the pillow that we embrace before we sleep for the last time."

"You are not like that."

"Not today, no. But I was. Until a few days ago, maybe even as late as yesterday, I was still trying to win the game. I hoped that with the right person by my side, I'd be the winner."

She blinks. "What about now?"

"I was playing the wrong game. I know now what I have to do."

SIXTY-SIX

— PETE —

I TOUCH MY grandmother's necklace. *Help me*, I think. Give me an idea.

"Are you okay?" Sophie asks. She and Robby plop into their seats.

"Fine. Fine. Absolutely perfect."

She lays her strong hand on mine. "What's wrong?"

She squeezes. Electricity and a jolt of lightning shoot through my skull and hair. Those fingers, her hand, her touch. I want to grab her and kiss her. And if she slaps me, or hates me, at least I will go down having tasted her lips again.

Instead, I look up and try hard, as hard as I can, to smile. "A lot on my mind. That's all."

"Yiayia?" she asks.

"That and other things."

I glance at Robby who is watching us cautiously. "Did you tell her?" Robby asks.

For an instant I think he's asking me if I told her how I really feel about her, but how would he know?

"The papers," he says.

She shifts from him to me. "What papers?"

I slap my head. "The most important papers since the magna-freakin'-carta," I say and pull them out. "You are free, Soph."

Her eyes go wide. She rises, flipping through the sheets, the stack of pages nearly touching her nose. "When?" she whispers. "How?" She looks up at me, her eyes are glassy and pink.

"I saw him outside. We spoke and he gave them to me."

She throws herself at me. My chair almost falls backward. With one arm, I embrace her, with the other, I hold onto the table to keep us from toppling onto the floor.

"Thank you. Thank you. Thank you," she whispers in my ear. She's holding me so tight, with so much passion and aggression that I imagine holding her like this forever. Her scent intoxicates me.

"What's going on?" Jen asks, a huge grin on her face.

Sophie pulls away. "This!" She shakes the papers in Jen's face. "Signed divorce papers. I'm going to take pictures of these and send them to my lawyer before I cry all over them."

She goes back to her seat and moves plates out of the way.

My heart is thudding in my throat. I rise. "Time to go to the boy's room," I say, and walk out.

"Thanks for the notice," Jen says.

I stumble to the restroom and wash up. I study my face in the mirror. I lean in closer. I'm losing my bearings. I splash more water on my face.

I step out and see Diana on the phone. I search my memories. What did I do at prom?

The plan had been Sophie's. Diana was Sophie's closest girlfriend and teammate back then. What had Sophie told me? *I really want you there at the prom.*

I hadn't asked why.

I'm running through the details, the little comments, the obscure looks. I study Diana, who is still on the phone. I march outdoors and tap her shoulder. She turns. "We need to talk," I say.

Her brow rises, she's not impressed.

"Please," I say.

Her eyes soften then she hangs up. "Did you figure it out?" she asks.

"She wanted me at the prom. Why was it important for me to be there? Is that why you're mad at me?"

Diana gets close. "Pete, you never heard this from me, because I made a promise." For the first time she sounds sincere, caring. "She didn't want to go to prom with Seth. When you told her you're going with Claire, she was forced into it."

I forced their first interaction?

"But then, the blonde queen disappears, you are dateless, but she's said yes to Seth. She had hoped that by setting me up with you, once my damn hot boyfriend arrived, you'd be alone and ready."

I swallow.

"Ready?"

"She knew Seth would be plastered. Even before we got to the after party he was smashed." She looks around then leans closer. "She wanted prom to be the night she'd... you know... she wanted you to be her first. She loved you, Pete."

I've stopped breathing.

"At the after party, when she tried to find you, she did. With Shannon. In the laundry room."

My heart drops.

"You broke her heart, Pete."

"She... loved me?"

SIXTY-SEVEN

— PETE —

DIANA AND I step into the hall together. I catch Sophie's eyes. She approaches us with a dubious look on her face. "This is a pleasant surprise," she says. "Are you two love birds all made up now? After ten years?"

Diana looks at me. "I forgive him. I don't know if he forgives himself." She winks then marches off.

Sophie's eyes shift quickly. She tries to read my expression for a hint of what I'm thinking. But I am a solid wall. After a few moments she asks, "What is she talking about?"

"I'm too drunk to understand," I say.

"Uh-oh. I've seen what happens when you get drunk."

I chuckle. "You're not that much better."

She blushes and a grin begins to form. Just as quickly, her faint smile disappears. She's not bending.

"Let's sit," she says. "Food's being served."

We sit, but I have no appetite. I thought Robby or Seth were my biggest challenges. I've been my own worst enemy. I feel old. Older, but not wiser.

Robby brings Claire to our table. Claire scoots next to me. "You're slouching," she whispers.

I laugh because everything is falling apart.

"Guys, watch the big screen," Sophie says. "A collage of videos and pictures of our school days."

The wall sconces go dark. The room's only illumination is temporarily provided by the dying candles. I look at Sophie's features. I want to touch her face. I want her to smile so that I can see her dimples again.

The screen turns gray. Then the video starts. "Hancock Prep: A family reunion." A few people whoop.

I brace myself.

To the backdrop of music that we grew up with, we watch the video.

A track meet in sixth grade where Sophie and Diana win first and second place.

Spelling Bee champion Claire.

I glance at Claire. She's touching Robby's shoulder. She's beaming, probably unaware of the physical contact she has with him.

The infamous dance. Robby and Claire dancing cheek to cheek. Sophie and me dancing, stealing the show.

I glance at Sophie as she covers her face, but laughs through it. Robby has a faint smile.

Raj winning the LEGO robotics challenge.

Tenth grade, varsity girls' volleyball winning the conference championship for small schools. Sophie and her teammates in a huddle hopping up and down in a ceremonial dance.

Erik on stage at the talent show.

The group produces a collective sigh.

Erik delivering one of his finest Elvis performances.

Frank and Robby head to head on the chin up bars. And when Robby ekes out one more, Frank nearly cries.

Frank yells out, "I want a rematch!" Everyone laughs. They exchange high fives.

Tenth grade varsity girls losing the basketball championship. Sophie on the floor, crying while I attempt to lift her to her feet.

Eleventh grade varsity girls winning the basketball championship when Sophie steals the ball and Diana seals the championship.

The first time I tasted her lips.

Twelfth grade, Claire and Robby hanging out in the gym holding up signs. We Remember 9-11.

Senior Ditch Day at the beach. Some are barbecuing, some are playing volleyball. Sophie is spraying suntan lotion on Raj's and my backs.

Prom night, I'm dancing with Shannon. Sophie is glaring at Seth. Diana looks ready to smack me on the head.

The song changes to Louis Armstrong's *What a Wonderful World.*

Fades in to a montage of clips from senior production of Grease. Claire and Erik the lead actors. One image after another of Erik singing, smiling, laughing. Alive.

The video transitions to Erik's senior yearbook picture. Claire cries on cue. I lay my hand on hers. She smiles and whispers, "Thank you."

I peel my eyes off Claire. Sophie's watching me. There's pain in her eyes.

Graduation day speeches. Sophie and I are hugging, our graduation caps askew because we had just exchanged them. Dozens of groups, hugging, kissing, waving.

Fade to black.

The video ends and the applause echoes through the hall. In the span of fifteen minutes, I've seen my life pass in front of me. All of those opportunities that I should have capitalized on, but hadn't.

I squeeze Yiayia's necklace.

SIXTY-EIGHT

— PETE —

I APPROACH THE DJ and ask for two songs. The DJ struggles for a couple of minutes, but when I slip him a tip, he identifies his source of motivation and downloads the songs.

I rush back to our table. Sophie is in the middle of a conversation with Robby and Claire, but I have to do this. I tap Sophie's shoulder just as the rhythmic horns and strings breathe a melody through the speakers.

She turns and studies my hand.

"Shall we *Sway?*" I ask.

Sophie tries to keep her face taught but can't. She grins, takes my hand, and rises without hesitation. She focuses on me.

"Yay!" Jen yells.

I will not make eye contact with anyone else. This is not about them and what they want. This is about us.

Dean Martin sings *Sway*, his voice gliding through my chest. The smooth and flowery nature of the music sways my body into motion. I take her to the center of the dance floor. Our bodies merge.

With his words on our lips, she holds me closer.

I slide one hand on her waist and with the other, hold her hand, allowing our intertwined fingers to swing gently at our side. When our hands squeeze, our bodies begin to sway and bend ever so lightly.

With each line of poetry, our movements become more pronounced, and our smiles fade into a mutual transfixed gaze.

Does she understand that his words are my words? Will she stay with me?

I lift her hand above our heads and slowly twirl her. Her sequin dress glitters against the dance floor. Millions of points of light explode across the hall.

Everyone's eyes are on us. But my eyes remain trained on her.

We move to the music, internalizing, mouthing the lyrics.

My knees go weak, I'm unsure if I can make it through the song. She moves into me. We are pinned to each other, swaying and moving to the song.

We've danced to this song dozens of times. But this time something feels different.

She moves closer, her body tight into mine. Our faces only inches apart. I no longer hear the music, I am with her and no one else matters. Her heart beats against my chest.

Her lips glisten.

Her eyes nearly close.

I lean in just as the song fades and the damn DJ mixes in a devilishly timed Caro Emerald song. A 50's style throwback Jazz. This is Sophie's favorite song. Our preferred music when we swing.

Her eyes pop open—wide open, with a mischievous glint. She's ready.

The powerful trumpets, the sassy voice, and smooth vocals are all we need. Sophie smiles, her dimples flare, and we both take a step back—an exaggerated pose we perfected for Raj and Jen's wedding.

She squeezes my right hand. The start signal. And so we begin. We spin then switch hands, she grins and we twirl, I laugh. The crowd gathers around the dance floor, clapping along.

I wink at her. Her eyes confirm and in that instant I spin her once, twice, three, more, more, and more. As she spins, I move her around the floor, claiming the dance floor as ours.

Then, in one powerful move, she stops and we move into quick hand switches, like snakes going in and out of each other's holds. We don't have to count, or think, or speak. Our hands do the talking, and our hearts keep the beat.

This is all natural.

We are natural.

We are one.

The steps come back instantly, innately. We've danced to this type of music dozens of times. We're recreating history. Suddenly, I realize what's different this time.

I am no longer the boy who was intent on making my moves to wow the crowd. I finally see what she's been doing—for all these years. She's been talking to me, communicating with her movement, her eyes, her smile. Has she been giving me an open invitation to come after her for all these years but I've been too young or too stupid to realize it?

I've wasted countless opportunities. No more!

We slide out of the movement and hold eye contact for a second. The end of the song is approaching. We go underarm and switch hands. I execute a quick turn as she spins around me. Her hand drags across my chest, and an explosion of goose bumps invigorate me. I hold, then turn her from her shoulder until we are locked in an embrace, face to face. I hold her neck and she holds mine. Our faces only inches apart as we spin until the song ends.

We breathe heavily, our chests rising and lowering in unison. Her bare shoulders glisten like satin. Our hands are wrapped around each other's neck until she moves in and hugs me. I lift her and her feet rise as I spin in place over and over again.

And when we stop, the crowd cheers and jumps, wanting more. But there is no more. This is our dance. Maybe our last dance. But if it's going to end, I will not go out gently.

I step into her to—

Our classmates encircle us

They're congratulating and talking, talking, talking. But all I care about is holding on to her eyes. Sophie and I drift a few feet apart. I don't want to let go of her hand, but in one instant, our tether snaps. She continues to look into my eyes.

Her soft eyes harden.

She shakes her head, then spins away.

SIXTY-NINE

— PETE —

SOPHIE'S WALKING AWAY. People have surrounded me. They're talking, but I can't hear anything. Sophie's eyes are downcast, but her stride is long and fast. She steps out and the door closes behind her.

It didn't work. I tried, but it didn't work. I run my hands though my hair, take a deep breath and consider my options. Someone grabs my shoulder and spins me violently. It's Jen. She's seething.

"Composure, Jen," Raj pleads. "Don't make a scene."

"What?" I ask.

"You were right there," she says, trying to whisper unsuccessfully. "Her face inches away from yours. You're holding her neck and hair. Bloody hell, Pete! You should've kissed her. That scene was written for a movie."

She's right, of course. "When we got pulled apart, I hesitated. I froze up, worried that I would screw things up."

"But you are screwing things up. Royally."

"I can't just grab her and force myself onto her."

"You bloody well can."

I yank the drink out of her hand. I finish her gin and tonic and hand her the empty glass. She's right. "Out of my way."

Action.

Velocity.

Acceleration.

I rush past the obstacles in the hall. People, chairs, tables, doubts, and fears. I confront them all. I acknowledge them, but continue to force my way through.

I slam the door open and spin to the right, then left. I don't see her. I jog through the hallways, glancing in all directions. Where is she? Why did she leave?

I'm a mouse in a maze, running around and around, getting nowhere fast. It's no use, I can't find her.

Even when I want to do the right thing... even when I want to fight for her, I can't do it properly.

I step back into the hall, scanning the people. Some are dancing. Some are talking or laughing. Some have a new beginning. Some will wake up tomorrow and wonder if there's more to life than this.

Our table is empty. Everyone is either dancing or at the bar. I slump on a chair. What now?

"Pete, I need help."

I look up. It's Pat. He's holding an iPad—Sophie's iPad. "How'd you get that?"

"Sophie gave it to me just before you guys started dancing. I'm supposed to start another picture show she put together for us, but I can't find Sophie. Do you know how to connect this thing to the AV equipment?"

"Sure," I say and take it out of his hands. "I need to find the right album."

We amble to the AV equipment. He's talking, but I'm not listening. I'm spent.

I lean against the wall and identify the cables I'll need. I'm about to plug it in, when I decide to search for the album before I connect it. She has hundreds upon hundreds of albums. I scan the names, looking for something like "Reunion." I see a few I recognize from past projects. "High Park," "Highland," "Hollywood." I pause. An album's name catches my eye. It's called "Him."

Him? Is it about Robby? Seth? I almost touch it to reveal who is behind that folder. But I don't have to. I know who "Him" is.

Me.

I'm "Him."

That's why she has never allowed me to look through her pictures.

"What are you doing?" Sophie's voice comes from behind me.

I turn slowly. "Pat asked me to find the reunion album."

Her eyes are red, sparkling. She takes the iPad out of my hand, studies it, then glances at me. Her lower lip nearly quivers. Without words, she confirms everything.

"Did you...?"

SEVENTY

— PETE —

I DON'T LIKE lying to Sophie, so I never will again. "I only looked at the album names."

Her shoulders sag. The tension in her forehead eases. She sets the iPad on a speaker, then exhales and drops her hands to her side.

"Soph, is your decision final? Did you decide to go to London for sure?"

She sinks deep into my eyes, then nods.

"When do you leave for London?"

She frowns. "In two weeks."

"Good, that gives me enough time."

She hesitates. "For what?"

"To quit my job and renew my passport."

Her back straightens. "Wait. What?"

I grab her waist and pull her to me.

"No more waiting," I say. "No more."

My fingers slide behind her neck and my eyes bore into hers. Her eyes widen as the distance between us disappears and our lips meet. A momentary hesitation, then she kisses back, her full lips accept mine. My lips smolder when I taste her sweet mouth again. But this time I am sober, aware, and in love. I am enveloped in the faint scent and taste of fruity nectar. My heart drums against my ribs, my lungs beg for her air, blood rushes throughout my body, and heat explodes across my legs. I want time stopped. I want this moment to be frozen. This is a new dance, our best dance.

But she pulls back and our lips part. I want to hold on to her taste forever. I want more. For a moment her eyes remain closed, her eyelids flutter until they finally open. She looks at me expectantly. Our eyes lock.

She opens her mouth and tries to speak. Then tries again. "Are you drunk?" she whispers.

"No."

"Are you sure?"

I cup her face and gaze at her like the precious jewel she is. "Sophie, for the first time in my life, I am completely aware of what I'm doing."

She blinks, then gently grabs my hands, her eyes crimson and hopeful. But just as quickly they turn hard with rage.

"Do you think I'm one of your conquests? Is that what I've become?"

"What are you talking about?" I try to connect the pieces.

"I am not one of those women. In all these years we've known each other, when have I given you the impression or the opening to disrespect me like that."

"I don't disrespect you—"

"You think I need your pity? You think I showed you my scar so that you'd feel compelled to bed me? Did you think—"

"I love you," I say.

Her face goes slack. All her energy and vitriol disappears.

"You are the one. It was always you." I bring her in tight. "I adore you. And I can't bear just being your friend. I need you completely."

A tear rolls down her beautiful face. I lean in and kiss the tear that streaks her cheek, tasting the salt, her essence. I am electrified.

"But Claire..." she stammers.

"Give me your hand," I say.

Her eyes search my face.

"Your hand," I repeat.

She places her hand in mine and I take her open palm and squeeze it against my chest. A couple of her fingers glide between the buttons and touch my skin.

"Can you feel it? This heart has always beat for you. It will only beat for you. If you're not with me, then I want it to stop. My story does not have to continue. Bring down the curtains. Send everyone home. If I don't have you in my life completely and forever, then I don't want to know how my story ends. It's meaningless."

She's silent for a few moments. Then her hand slides over my chest until she caresses my face.

"I thought you'd never give up on Claire."

I blink.

"I didn't want to love you," she continues. "I tried to love others, even forced one. But every time I imagined a happy, complete life, it was your face I saw."

Her fingers glide through my hair.

"I had to deal with a simple fact," she continues. "I would always be your buddy—one of the guys. You would never be interested in me romantically. Unless you were drunk." Her eyes harden. "You're sure you're not drunk, right?"

"I could be drunk, sober, awake, or asleep. My state does not change what I feel. I came to this reunion, convinced that it was about second chances. About righting those things which went wrong. Yiayia said I'd find my true love here. I found mine. I don't pray much, but I pray that you've found yours, too."

She smiles. "I found it sixteen years ago."

I pull her into my arms and hold her tight, not wanting to chance it. I will not lose her. Not now, not ever. I take her chin and look into her eyes. "Sophie, will you be my prom date?"

She sniffles, then chuckles as she gently wipes at her eyes. "I suppose," she says. From her purse she takes out the snapped leather wrap-around wristband. "Frank found it. He's an amazing detective. Do you think it can be repaired?"

I nod. Anything can be repaired. I take it out of her hand and slip it in my pocket. "Sophie," I say, then reach behind my neck and unclasp Yiayia's necklace. Sophie's eyes go wide when she sees the chain. I pull out what has served as the pendant on her antique necklace.

"That's Yiayia's," Sophie says, her eyes bright.

"No," I say. "It's yours now." I take her right hand. "You really need to marry me. I have a nice smile and a firm handshake. I know how to dance, particularly when I feel your heartbeat against my chest. I can even design your dream home."

She just stares at me.

"You need more? Fine! I'll even wear yoga pants and eat wheat germ if that's what it takes. But I need to know that each time you smile and produce those dimples of yours, they are there because you're with me. Because I make you happy, because you love me. I'll even throw my family into this deal." I touch her face. "This really is a good deal, Soph. So what do you say? Will you marry me?"

I slip my grandmother's wedding ring onto Sophie's slender finger.

Sophie grabs my face and kisses me. Hard. Her mouth on mine, her hands in my hair, her body tight against mine. She pushes me against the wall. Her body writhes into mine, igniting the thunder within. My body shivers, my skin's ablaze. Everything's on fire.

I lose myself.

Almost.

The explosion of cheers and applause and catcalls freeze us instantly. Our eyes open and our gazes lock onto each other. We don't dare look around.

Her lips still on mine, she asks, "Are people watching us?"

"What people?"

SEVENTY-ONE

— SOPHIE —

HIS FIERY LIPS find mine again, to the backdrop of friends cheering and laughing.

He's mine.

Finally.

EPILOGUE

- SOPHIE -

One Day Later

One of our phones chimes. I hope it's Pete's. I don't want to move. I want to stay like this forever. I am draped in Pete's body. His flesh against mine, sparsely covered.

The phone chimes again.

"I think it's yours," I say.

"No, thank you," he whispers, but he's more asleep than awake.

As much as I hate to, I untangle myself from Pete and the bed sheets, and reach for my phone. Not mine. I study the remnants of our clothes on the floor. Hanging over the side of the bed, I rummage through his pants and pull out the phone.

"It's yours," I say. "It's from your assistant."

"Ur ght," he says, whatever that means.

I lay back on the bed and he drops his arm around my chest as I unlock his phone to read the complete message. "Sandy has scheduled a call for tomorrow at 10:00 a.m. with the client."

"Okay," he whispers, directly into my ear, shooting goose bumps all over my neck.

I read the next line, then pause. I rub my eyes and read it again. My eyes go wide. "Holy shit!" I scream and leap to a sitting position.

He jolts up and falls to the floor. "What? What happened?"

"Your client," I say. "The client you're meeting with tomorrow!"

"Ten o'clock. I heard you." He rubs his bloodshot eyes. "But why are you yelling?"

"Your client," I repeat, as I scramble to him and show him the client's name.

He reads it. No reaction.

"Well?" I ask.

He looks at me and shrugs. "Okay, I give up. Who's Gemma Lennon?"

— THE END... For Now —

If you liked this story of second chance, sporty romance, then you'll want to check out **15 Days With You**, *Book 3 in the Second Chance Coast series. Take a surfing journey up and down the Pacific Coast Highway with best friends Shep, Sam, and Carmen in a coming of age, second chance redemption story.*

PLEASE LEAVE A REVIEW!

If you enjoyed this book, you can make a big difference by leaving a review.

Honest reviews of my books help in getting the attention of new readers.

To leave a review, click below:

To leave a review, return to the retailer's website search for TEN YEAR DANCE and leave an honest review.

Thank you!

Join Ara's V.I.P. Club

Ara Grigorian's VIP Club members receive free behind the scenes content to accompany the book.

Members are always the first to hear about Ara's new books and publications.

Click to Join my VIP Club:
www.AraGrigorian.com

BOOKS BY ARA GRIGORIAN

Pacific Coast Sunrise Series

Game of Love

Ten Year Dance

15 Days With You

Fortuny Bay Series

Reunion at Fortuny Bay

Secrets of Fortuny Bay (coming in early 2023)

AUTHOR'S NOTES

A Christmas gift and Garth Brooks

The number one question I'm always asked, "How did you come up with this idea?"

In August of 2011, I was waiting for the literary world to discover me (Spoiler alert — it would take a few more years until they would). While waiting, my mentor at the time advised that instead of watching my nails grow, I should write the next book. Brilliant advice. I just needed an idea.

Nothing great came to mind so I did what all self-respecting writers do: I turned to organizing my bookshelves — alphabetically, by genre, by color, by theme (don't ask). Embedded in the shelf was a red, hardcover journal. The spine declared "1985."

It was my diary from 9th grade. I think either my brother had bought it for me for Christmas, or in an attempt to be like my brother (who had been writing journals for years), I had gifted it to myself. This was a short-lived diary, but a definite attempt at capturing my pitiful life as an awkward teenager trying to find a place in this world.

It ran from Jan 1 through April 25. The very last line in the diary read: "I really love her, more than any other girl in my life." Clearly, I had the gift of melodrama at a very young age!

Honestly, I couldn't even remember who I may have been in love with. But I had four months of material to read through. Needless to say, it all came back to me. I was a mess. No, no. I'm serious. I had a mad crush over this girl and each time we made eye-contact, or chatted, I would hold on to that for the entire day. If the next day we didn't speak, my life was in ruins. As I flipped through the pages I recalled what some of my friends had noticed at the time — "I think she likes you," one would say. Or, "You should ask her to the dance."

I felt for Ara. He was a good kid, but clueless, really. I continued to flip through the page, recalling little details, when, as is always the case, the muse decided to step in. My playlist, which had been playing in the background, kicked off a Garth Brooks song about unanswered prayers. [Note: Yes, Armenians are HUGE country music fans... okay, fine they are not, but I am.]

With the diary in my hands, and the strumming of chords in my ears, questions popped into my head. What if my character had a mad crush over the "perfect" girl? What if in his blinded state, he never saw what was always in front of him — the real perfect girl — his best friend? What if things got ugly right before prom and what if at the high school reunion they all returned with the hope of putting right what had gone wrong?

The first draft happened in ten days. The finished novel took another four years. Now you know the rest of the story.

ACKNOWLEDGMENTS

Writing is a solitary sport. Publishing on the other hand is a massive, multi-player sport. And I have some of the best on my side of the field

My agent, Stacey Donaghy, who asked me not to give up on Pete and Sophie when I was tempted to scrap the story. I am fortunate that I have a partner like you on my side. I could not have asked for better.

My alpha readers: Demetra Brodsky, Diana Gardin, Aline Ohanesian, and Robin Reul. Your honest (sometimes colorful) feedback helped me work harder *before* I embarrassed myself.

My beta readers who read multiple versions of the manuscript: Andreh Anderson, Norm Thoeming, Kendall Roderick, and Janis Thomas. You guys are the best anyone could ask for. Each of you insisted on reading it "one more time." I am fortunate that you like punishment. Thank you.

My friend, editor, and guru, Jean Jenkins. You are extraordinary.

My cover designer, Tracy Van Dolder of Virtually Possible Designs. You are what every author needs — a true and genuine friend. And an amazing talent. Thank you for all you do!

My sisters of the NAC who are always there for me: Missy Belote, Marnee Blake, Diana Gardin, Sophia Henry, Jamie Howard, Kate Lynn, Marie Meyer, Sribindu Pisupati, Jessica Ruddick, Meredith Tate Servello, Laura Steven, and Amanda Stogsdill — It's an honor to be one of the girls :)

My wolfpack: Chase Moore, Trey Dowell, Norm Thoeming.

Three reasons why the Santa Barbara Writers Conference will always be near and dear to me.

The conferences that make it possible for me to connect with my people: Southern California Writers' Conference, Santa Barbara Writers Conference, and the Writer's Digest Novel Writing Conference. The staff, the volunteers, and the workshop leaders — you make the literary world better.

My classmates from Ferrahian High School who come out in droves to support me at my book signings. Our stories together are the reason I wrote about a high school reunion.

My Second Chancers — this book launch could not have happened without you! My sincerest gratitude.

My friends and family: life without you is... well, truthfully, life without you is pretty good too, but I still prefer having you in my life :)

Last but never the least, my fans. It is always a humbling experience to meet and connect with you. Your words of encouragement mean the world to me. I still think you've mistaken me for someone else, but I don't want to break your heart or mine :) You are the best. Thank you.

Fight the good fight!

ABOUT THE AUTHOR

Author's photo courtesy of FlashCube Photography © 2021

Ara Grigorian is a USA Today Bestselling author whose novels include the international award-winning Game of Love, Ten Year Dance, 15 Days With You, Desire After Dark (anthology), and Reunion at Fortuny Bay, his latest series. Fascinated by the human species, Ara writes about choices, relationships, and second chances. Always a sucker for a hopeful ending, he writes contemporary stories targeted to adult and new adult readers.

Ara is also a technology executive in the entertainment industry. He earned his Master's in Business Administration from University of Southern California. True to the Hollywood life, Ara wrote for a children's television pilot that could have made him rich (but didn't) and nearly sold a video game to a major publisher (who closed shop days later). Ara and his wife are the proud parents of two teenage boys and two senior cats. They have laid roots in both Los Angeles and North Dallas.

Ara is a story coach and a workshop leader. He has taught at the Southern California Writers' Conference, Santa Barbara Writers Conference, and the Writer's Digest Novel Writing Conference.

Ara is represented by Stacey Donaghy of Donaghy Literary Agency.

www.AraGrigorian.com

www.ingramcontent.com/pod-product-compliance
Lightning Source LLC
Chambersburg PA
CBHW031022120726
47905CB00007B/2013